Home

By Kate Hughes

For Lyndsay

Prologue

It was that word again.

"No."

Why? Rosie knew it was there. It was always there, sitting in the cupboard right in front of her.

Frustration surged through her body as she tried desperately to make them understand. Again and again she attempted to form the words she needed. After all, it was so simple. It tasted good, it was something she was allowed to eat, and she wanted it now. Why were they saying no, then? It didn't make any sense to her.

It had been building all morning. The agitation, the uncertainty, the anxiety, the jumbled thoughts. Now Rosie could feel the familiar climax arriving. She clawed at her clothes. The itching from the fabric seemed to be piercing her skin. She grasped her hair and pulled. Anything to take the feelings away.

The lights were suddenly too bright. The sounds were far too loud. She saw mouths. She heard voices. Too many, too loud. Piercing her head. It hurt. It hurt too much. She thrust her hands over her ears, trying to shut it all out. Everything was just too confusing.

Her heart began to beat faster. She could feel it pulsating, each throb stronger than the last, moving towards the moment when it would explode from her rib cage. Her head felt like it was full of bees falling over each other in the tight space, the buzzing deafening her. Her body could feel every tiny movement and sensation in the room. It was as if her bones were vibrating.

Rosie tried to tell them. She tried to explain that her entire body was a volcano with the pools of lava bubbling louder, higher, faster, about to erupt.

Overwhelmed and frightened, she threw her arms out, frantically trying to grip something, anything to make her feel safe. All at once, she was aware of shouts. Loud, so loud they seemed to penetrate her brain. Hands were now on her arms trying to pin them to her side. It felt as if an electric shock had shot through her entire body. Rosie struggled to break free, arms flailing in front of her grabbing. Her nails dug in. She heard a scream.

Rosie looked around her. Everyone seemed to be angry. More loud voices. Too loud. Too loud. She searched frantically for an escape. Finally there was an open door. Freedom, space, quiet. She ran. Hands over her ears. Eyes tightly shut. Up the stairs, two at a time.

No more noise.

Why couldn't they understand?

1

Gripping the steering wheel until her knuckles were white, Sophie let go of the tears which had been threatening to escape since the call.

Why her?

She started the car and swung out of the hospital car park with the force and flourish of someone who just at that moment didn't care if they hit another car or, in fact, a brick wall. It might be a blessed release from the constant worry of this nightmare world she had been flung into ten years ago.

Rain was battering the windscreen and her wipers were having to work at full strength to clear it. What was it that people said about the weather mimicking how people felt? Should be bloody raining all the time then, she thought. Anyone else might find driving with a constant stream of rain and eyes full of tears very difficult; it certainly did blur your vision. Sophie, however, was an expert at it now. The car was one of the few places where she could really scream and rage against the world.

And cry.

The call had come just as Sophie had sat down for a much needed lunch break. After the usual busy morning, she had been looking forward to a little time to eat and gather her thoughts. Everything in her head these days was a jumble, worry upon worry all knotted together so that she couldn't think clearly most of the time. It was just exhausting. Sometimes she thought she would never truly relax again.

So, daft as it was, she looked forward to her small breaks at work, since it was the only place she managed to get some head space. She could at least sit still and finish a cup of tea for once. It was not to be this lunchtime though. Just as she was about to take a second bite of her hastily put together ham and cheese sandwich, the voice of her friend Anna had boomed across the room.

"You've got a call, Soph – it's your mum."

Sophie had stopped mid-bite and looked up anxiously. From experience she knew that calls from home when you were at work were never good news; in fact it usually signalled a crisis.

Especially in her life.

Putting her sandwich down quickly, next to the cup of tea that she hadn't even started, she'd hurried to the staff phone that Anna was cheerfully waving in the air. A few of the other nurses looked up with mild interest as she hastily brushed past them.

"Hi, Mum," she started brightly, trying desperately to avoid whatever bad news was coming, "everything okay?"

"Oh Sophie, it's Rosie…" her mum, Diana, sniffed. Sophie felt her heart sink. Knowing the words which followed weren't going to be great, she braced herself.

Diana began to talk quickly, each phrase punctuated with a sob, "I can't believe it… you know I try so hard to keep her happy… I just can't control her now… she's so big… when she was little it was different… I just don't know what to do anymore -"

"Mum, just tell me what's happened!" Sophie didn't mean to be so sharp but these days she didn't have much patience with anyone, even her own mum.

"Rosie's hit me, Sophie." She was still crying. "She had a huge meltdown and I just couldn't stop it. She wanted some sweets out of the cupboard and I tried to ignore her like you said, but then she just went for me!"

Oh God.

"Where is she now, Mum?" Sophie felt herself breathing way too fast.

"She's in her room; Chloe managed to get her in there."

Chloe. Sometimes Sophie didn't know what she would do without her beautiful older daughter.

"But she's banging quite a bit you know; it sounds like she's going to come through the ceiling… "

Sophie really hadn't wanted to hear anymore. What she actually wanted to do was throw the phone on the floor and run away, sit in a corner somewhere and cover her ears. She didn't though, instead she clutched the phone tighter and kept listening.

"She was just so angry. You should have seen her, she just flew at me, like a wild animal. I've truly never seen her like that before."

Unfortunately Sophie had. Many, many times.

She'd almost expected something bad would happen today. The way things had been recently, she knew it had been a risk leaving Diana at home in charge, but during half term there was no other option. She *had* to work so she needed childcare and her mum was the only person left who would look after Rosie.

"Look, Mum," Sophie sighed, "don't worry. I'll explain to my manager and I'll come home now. Okay? Just make yourself a cup of tea, put the telly on and try to calm down."

"I'm so sorry. I didn't want you to have to leave work, Sophie, I just didn't know what to do for the best. I'm really worried about what she'll do next. Do you know… it was almost as if she hated me today?" Diana started sobbing again. With the phone still pressed to her ear, Sophie put her head in her hands and thought how awful it was to hear your mum cry especially when it was your own child who had been the cause.

After what had felt like an age reassuring her distraught mother that it wasn't her fault, that she hadn't done anything wrong and that she would be there as soon as she could, Sophie had finally got off the phone. She had glanced at her half-eaten sandwich, suddenly not at all in the mood for it anymore. The hunger pangs that she had felt at the end of the operation had now been replaced by a terrible sick feeling right at the bottom of her stomach. A feeling she was growing quite familiar with.

Trying desperately not to draw attention to herself, Sophie had quickly put the remains of her lunch in the bin, poured her now lukewarm tea down the sink and gathered up her book and bag.

Anna had looked up concerned, "You okay, mate?"

Sophie had wondered whether to answer that question honestly.

Instead she had gone for the easier option which required less explanation and wouldn't have everyone tripping over themselves to feel sorry for her. She had forced herself to smile, "Yeah, but I've got to get home – minor crisis. Nothing to worry about."

"Oh, alright," Anna smiled warmly. "Well, I hope everything sorts itself out. You know where I am if you need me. See you tomorrow, lovey." With that she had gone back to her glossy magazine, her healthy food and her normal life. In fact, looking around the room, Sophie had noticed how everyone was sitting enjoying their lunch, reading or quietly chatting. She had taken a deep breath and tried to suppress the feelings of jealousy that always surfaced when she had a glimpse of other people's lives. Sometimes she felt like she was living in a completely different world to the one they inhabited.

A world with autism.

2

Feeling the familiar panic beginning to bubble, Sophie had found her manager quickly and explained the situation. Although she wasn't particularly happy about losing a member of staff at such short notice, Caroline had had no choice really but to let her go. Sophie had made it quite clear she was leaving anyway.

Ten minutes later, she had been heading out of the door.

Walking quickly and looking down, busily trying to locate her keys in her way too full bag, she had collided with a slightly familiar figure. Mark, a recent addition to theatre recovery, was just starting his shift. Her bag landed at his feet and most of the contents tumbled out.

"Sorry, I… " Sophie whispered and crumpled on to the floor to pick everything up.

"Whoa! Watch it, Sophie!" Mark had chuckled as he'd bent down to help her pick everything up. "Rushing like that and you could have lost your… " he'd examined the packet in his hand, "…your very important pocket tissues with aloe balm." He'd winked and laughed. "Hey, actually you're rushing off a bit early aren't you? Not skiving are you?" he had grinned.

Sophie had retrieved all her belongings and stood up. She had looked up at his smile and struggled to see how anything could be funny today. The way she was feeling, she had just wanted to scream at him, "No, I'm not bloody skiving! If you must know I'm going home to my autistic daughter who just happens to have punched my mum in the face. I bloody well wish I was *skiving*!"

She hadn't though. Exhausted, Sophie had suddenly found herself wishing with all her heart that she was simply a normal woman with time to have a joke with a fairly good-looking bloke. Wishing that she didn't have this life.

She had sighed and tried to explain. "I… well… my daughter's autistic and… " However the words wouldn't come. Where would she start? She had felt the first tear starting to form. She knew she had to move now in order to escape from a situation where she would be stuck crying on the shoulder of a virtual stranger and unloading all the trauma of the last few months. She turned to go.

Bewildered, Mark had by now realised that his humour hadn't had the reception he'd obviously intended. A frown settled on the previously smiling face and an arm reached out and rested on her shoulder. "Oh Sophie, don't, hey I'm sorry I…"

His kindness had just been too much. All at once she'd had an overwhelming need to escape to a place where she could let everything out. So Sophie had shrugged his arm off and snapped, "Just… look… just leave me alone!"

She'd left a shocked looking Mark staring after her and got into her car. It suddenly occurred to her, as she'd roughly yanked her seatbelt on, that the soft, kind Sophie which had existed years ago would never have spoken to anyone like that. She constantly wondered just when she had turned into this bitter, cross person.

So, here she was on her way home having completed the shortest shift in history. Still gripping the wheel as she negotiated the heavy traffic, she wondered if there was anyone on this earth who felt like she did today.

After a swift drive home - she wouldn't be surprised if she'd broken a few speed limits - Sophie pulled into the drive. When she turned the engine off, she sat there for a moment. It was so peaceful. All she could hear was the quiet rhythmic tapping of the rain. Although realising that she should really be running straight in, Sophie felt as if she just needed to savour the silence and breathe, because when she did step through that front door there would be so much to sort out.

After many years of living with autism, Sophie had thought she could take whatever was thrown at her, but this violence was becoming increasingly harder to deal with. Oh, there had always been tantrums – or meltdowns which much more accurately described them – everyone agreed it went with the territory with autistic children. These days, however, it was different. Each time Rosie lost her temper, it was as if, very briefly, someone had replaced her sweet, smiling child with another person that she barely recognised.

Finally able to move, Sophie locked her car and walked into the house.

"Hi, I'm home!" she shouted, trying to sound a little cheerful despite the completely dire situation. Waiting for a response, she caught a glimpse of her reflection in the hall mirror and winced.

It really wasn't a pretty sight today.

Her hair felt and looked greasy. It had been such a busy morning trying to get all her jobs done before Rosie woke up and grabbed her attention, that she'd only had time for the quickest of showers, certainly no time to wash her hair. So, she'd shoved it up into a messy bun with various pieces sticking out. Sophie looked closer and noticed that there were a fair few grey hairs peeking through now too. Thankfully, being a natural blonde, it might be a while before anyone else noticed. Her pale skin was dry in places and there were dark patches under her eyes, a mix of smudged eyeliner from her recent bout of tears and too many sleepless nights.

All in all she just looked tired. And old. For probably the hundredth time that day, Sophie sighed. Where had that young, once vivacious, blonde gone? When had her body been taken over by this old hag? She was only thirty-eight but felt about fifty.

Standing at the bottom of the stairs, she could hear the noises that Rosie always made when she was busy concentrating on her books. Of course, always the same books and always the same pages. Sophie loved it at bedtime when they would snuggle up and look at them together. Her daughter's throaty chuckle when she recognised particular pages was deeply infectious and could cheer Sophie up even after the worst day.

She was shaken out of her daydream when Chloe called down cheerfully, "Hi Mum, I'm up here with Rosie, she's okay now so don't worry!"

"Thanks so much, Chloe," Sophie shouted, "I'll be up in a minute. I'm just going to check on Nanny."

Just then Diana appeared in the hallway; eyes red rimmed. She rushed over to Sophie and wrapped her arms around her, clasping her tightly. "Oh sweetheart, I'm so sorry to have had to call you at work." Sophie felt her body become limp, as if all her energy had drained away. She rested her head on her mum's shoulder for a moment, wishing desperately that she could simply stay there and be looked after again, just like when she was a child.

It was impossible though. There was too much to sort out.

"Mum, it's fine," Sophie answered, trying to reassure her yet again. "Rosie's more important than work." She pulled away to look at Diana's face and despite the many bruises and horrible injuries she had seen as an experienced nurse over the years, she couldn't help wincing when she saw what her adored daughter had done to her own nan. "Oh, Mum, that's going to bruise badly, let's get some ice on it."

"It's fine, darling."

"Mum! I *am* a nurse you know. Now sit down and let me look after you for a change." Diana smiled sadly, gave in and dropped on to the settee. She waited patiently while Sophie quickly fetched a bag of ice from the kitchen and anything else which might help to make her mum look less like she had just done a round in the ring.

Just as Sophie was finishing patching up a subdued Diana, who was finding it hard to shake the feeling that she could have handled the situation with her granddaughter much better, Rosie made her entrance. She came running in at full speed and despite the terrible events of the day, when they spotted her, neither Sophie nor Diana could help but burst out laughing. It was clear that while no one was looking, en route to the living room, Rosie had decided to help herself to the rest of the chocolate cake and had managed to get it over most of her face and hands. The whole family believed that this child actually had a sixth sense when it came to locating chocolate. It didn't matter where you hid it, she would find it. Sophie had lost count of the number of times when the chocolate decorations on the Christmas tree had all mysteriously disappeared; whole advent calendars had been demolished or Easter eggs had been wiped out, leaving only bits of crumpled foil behind.

Rosie really was a force of nature.

But Sophie adored her.

Chocolate aside, Rosie was a beautiful child. With her round face and dark eyes, which lit up when a huge grin spread over her face, she melted everyone's hearts. It certainly allowed her to get away with much more than she should. Her lovely face was framed by thick, dark hair cut into a long bob and Sophie saw that as usual, disliking the feel of the tight hair bobble, she had pulled it out of the neat ponytail that it had been put into before work. Rosie had also taken off her socks, which for her was another source of constant irritation. She often left a trail of discarded socks around the house. It never failed to surprise Sophie just how many things annoyed her little girl though 'little' probably wasn't such an accurate description these days. She was growing up fast and was now quite tall, but unlike her older sister's slight frame, she had a much bigger build.

A chocolate coated Rosie swiftly proceeded to jump on to Sophie's lap, wrapping her arms around her and burying her head in her shoulder. It didn't matter that her clothes were now probably smeared in chocolate too, Sophie savoured these moments when her baby came to her for a cuddle. Her baby.

It all changed suddenly when Rosie started asking in stilted speech for yet more chocolate. Constant eating seemed to be her latest obsession.

"Oh Rosie, no more chocolate!" Sophie groaned wearily.

Hearing the word 'no' was like a red rag to a bull and Rosie's hands immediately went to Sophie's face to hit her.

"No! No!" Sophie shouted, trying desperately but failing to hold her daughter's arms down. The trouble was, at twelve years old, she was getting so much stronger now. Rosie started to claw at Sophie's face and almost growled in anger. This sudden display of fury was happening more and more often these days and seemed to come out of nowhere. Diana moved over to help, but Sophie, who didn't want her mum injured anymore today, stopped her.

"No, Mum, leave her! I can handle it!" she shouted. Finally managing to hold Rosie's arms down like the well-meaning professionals had shown her, Sophie got up and backed towards the door, still clutching her child tightly. Rosie struggled, spitting fiercely in Sophie's face, completely unable to control her frustration at not getting what she wanted. Sophie loudly shrieked, "No!" She knew it was better to remain calm in these situations, but she defied anyone to remain calm when their own child was lunging at them like a crazed animal.

Eventually with the help of Chloe who, hearing the commotion had charged down the stairs, Sophie managed to get Rosie into her room so that she could at least be contained until the meltdown was over. Sophie held the door for a minute to stop her furious daughter charging out again. Feeling, not for the first time, a lot like a jailer, she stood there trying to stay quiet and breathe normally. She could hear things being thrown about and it sounded like the curtain rail had been pulled down again, but at least she knew Rosie was safe there. Wasn't that the most important thing for your child, *to be safe*? Sophie's face crumpled with the awfulness of it all.

Why her?

The worry of it all never left her. From the moment she woke, to the time she fell into a weary sleep, the uncertainties whirled around, burrowing deep into her brain. What would happen to Rosie? Who would look after her when Sophie wasn't here anymore? Would anyone care about her like she did? Would her daughter ever speak to her? Would she ever have peace of mind again? Round and round they went with no answers ever coming. It was exhausting.

After a while the banging stopped and they heard Rosie go back to her books. Finally, Sophie and Chloe trudged back downstairs.

"Interesting day eh, Mum?" Chloe smiled weakly at her. "Shall I put the kettle on?" Not waiting for an answer, she disappeared into the kitchen.

Diana was still on the sofa, looking worried. She looked up as Sophie trudged back in and sank into the sofa. "Are you okay? Has she hurt you again?"

Sophie sometimes worried that her mum forgot that it wasn't intentional. "You do know she doesn't mean it don't you, Mum? You do know she isn't some monster?" she couldn't help snapping.

Diana's face fell. "Well of course I do!" She sounded hurt. Sophie immediately realised that she'd misjudged her and felt bad.

"Oh God, I'm sorry, Mum, I don't mean to get cross with you. I don't really know what I'd do without you. It's just that... I worry everyone forgets that it's her frustration that makes her act like that and not that she's some evil child. She's just a twelve year old having a three year old's tantrum. The trouble is a three year old doesn't have the strength she's got. If she could just talk, you know, communicate with us properly, it would be so different. She could tell us what's upsetting her and we could explain things and I don't know… "

It had all been said before.

Diana took her hand, "You do know that I love her, don't you, Sophie? I always will. She's my grandchild, for goodness' sake," she started to weep, "but I'm just not sure that we can all cope with this much longer. Have you given any more thought to - "

"I know what you're going to say, Mum!" Sophie felt herself getting angry again, "You all just want me to send her away, don't you?"

"Sophie!" Diana sounded shocked. "No one *wants* to send her away; we all love her for goodness sake! We're just thinking of you. Look, you have done an amazing job, darling. You've managed all these years and, I know I'm biased and bound to say it, but I don't think I've ever seen a more patient, caring mum in my whole life." Diana sighed, "The thing is, Sophie, she's getting bigger and stronger all the time and look at the damage she's doing to the house - and us."

Sophie looked round at the broken curtain rail, the door with a chunk out of it and the cabinet with the broken glass. All evidence of Rosie's rages.

Diana continued, "That social worker, what's her name… Jane… you know the one that came round when we had that bad phase before… well she was lovely and helpful. Why don't you have a chat with her?"

Sophie groaned. Why did everyone seem intent on locking her child away somewhere? She took a deep breath and tried not to scream.

"It's not that bad, Mum, I can cope. Chloe helps me and it's not always this awful is it?"

Diana looked straight at her.

"I know Chloe's brilliant, but is it really fair on her? She's only just sixteen. She should be out having fun, but most of the time she's here worrying about you."

17

Sophie put her face in her hands and closed her eyes. Her head hurt. God, she could do with a cup of tea. Actually something stronger might be better the mood she was in. She wasn't an idiot; she knew her mum was right. She knew it was getting harder every day and that at some point the decision might be taken out of her hands. As her mum had reminded her, the idea had already been discussed reluctantly with her social worker a few months back following another difficult patch with Rosie. Things had got better though for a while and with a massive sigh of relief, Sophie had managed to forget all about the horrible idea. Send her little girl away? The beautiful smiling girl who woke her up with a hug and kiss every morning?

No.

It just felt too huge and she just felt so sad.

3

Later that evening, after her mum had finally gone home, Sophie sat down with a big glass of wine and wondered what to do. She'd just had bath time with Rosie and it had started so well. Sophie had run a deep bath with bubbles for her just the way she liked it, a little on the cold side. Then she had sat down by the side of the bath while Rosie played with the cups filling them and tipping them out over and over. Anyone else might have considered it boring, but to Sophie it was always wonderful to see Rosie enjoying herself. She loved to hear her giggle when something had amused her. Sophie wasn't always sure what had made her laugh but then, as she had decided long ago, that was autism, most of the time spent floundering around in the dark trying to understand what was going on inside her child's head.

Unfortunately, as was the pattern recently, the good mood hadn't lasted.

The two of them had been lying on the bed sharing a book, just like they did most evenings. Rosie loved pointing at the pictures and getting Sophie to repeat the words over and over. A picture of a school building was on the page and Sophie had mentioned that she needed to get Rosie's clothes ready for school. Rosie had become enraged. On reflection it was probably the 'school' word. It was as if a magic button had just been pushed.

Rosie had flown at Sophie digging her nails into her stunned face with the force of an adult not her twelve year old baby. Chloe had as usual dashed in and between them they had managed to calm her down and prevent her from inflicting more damage to them or the house. She was now fast asleep looking as angelic as she always had. Her beautiful girl.

Sophie felt the marks on her face. Rosie had managed to draw blood this time and with her luck she would have an awful mark there tomorrow. Good job she wasn't going in to work then. If anyone had told her, when she had first held Rosie all those years ago, that any of this would even have been possible, Sophie would have shrieked with laughter. The thing was, it just wasn't funny.

Sophie remembered clearly, so clearly, the birth of Rosie. Entirely different to Chloe, whose birth had been long and laborious in the truest sense of the word, Rosie had tumbled out, all nine pounds of her. Ready to meet the world at last. What an easy baby she had been too, completing Sophie's family. The two gorgeous children that she and Liam had always wanted.

Everything had been fine for a while. After the initial shock of being a mum of two, Sophie had managed to get her life into a routine. She went back to the job she loved part-time and, even though it was hard to juggle work and motherhood, she was so glad she had. She enjoyed having a balance, time with adults and feeling that she was contributing to the finances, and time just being a mum.

Rosie had flourished. She met the required milestones and had been a smiling, happy baby. Chloe had adored being an older sister and Liam had constantly told her how proud he was of his family. Sophie had felt that life was turning out well. She even indulged in a little feeling of smugness when she looked at some of her childless friends. Wasn't she lucky to have a smiling, handsome husband, two wonderful little girls and a comfortable home?

Just perfect.

For a while anyway.

But as in most fairy tales dark clouds suddenly appeared on the horizon. Cracks in her 'perfect' marriage began to widen until the damage was irreparable. That had been hard but nothing compared to the huge storm cloud which soon emerged in Sophie's world.

Gradually Rosie's development stopped and Sophie started to notice some odd behaviour. Her adorable baby became a tumbling toddler who ignored her; played around other children rather than with them; flapped her hands; didn't speak. Sophie had listened to everyone's reassurances, tucked each one into her pocket carefully. There couldn't be anything wrong, not with her child. She had done everything right hadn't she?

Then came the diagnosis which couldn't wait any longer; things were just not right.

Autism.

Her child was autistic.

Rosie was on the Autistic Spectrum.

Suddenly her head had been filled with so many questions.

Why her? How could that be? Was it her fault? Had she done something wrong when she was pregnant? What would it mean? Would she be rocking in a corner? Would she be amazing at art? Some sort of maths wizard? What would happen in the future? Was there a cure? Every day a new set of questions would make their way in to her tired brain, whirling round and round, tormenting her.

After the initial devastation and the endless weeping, Sophie dusted herself down and became motivated. A capable nurse of many years, she was nothing if not organised in every area of her life. So she could sort this out, couldn't she? With Liam long gone, it was up to her. She would make her little girl better.

So how could she do it?

Sophie researched thoroughly. So many different treatments to try; some English, some American, but all promising to get through to this uncommunicative child who Sophie so desperately loved.

But nothing worked. Everything she tried failed. Simply many years of hopes dashed, dreams trampled on.

Finally, with an enormous amount of pain deep down inside, Sophie had to accept the hard fact that she would always have an autistic child. Rosie wasn't a problem that could be solved. She was simply her child and she needed to be loved just as she was. It wouldn't be that bad would it? This new acceptance and determination had made her strong, this was her Rosie - whatever she was, however she behaved, Sophie would cope. Because she loved her.

And she had actually managed well. She had kept working with the help of her mum, who thankfully she could always turn to for help, and she had built a life. A good life with lots of happy times. Times when Rosie had made her and her big sister laugh so much they cried.

Rosie wasn't this silent child who opted out of the world, which seemed to be everyone's idea of autism. She was warm and affectionate and would often hug you so hard you couldn't breathe. If anything, Rosie felt everything too deeply. Her overloaded senses, trying desperately to deal with a confusing world, had led her to this point. Where slowly she was becoming uncontrollable.

Sophie lay back and put her feet up on the coffee table. This was literally the only time of the day when she came close to actually relaxing. A time when she wasn't constantly worrying where Rosie was and what she would be doing or wondering whether she was going to be aggressive or in a good mood. Sophie realised that life had become pretty gruelling.

Just at that moment, Chloe appeared at the door.

"Want to watch a film, Mum?"

Kind, lovely Chloe. Her saving grace.

At sixteen she was growing into a beautiful young woman. Like Rosie, Chloe had her father's olive skin and flawless complexion, a complete contrast to blonde, pale Sophie. When people looked at Chloe, a pair of beautiful brown eyes was what they noticed first; eyes just like dark mysterious pools. Her soft, sleek brown hair fell over her shoulders and was her pride and joy and, just like many other teenage girls, Chloe would spend hours washing and styling it. However, very unlike others of her age, Chloe's short life so far, peppered with divorce and the trials and tribulations of a special needs sister, had filled her with a kindness and compassion for others which seemed to be limitless.

Sophie beamed at her.

"That would be brilliant – something funny though. God knows, I badly need to laugh." She smiled, but was surprised when a few tears rolled down her tired cheeks. Tears seemed to come so easily these days.

"Hey Mum, you okay?" A concerned Chloe rushed over to the sofa and put her arm round her.

"Fine love, just tired."

Chloe rested her head on Sophie's shoulder. "It'll all be okay, Mum, she'll grow out of it. I'll always help you, you know."

Sophie brushed her tears away. She really needed to pull herself together. She was the adult here.

She kissed the top of Chloe's head and breathed in the smell of her hair. It was amazing really, it didn't matter how big your children got, they still smelt like your babies. "Everything'll be fine, honey. Now what shall we watch?"

4

Of course it wasn't going to be fine and that became quite apparent the next day.

Sophie had always thought it was weird how a day could start off like any other and then quickly turn into one when monumental things happened. It had been like that the day of Rosie's diagnosis really.

Sophie lay in bed as the sun fought to get in through the curtains and remembered back to that momentous day in April ten years ago. She'd been another person then, a normal 'rushed off her feet' mum of two, with nothing more to worry about than whether there were enough clean socks in the drawer.

On that day, just like every other day, Sophie had got up, showered and given the girls breakfast. Everything had been absolutely fine. The girls were in good moods and the morning had run as clockwork. Sophie had pushed any worrying thoughts about the impending appointment right to the back of her mind and managed to convince herself that nothing much would actually be said. She had been more concerned with deciding what they would have for tea. Privately, she'd thought the health visitors were just ticking boxes when they referred her to the specialist and it would be another 'let's wait and see what happens' type of appointment. Surely, there was no way she could have an autistic child.

Could she?

Her?

No.

In her head these days, Sophie divided her life into two halves. The first half existed before she went into the consultant's room on that murky day in April and the other half began when she came out. Everything changed with the diagnosis. It had been a good thing that her mum had been there because, with tears streaming down her face, it had been difficult to take anything in.

While the consultant was talking, Sophie had simply fixed her eyes on Rosie, watching her every movement in the room. Devastated and overwhelmed, it was as if someone had taken off her goggles and she was seeing Rosie for the first time; seeing her as everyone else saw her. It was completely obvious now that Rosie was not a normal child after all. Sophie just hadn't wanted to believe it. She realised that she had been hoping desperately that the lack of speech, the repeated sounds, the flapping, everything was going to have been explained away today.

And so, here she was, ten years later, living alone with the diagnosis every day.

Sophie lay back in bed and sighed. After the events of the previous day, she had got up early and called the hospital to take a day's annual leave. There was no way she could face all the stress at work, she had more than enough here thank you very much. Anyway, her head throbbed and she couldn't trust herself to concentrate fully on her patients today.

After the phone call, Sophie had crawled back to bed. Although she felt guilty, she had to admit that it was comforting to be in a warm place for once instead of battling the busy roads to work. It was one of those bright but crisp October mornings when you just knew winter wasn't too far away. So, as there was now no rush to get up, Sophie wrapped herself in the duvet and tried to sleep a little longer, though that was getting harder and harder to do.

When sleep wouldn't come, she pondered on what she should do today instead. Chloe was still fast asleep and so far she hadn't heard anything from Rosie's room. She could take the opportunity to tackle the huge pile of ironing, though it was always difficult getting the ironing board out while Rosie was jumping around. Or she could get some shopping in, though of course she would have to get Mum round to look after Rosie if she wanted to avoid a major meltdown at the shop. It was getting more difficult to take Rosie anywhere.

Maybe, she thought irritably, it would just be safer to sit on the sofa all day instead and pander to Rosie's every need. Sophie took a deep breath and tried to stop feeling sorry for herself.

Just then she heard the familiar heavy footsteps on the landing and her door abruptly swung open.

With hair tangled and eyes still only half open from just waking up, Rosie trotted over to Sophie and jumped into the bed with a giggle. Sophie felt her heart leap as her baby nestled into her with obvious happiness. She looked into her daughter's smiling face and deep brown eyes and wondered, not for the first time, what was going on in her head. Did she love Sophie? Did she know who she was? Had she any idea that she was her mum? Did she understand what a mother was? So many questions – the trouble was nobody could ever answer them.

At that moment, Chloe wandered in rubbing her eyes. Her older daughter seemed to have a sixth sense when it came to knowing her little sister had woken up.

Without a word, she too climbed in next to Sophie and gave her a hug.

Sophie lay there for a while content with the world. There was nothing better than being with her two precious girls. Why couldn't it always be like this? She sometimes wished she could run away to a desert island with them and just shut the rest of the world out.

"Aren't you going to work today, Mum?" Chloe asked sleepily.

"No, love, taking the day off. Want some breakfast?"

"In a minute… " Chloe mumbled, closing her eyes again.

"Look, why don't you stay here and have a doze while I go and get Rosie something to eat?"

As Chloe slowly nodded, Sophie got up, followed by a chuckling Rosie and made her way downstairs. The phone rang as she was busy making some toast.

"Hello?" she answered, preoccupied with trying to keep an eye on Rosie in the kitchen. It was only a matter of time before her clever daughter located some chocolate and decided that that would be a much better breakfast than marmite toast.

It was Mark.

Now, what the hell was someone she had only talked to a handful of times doing ringing her at home?

"Hi Sophie, I know this is a bit strange, me ringing you, but I found out you weren't in today…"

"Hang on, how did you get my number?" Sophie asked curtly.

"I begged Anna for it, don't blame her. I think she was worried about you too."

Sophie tutted. Typical Anna, she thought, probably grabbing a chance to set Sophie up with someone. Just because she was loved up with her new husband, she wanted everyone else to be in a cosy relationship too.

"Anyway, I rang because, well you seemed upset yesterday and I hope… well I was worried that… I… I hadn't upset you more by what I said about you skiving. I was only joking. I sort of do that too much probably. So, well, I really didn't mean to make the situation worse. I honestly had no idea that your daughter… um… well that she had… "

"Autism?" Sophie finished off his sentence crisply, unable to bear his awkwardness a minute longer.

"Yes - "

Sophie interrupted what was probably going to be a 'so sorry for your loss speech'. She really didn't want to hear it today.

"Look, forget it, Mark. Believe me, you didn't make anything worse. That would actually be impossible at the moment." She laughed bitterly. "Anyway I've got to go; I'm just in the middle of making breakfast and Rosie won't wait."

"Oh, okay… yes… so sorry… well, I'll see you at work then."

"Yep. Goodbye then." Sophie put the phone down.

She had the feeling she had been a bit too sharp with him. Again. After all it wasn't his fault that she was having a bad day, month, year, life. She should probably say sorry when she saw him, except she didn't actually feel sorry. Frankly, the feelings of some bloke she had only known a few months were really the least of her worries right now.

Finishing the toast off hastily, Sophie sat down to a leisurely breakfast with Rosie. Well sort of. As she nibbled her toast, every now and then Rosie would look and point longingly at the biscuit tin. Sophie carried on sipping her tea and smiled. Experience told her that if she ignored it, she might just avoid any confrontation.

Just then there was a tap at the back door and a familiar face, framed in bright red hair, peered round.

"Hiya hon, this a good time?"

"No good time in this house," sighed Sophie. "Come in, Gem. Cup of tea?"

"No, it's ok, I can't stop love, I've got to go to work in a bit."

Her next door neighbour of many years wandered in and sat down next to Rosie.

"Hi Rosie," Gemma gave her quick smile and a brief hug. Rosie wriggled away but, seizing the opportunity of there now being a different person in the house to get her what she wanted, started pointing to the chocolate tin. "Choc-choc?" she said hopefully.

"Quick, talk to me about something! Don't answer her!" warned Sophie with a frown.

"Okay," agreed Gemma grinning. Sophie was always grateful that Gemma was one of the people that she didn't have to explain things to. Having lived next door for so long and seeing Rosie grow up, she knew how to handle Rosie better than most.

"Well, what are you doing home anyway? Thought you were at work today?"

With a sigh, Sophie relayed the events of the previous day to her concerned friend. Why did it always sound worse when you told someone else? She thought. Surely Rosie wasn't that bad really?

Gemma, head on one side, squeezed her hand.

"So, how's Diana?"

"Oh, Mum's fine, just a bit shaken up. I think she'll have quite a bruise though. Actually I'd better ring her in a bit. The problem is I don't think she'll be looking after Rosie again and I'm not sure what I'm going to do for childcare now really. I'm going to ring the school later and see if they know of any specialist childminders or something." Sophie put her head in her hands.

Gemma sighed, "Tough times eh, love?"

"The worst, Gem. I just don't know what to do next."

"God, wish I could help. I think you're just going to have to go day by day and see what happens. You've had rough times before though, Soph and she's got better. Remember a few months back?"

"I don't know. I think this is probably the worst it's been." Sophie felt the tears coming. "Anyway, enough about my sad life, it depresses me just hearing myself talk about it. What about you? Where's your kids and did you want anything in particular, my dear neighbour?"

"Well, the kids are at their dad's for a few days, probably being indoctrinated by the beautiful Helen," Gemma swept her hair back dramatically in the style of her ex-husband's wife.

Sophie couldn't help laughing at this. There was certainly no love lost between Gemma and her children's stepmother. Helen was a catalogue model blessed with a body that had never had to endure the agony of childbirth and didn't she know it. She could never be seen without a face full of make-up and the latest designer clothes. The trouble was she tried just a little bit

29

too hard and ended up looking like a parody of every wannabe supermodel. Sophie and Gemma's favourite pastime, after a glass of wine, was sniggering over the many pictures Helen had plastered on Facebook.

"Actually, I'm praying for rain tomorrow." Gemma grinned wickedly. "Alex has a football match and, as she is still trying to be absolutely the *best* step mum in the world, she'll be forced to stand on the side line with wet hair cheering him on. *And* if God really does love me, she'll be wearing heels which will sink slowly into the mud. I told Jess if she looks really bad to take a sneaky photo on her phone."

Sophie almost choked on her tea.

"Gem, you're terrible. There won't be a place in heaven for you!"

"Yeah well, she shouldn't go round pinching other people's husbands then," she scowled. "Anyway, I think my place in heaven may have been lost quite a few years ago. If indeed I ever had one in the first place."

Despite the jokes, only Sophie knew how devastated Gemma had been when her marriage had ended with a bang some years back. A weekend with the boys for her husband, Joe, had turned out to be the start of a life with a girl almost half his age. The day he had finally left was not long after Rosie's diagnosis. That morning, Sophie, who had been busy having a weep herself, had spotted Gemma from her bedroom window. She had been sitting in the garden with tears streaming down her face, unable to move but still clutching a basket of washing. From that day on, the two women, who until then had only really exchanged pleasantries, had been united in their different versions of grief.

Gemma's oldest, Jess, was the same age as Rosie and, if it had been anyone else, Sophie would have hated her for having a 'normal' daughter, passing all the milestones that Rosie should be flying through. But Gemma was Gemma and, although Sophie could be a tiny bit jealous at times, she could never hate her.

"Anyway, I came round to see if you fancied nipping out for a few drinks at the weekend?" Gemma asked smiling. "It's karaoke at the Queen's and that's always a laugh. Might even be some lovely men to look at, you never know…"

Sophie grinned. "Lovely men at the Queen's? Are you mad? No, sorry I can't mate. I just daren't leave Rosie with anyone at the moment."

"Aw mate…" Gemma's put her arm around Sophie's shoulders. "You sure, you can't persuade your mum to let you out for an hour? Rosie might be better in a few days."

"Really, I can't, Gem. You didn't see how upset she was yesterday. I don't want to go through that again."

"Oh, all right then, honey," Gemma reassured her, "we can do it another time. Though of course, you do realise you could be missing out on meeting the man of your dreams!"

"I repeat, Gem, *at the Queen's? Are you mad?* Anyway, he doesn't exist. The only men I meet live in my nightmares."

Gemma laughed, "Right I'd better get back and get ready for work. It's really busy this week with all the kids off school and being dragged in for their holiday trims. I just hope none of them have got nits this time!" She got up and gave Sophie a hug. "I'm sure it'll all be fine you know. It's probably just another one of her sensory phases; this time next week she could be different again."

Sophie smiled at her friend. She always tried to make it better and she loved her for that.

"I'll pop in tomorrow and see how things are, love, ok?"

"Cheers, Gem."

And she was gone.

Chloe sauntered down and sat down at the table next to giggling Rosie.

"Cup of tea?" asked Sophie, as she got up to flick the kettle back on.

"Yes please, Mum. Is it okay if I meet Megan and the others in town today?"

"Of course. Why wouldn't it be?"

"Well, I just wondered if you needed me to hang round here after Rosie kicked off yesterday."

Sophie gave her a reassuring smile; just like Chloe to worry about her. "No it's fine love. You go and enjoy yourself with your friends; I can cope here. Rosie and me will have a much needed chilled day won't we, darling?" Rosie grinned at her with her marmite covered mouth.

The worried look fell from Chloe's face and she beamed. "Cool. I'll just have some brekkie then I'll go and get ready."

As soon as Rosie had finished her toast, she made a dash for her bedroom. Sophie, wanting a quiet day, decided to finish her tea and leave her up there for a while before she began the daily battle of the tooth and hairbrush. After all, there was nowhere she needed to be or anyone she needed to see.

For a while, she enjoyed sitting there listening to her oldest daughter chatting about her friends; who was going out with who, who was in trouble at school etc etc. God, life was so simple when you were a teenager, Sophie thought with a pang back to when she was that age. It was a damn good job you didn't know what was in store for you when you were that age. If you did you'd never bother getting up after your sixteenth birthday.

Suddenly, she heard Rosie running downstairs and a moment later she exploded into the room with the force of a tornado. Rosie threw her arms around Sophie, put her face close to hers and started her daily chant.

"Choc-choc."

Sophie just smiled.

"Choc-choc."

Sophie did *not* want to say the word 'no' so she smiled and hugged her tightly trying to ignore it.

"Choc-choc."

She tried to change the subject. "Shall we get a book, Rosie?"

"Choc-choc." Nose to nose, Rosie looked intently at Sophie.

"Choc-choc." More urgently now.

On and on and on.

Finally, feeling defeated, Sophie tried to make her voice into a sing song, sometimes it could defuse the situation. "Finished, Rosie. Choc-choc finished."

Suddenly, her face contorted with rage, Rosie gripped Sophie's hair and pulled. A familiar growling noise burst from Rosie's mouth as she went to bite her. Not believing it was possible to be this frightened of what your twelve year old child could do to you, Sophie pulled away and screamed loudly, "No!"

Chloe managed to grab her arms while Sophie shrieked, "Upstairs now!"

Now sobbing, clearly not understanding what she could have done wrong, Rosie thundered up the stairs to her room, slamming the door loudly behind her.

"You okay, Mum?" Chloe asked quietly, "Did she get you?"

Sophie rubbed her arms where Rosie's nails had dug in to her skin. Blinking back tears she smiled at Chloe, trying to reassure her.

"Not really, love. I've had worse. Come on, go and get ready to meet your friends while I wash up."

"Are you sure?"

"Yes!" Sophie said, a little more sharply than she meant to. The stress was getting to her already and it wasn't even lunch time. Immediately sorry for snapping, she hugged her daughter tightly. "Sorry, sweetheart, I'm just tired. I want you to go out and have fun, okay?"

Chloe smiled sadly, "Well, it's only town, but I'll try."

She ran upstairs, while Sophie started on clearing up the kitchen. Plunging her hands into the washing up bowl, her eyes travelled to the pictures on her fridge. One of her favourites was the one in the centre, of Chloe with her arms round a grinning Rosie on the beach. Sophie remembered exactly when it had been taken. They had been on holiday in Norfolk quite a few years ago and it had been one of the hottest days they had had that year. Rosie had been in a great mood as she had just finished a huge ice cream and Chloe had built a beautiful sandcastle, covered in delicate shells, which she had been so proud of. Funny thing was, there must have been difficult moments on that holiday. Nothing was ever problem free where Rosie was concerned, but they would pale into insignificance next to what she had to face now. Sophie tried to stop herself wishing her daughters were both small again as that was the sure way to end up in tears. Again.

A few minutes later, a loud shriek, followed by sobs brought her back to the present.

Sophie ran up the stairs two at a time. Chloe was standing at the top, shaking and crying.

"She hit me, Mum. I thought I could get her dressed, to save you a job, but she just went mad. She kept hitting me and wouldn't let go. I just had to run away from her."

"Oh, Chloe… She probably thought she was going to school when you mentioned getting dressed." Sophie took her older daughter's face in her hands and looked sadly at the big red mark there. She noticed there were also scratch marks on her arms.

"Oh God. Where is she now?"

"In… her… room," Chloe managed to get out between sobs.

As she tried to move away to make sure Rosie was ok, Chloe continued to grip Sophie.

"Mum… I don't… want to… hate her but… "

"I know, darling, it's hard. Look, let me just check on her, ok?"

Leaving her crying on the landing, Sophie swung open the door to Rosie's bedroom. The sight that met her eyes sent panic through her entire body; she felt as if she could actually hear her heart beating.

Her younger daughter had managed to pull down the curtain rail and was now standing sobbing on the window sill, banging on the glass and tearing at her hair in frustration. When she turned and saw Sophie, she started to spit too. Terrified that the glass would not be strong enough to withstand all the pounding, Sophie trying desperately to remain calm, attempted to coax her down. Rosie took no notice, but carried on, battering the window with increasing force. Meanwhile, Sophie could hear Chloe still crying.

"Rosie, stop it! Get down now!" Sophie couldn't stop herself screaming now.

It was no good. Rosie, totally oblivious to the terrifying risk she was taking, fuelled by the anger at not getting what she craved, continued to alternate between spitting across the room and hammering on the window with increasing force. Watching in horror as the glass vibrated, no more words would come out of Sophie's mouth. Sheer terror rendered her immobile as her frantic mind pictured the possible horrible end to this situation in chilling detail. Rosie, her baby, sprawled on the hard concrete below amidst a mass of shards of glass, blood seeping from her lifeless body.

Mercifully, after what seemed like hours, but was, in fact, only a few minutes, Rosie finally jumped back on to the carpet, deciding that pulling the books off her shelf and throwing them across the room might be a better way to get what she wanted.

Tidal waves of relief coursing through her, Sophie slumped down on to her Rosie's bed. Rosie, with cheeks still wet from crying, sat down next to her.

"Choc-choc," she said hopefully.

Sophie smiled through her tears and realised that the final straw had just been reached.

"Okay, Rosie," she sighed, "choc-choc."

***

By lunchtime, Rosie was sitting happily in her room; still in her pyjamas, hair not brushed, teeth not brushed and chocolate plastered round her face from the biggest bar that could be found in the house. She was flicking through her books making the usual loud repetitive sounds. Meanwhile, at Sophie's insistence, a calmer Chloe was on her way to town.

Sophie sat quietly in the living room. She looked down at her arms. The bruises on them were of varying ages. Some yellow, some blue. Some pinch size, some huge. The bite marks further up were perhaps more vile looking. She thought of Chloe vigorously rubbing copious amounts of foundation on to her face to cover the marks from this morning. She imagined how her mum's face would be looking now. She remembered the terror she'd felt just a few hours ago seeing Rosie perched on the window sill, her face full of rage, mouth twisted and eyes flashing.

Sophie made the most difficult decision she would ever have to make in her life. One that had been coming for a long time.

She picked up the phone and dialled the number on her lap.

Keeping her voice calm and trying desperately not to cry, Sophie asked for Jane. When she eventually came on to the line, Sophie spoke steadily and clearly, so that there could be no misunderstanding.

"You need to come and get my daughter. She's not safe anymore."

5

The next few days went by in a blur.

Once she had made the phone call, everything seemed to move quickly. Her social worker arranged to see her and called an emergency meeting with all the key people in Rosie's life.

Before she could focus on anything though, Sophie needed to go into work and explain that she would need some time off to sort things out. It wasn't a conversation that she was looking forward to. Her manager, Caroline, could be quite sharp and had been known to sigh fairly loudly and impatiently when presented with any kind of difficult situation. Sophie was worried that one wrong word from anyone at the moment could send her over the edge. After all, she was already standing on the precipice. By the end of the morning she could possibly be either on the floor in floods of tears or have ended up punching her manager and having no job anyway.

Walking into the hospital but not actually going to work made Sophie feel more of an outsider than ever. The hustle and bustle was the same, yet she wasn't part of it. The feeling was one she was getting used to though, her world was a place most people would never glimpse.

In the end, the meeting had been fine and it turned out that Caroline was more sympathetic than she had given her credit for. Her manager's face had worn a fairly sympathetic expression as she had listened patiently and agreed that Sophie could have as long as she needed. She left the office feeling that at least work was one thing she wouldn't have to worry about.

Sophie had intended to see Caroline quickly, then head out of the door as soon as possible. After all, she had left Rosie with Gemma, who'd bravely volunteered to look after her for an hour. Sophie had instructed her to give Rosie anything she wanted. She didn't want any more battles and anyone else getting hurt. She felt guilty enough about everything anyway. The trouble was as she walked down the corridor, she bumped into Anna who dragged her into the staffroom for a coffee. If it had been anyone else Sophie would have refused, but she'd worked with Anna for years and even though her life was completely different to her friend's, Sophie knew she cared.

For a while it was just the two of them so Sophie managed to explain the events of the last couple of days. She felt sorry for Anna really, as clearly her friend of many years didn't quite know to say. Like most people, she just put her head on one side and interjected with the odd 'really?' or 'oh no'. Sophie was just grateful that at least she didn't try and give her any advice. There had certainly been enough of that over the years and it hadn't helped one bit.

Just as Sophie got up, about to leave, Mark came in. He smiled in surprise when he spotted her.

"Hey Sophie, good to see you. I'm getting a tea, want one?"

His friendliness made her feel guilty for the way she had been with him on the phone. Some sort of apology was obviously in order. As he filled the kettle, she dug her hands in her pockets and took a deep breath.

"No thanks, Mark, I've just had a coffee with Anna. Look… um… I think I owe you an apology for the way I was on the phone. Things haven't been great for a while and … well… actually they've now got incredibly bad, which I don't really want to go into. Anyway, I was probably a bit sharp with you the other day so… well… I'm sorry."

Mark turned to face her. "No… God, Sophie, there's absolutely no need to apologise. I'm so sorry for phoning you at home. I just didn't want you to think I was completely thoughtless." He grinned, "I'm really only the average amount for a male."

Sophie smiled, "Well, I think that's more than enough apologies for now, don't you?"

"Yeah, definitely." He was still smiling and Sophie couldn't help but think that sometimes it was worse when everyone was kind to you. What she really wanted to do was have a good rant at someone.

Anna glanced at her watch. "Sorry Soph, got to go." She hugged her friend tightly. "Now listen, I'll give you a ring to see how things are, okay? In the meantime, you know where I am if you need me."

Sophie sighed. Everyone meant well but no one could help her with this.

As Anna left, Sophie began to put her jacket on. She really needed to get back as she'd left Rosie long enough. World war three could have easily broken out by now and poor Gemma, as capable as she was, didn't deserve that. As she passed him to get to the door, Mark got up from the chair and placed his hand delicately on her arm.

"Hey Sophie, I know this might be the wrong time, but I wondered if you wanted to go for a coffee at some point - "

She didn't let him finish. Shrugging Mark's hand off angrily, Sophie whipped her body round to face him and only inches away from his face, she shrieked.

"Absolutely right this is totally the wrong time. Do you know what's going on in my life at the moment? Do you even have the slightest idea why I'm here? The last thing and I mean the *very last thing* on my mind is starting any kind of relationship."

"But I - "

"God. And to think I felt I had to apologise to you!"

Mark's smile had left his face now. "Actually, I was going to say *as friends*. I'm not completely stupid, you know. You just look…"

"What?!" she snapped, hovering by the door. "I know I look like hell!"

"No," he said softly, a slight frown on his face, "you just look like you could do with some looking after, that's all."

Probably true, she thought as she stormed out.

6

Now that work was no longer in the equation for the moment, Sophie knew she had to make the phone call she had been putting off and simply dreading.

Liam. The man who she had been married to for six years.

Liam had escaped to Ireland in the wake of the destruction of their marriage. In the years since, he had been a distant figure, very much in the background of anything that happened in her children's lives. In truth, Sophie couldn't really believe she had ever been married to him at all. Such a short amount of time really but in that time two amazing things had happened, Chloe and Rosie.

When he had fled so suddenly, it had left Sophie wondering if Liam would turn his back on them all forever. She had worried that his fury towards her would make him want to leave his past behind completely and start again.

To his credit he hadn't.

As well as contributing generously every month, Liam kept in regular contact with his girls. Most of the time Chloe went over to visit him, but a few times a year he would return to England to see Rosie. Sophie knew that he had struggled with Rosie's diagnosis which came shortly after he'd left. For Liam, it had all come out of the blue. In his mind, he had left behind a normal toddler and the next time he saw her she was autistic. Sophie now realised that the symptoms had been there for a long time, they just hadn't recognised them for what they were. She often wondered if they were both just too preoccupied with everything else which was going on at the time.

Sophie didn't really know much about his life over in Ireland, only the bits which Chloe told her about. For the girls' sake, when they saw each other during his short annual visits, they kept it civil and tried not to rake over the past. It was never easy though, Sophie knew that he still blamed her for the fact that he wasn't there, in the family home anymore and she was furious that he had gone so far away.

Chloe adored her dad and despite the distance, they had a good relationship really. She loved her dad in a way a child loves a distant enigmatic figure. He was her hero and she put him on an extremely high pedestal. Sophie tried to suppress the feelings of jealousy when she saw them together and see it as the positive thing it was. She knew it was so important for Chloe and Rosie to have two parents who loved them.

Sophie couldn't remember the last time she had talked to Liam. She tried to keep him updated, after all he was Rosie's dad, no matter how far away he was.

The phone rang quite a few times before it was picked up.

"Hello, Liam, it's Sophie."

"Sophie?" Liam sounded puzzled. She hardly ever rang him. More often they simply exchanged stilted texts. Everyone found it easier that way. She could hear the anxiety in his voice. "What is it? Is everything okay?"

"Not really… " Where would she start? How to sum up the agony of the last few months? "Thing is… "

"Are the girls okay?" His tone was a little more urgent now. She knew he felt as uncomfortable speaking to her as she did to him. She just had to get through this call. Sophie sighed and went through it all again. Listening to herself speak, she thought that if this was happening to someone else she would be feeling incredibly sorry for them at this point. Liam sounded shocked when she'd finished.

"God, that's awful!"

"Yep." Was all Sophie could say.

"How can you send her away? Are you sure you can't keep her at home?" His shock had been replaced with an accusatory tone that Sophie recognised from the past.

"Well if I could, don't you think I would be? How can you even ask that? Don't you know me at all?"

"I thought I did once… " His voice trailed off.

"Liam, I… " Sophie began, fighting back tears. Is this what everyone would think of her? That she had taken the easy option. Because if this is what easy felt like she would hate to see difficult. She was just so very tired of explaining everything over and over again.

"Look, can't you get some help or something? I mean I could pay if that's the problem. It just seems so extreme to send her away. For God's sake, she's our little girl… " Sophie could hear his voice beginning to crack.

"Liam, don't you think I have done absolutely everything? Do you really think I would do this if there was anything else?" Sophie felt herself getting defensive. How dare he? "It's alright for you over there with your problem free life. I mean, you're hardly here for God's sake and you don't have to deal with it every day. You just don't know how it's been the last few months."

"Well, we all know whose fault that is, don't we?" Sophie imagined his face screwed up in anger, hurling the words down the phone at her.

"If it makes you feel better to say nasty things to me, go ahead." Sophie hissed back unable to control herself anymore. "To be honest, you can't make me feel any worse that I do right now. I mean if you believe in Karma, then I'm certainly getting my share right now."

Sophie took a deep breath. What was the point in this?

"Look, Liam, let's just stop." She could hear his deep breaths on the other end. "Can you come over? It's just too hard doing this all on my own," Sophie braced herself for a refusal.

"Of course I'll come," he said quietly.

***

42

Later on that day the meeting with her social worker didn't do much to improve Sophie's mood. Even though Jane was nice enough, smiley and pretty with a lilting Welsh accent which made even the worst news sound like a song, she was young and childless. So despite her protestations that she completely understood what Sophie was going through, it stood to reason that the poor girl didn't have the faintest idea of the enormity of it all. When Jane tried to make sure that Sophie was 'absolutely sure about the decision she had made', Sophie felt like screaming back, "Well of course not! I've made the worst, crappiest decision of my life." Although she didn't actually scream, Sophie knew she was being extremely sharp with this poor young girl.

Tough.

Jane patiently explained that the emergency meeting had been scheduled for tomorrow with all the key people in Rosie's life; paediatrician, head teacher, social workers and so on to make the final decision about residential care. When it was over Jane would ring Sophie and let her know the outcome. She soon left carrying her big bag full of folders and paperwork containing all the details of people's lives. One of which was Rosie.

When had this happened? When had a group of people that she didn't know very well, some of whom she had never met, when did it happen that they would have such a huge say in the life of her little girl?

Sophie thought back again to when she had been holding her beautiful new baby in the hospital, happy beyond words. If someone had told her then that one day she would be waiting for a group of strangers to decide whether to send her little girl away before her thirteenth birthday, she may just have hit them with the nearest heavy object.

So now all Sophie had to do was wait for the final say.

How easy it was really to give your child away.

7

The call came the following afternoon as Sophie sat next to Chloe watching some mindless lunchtime telly. Rosie was upstairs furiously throwing heavy things around in her room after Sophie had dared to try to brush her hair. Sophie knew she should go and sort it out but she just didn't have the energy right now. What did it matter if there were yet more holes in the wall?

The call was short and sweet. The panel had all agreed. Apparently all the important people had decided that 'yes' Rosie could go and live somewhere else.

That was that then. Decision made. There were two possible homes for her to look around. Homes for Rosie without her family.

Sophie cried.

Chloe cried.

Rosie carried on destroying her room.

8

Sophie knew she was staring into space but she couldn't seem to move her eyes from the wall. It was only early afternoon but she felt absolutely shattered and had done since the life changing call came yesterday. Of course, the morning she'd had today hadn't helped much.

Sitting happily next to her was her Rosie. In her hand was the DVD remote control which she was using to flick the film back to her favourite part over and over again. Sophie turned to her and smiled as her daughter wriggled excitedly whenever she saw the dragon appear on the screen again. For a few precious moments Rosie was calm, so Sophie tried to savour it. Something she found increasingly hard to do as she was always waiting for the next meltdown which was usually just round the corner. What had it been like, she wondered to actually sit and relax with her? Sophie just couldn't remember.

Rosie had no idea what was happening. Or did she? Sophie had always thought that her daughter understood much more than people gave her credit for. In her heart she believed, that like many autistic people, Rosie was intelligent, it was just that she existed on a different plane to everyone else. For the first time in her life though, Sophie hoped to God Rosie was oblivious of the momentous events going on, because if she understood what was going to happen that would make it so much worse. What on earth would she think of her mum? Sending her away to live with strangers.

Looking at her now, giggling and clearly happy, no one would ever believe that this was a child that Sophie was finding so hard to control. However, if anyone had seen Rosie in the shop earlier they might have understood why Sophie was doing what she was doing.

***

It had been a stupid decision.

Sophie realised that now, however, this morning she had desperately needed milk, amongst other things, and was getting fed up of having to rely on other people to do her shopping. It felt as if she spent her whole time asking people for help of various kinds. Besides, her mind had reasoned, Rosie had actually seemed to be in a good mood and Sophie had by now perfected the art of shopping at high speed.

Acting quickly while the good mood lasted, she had given Rosie her phone to play on and quickly bundled her into the car. Even though it wasn't far, Sophie had thought driving would be a better idea. Rosie had always loved the car and for the last few days, Sophie had tried anything to keep her unpredictable daughter happy, even if it meant indulging her. She just couldn't face another episode like the one a few days ago.

Anyway, everything had been manageable – nothing apart from a few moans and shouts - until they had got to the checkout and Rosie had spotted the chocolate. The usual mantra of 'choc-choc' had begun and with a sinking feeling that didn't stop at her stomach but went right down to her legs, Sophie had suddenly recognised that she was on a very short time limit.

She had hastily taken a bar off the shelf and given it to Rosie. However, her anxious daughter was in such a state that this didn't seem to appease her this time. In a few minutes, Rosie had managed to wind herself up completely and had started whimpering and crying with increasing volume while frantically pulling at Sophie's jacket. Realising that Rosie didn't really know what she wanted except that she definitely wanted to get out of the shop now, Sophie had looked anxiously at all her much needed shopping that was now on the conveyor belt about to go through the till.

Nervously, she had weighed it up. Could she keep Rosie under control for the few minutes it took for her to pay for the shopping or should she leave now? The woman on the checkout had been fairly quick with other people in front of her, so Sophie had decided she could probably wait.

It turned out she had made the wrong decision.

Rosie had begun jumping up and down and shouting loudly, as if she simply couldn't control the anger she felt just being inside the shop. Her face had become contorted with increasing rage and she was pulling at her own hair. Everyone in the vicinity had started to stare, something which Sophie had got used to over the years but it didn't stop it feeling horrible. She had just wanted to shrink into a corner and let somebody else take over for once.

An old woman behind Sophie had started to tut and had made a face at the checkout operator as if to say 'why can't she control her child?' Sophie had felt the tears, of frustration more than anything else, begin to fall around the time that Rosie had begun to spit. Unfortunately, it hadn't just been directed at Sophie, it was at anyone around her, including the charming old lady behind.

If this had been happening to anyone other than her, Sophie might have stifled a giggle at the lady's look of utter shock, when a globule of saliva had landed on her furious face.

"Well that's just disgusting!" she had shrieked, wiping her hairy chin with a tissue. "What on earth is wrong with that child?"

While trying desperately to keep Rosie's flailing arms down before they could scratch her face again or indeed anyone else's, Sophie had spun round to face the angry woman, feeling that familiar anger rising, "Actually," she hissed, "my daughter is autistic and she can't help it!"

"Well, maybe you shouldn't bring her out in public then!" the woman had snapped back, picking her basket up and joining another queue.

Feeling like someone had hit her with a brick, Sophie had just stood in shock for a moment. Sod the milk, sod everything. She had decided that she needed to get out of there immediately.

"Sorry I –" she had begun to say. But when she had suddenly caught a glimpse of the old woman scowling and whispering to others in the nearby queue, Sophie had given up and just dragged a howling, spitting furious Rosie outside. To anyone else it had probably looked as if Sophie was fighting off a violent teenager rather than trying to get her daughter into the car. By the time Rosie had been belted back in, Sophie had a new collection of scratches on her face, red marks on her arms and spit all over her face.

While Rosie had continued to kick the back of Sophie's seat, still trying to grab her hair in a screaming rage, Sophie had simply put her head down on the steering wheel and wept.

Again.

***

At long last, when it had been safe to drive, Sophie had made it home. Once through the door, placated with crisps and her favourite DVD, Rosie had calmed down. She was now a completely different child.

Sophie picked up the phone and rang Gemma. She desperately needed someone to talk to. Although Chloe was only upstairs finishing off the last few bits of her half term homework, Sophie didn't want to burden her anymore with it all. The truth was that she was worried about her oldest daughter. Since she had made the decision, everyone had been fussing over Sophie. Her mum had been constantly ringing, Gemma had been regularly popping in and even Anna from work had been true to her word and called to check on her.

But what about Chloe?

She had been extremely quiet and whenever Sophie had tried to talk to her about the decision, Chloe had simply gone to do something else. It just wasn't like her. She had always been an open book and had always told Sophie that she 'could tell her anything.'

Sophie was snapped out of her trance when there was a knock at the door. A few moments later her friend let herself in.

"Hey Soph, you okay?" Gemma came over and gave her a hug.

"Not really."

"Right, let me make us a cuppa and get you a few tissues because I can see you need a good cry, honey."

After Gemma made the much needed tea, Sophie gave a sobbing explanation of her awful morning. Her friend listened with a pained expression on her face. Sophie knew that Gemma understood how she felt more than anyone else but she still probably hadn't a clue what to say because there wasn't anything anyone could say really. This was just Sophie's life and that was it.

She slumped in her chair. "Oh, Gem, I feel so old and such a bloody failure."

"Thing is, Soph, this is why you've made the right decision. At the moment it's like you're a prisoner and can't go anywhere with Rosie, just in case she kicks off. Look at how awful you're feeling now after a simple trip to the shops. God, and it's not as she just kicks off outside, it's here too. Look at your arms and your poor face." Gemma held her hand.

"But it's my baby," Sophie managed to get out through tears. "I'm sending my baby away. It's not right; she should be here with me so I can look after her." Her face crumpled and a feeling of complete despair took over. "I just can't stand it Gemma, I just can't!"

"I know, mate." Gemma put her arm round her and pulled her close. "It's just crap."

Sophie looked at her friend. "What if it was your Jess? Could you do it?"

Gemma stared back and was silent for a moment. Sophie could tell she was searching for the right thing to say. "Do you know what? To be honest, I just don't know. You're right it's horrible and I can't imagine being in your place right now." She sighed. "All I can say is that it wouldn't be me I'd probably be thinking of first, it would be Chloe. I think you need to do it for Chloe. That girl is a saint, but she really should be worrying about other things at her age and not her mum being so upset all the time. At least this way you're going to be able to find a good place for Rosie to be where you can see her lots. You'll be able to spend time with Chloe too, take her out and do normal stuff. And actually you know this might be what Rosie needs too. God, you've told me so often that autistic children need routine, haven't you? Well, you just can't give her that here with your shifts and everything else, can you? Really, if I'm honest, and I know I'm not an expert or anything, but I don't think you really have a choice anymore, do you?"

Sophie leaned back on the sofa and stared at the ceiling. She knew Gemma was right. Everything she and her mum said made sense. She couldn't go on like this; she was no good to anyone. Crying all the time; not able to go out like normal people. It wasn't as if anyone could say things would get better soon. If Sophie thought anything was going to change, for the sake of her little girl, she would put up with all these problems in a heartbeat. The truth was, as Rosie got bigger and stronger, everything was more than likely going to get worse. Sophie never thought she would find herself in this position. Whenever anyone had raised the idea of residential care over the last few years, she had immediately silenced them, knowing that she would never ever send her daughter away. That was before all the recent horrors that life had thrown at her.

"Where is Chloe anyway?" asked Gemma.

"Upstairs doing her homework before she goes to Megan's." Sophie frowned, "I'm a bit worried about her actually. She's been really quiet since I phoned the social worker and she seems to want to be anywhere else but here. What if she hates me for what I'm doing? I mean it is her sister after all. I've tried to explain loads of times but I'm not sure she thinks I'm doing the right thing."

"Aw Sophie, she has been living here too, you know. Of course she understands. I bet she's just gutted like you. She's bound to be, love. Look, just give her lots of hugs. She loves you and she knows you wouldn't do anything like this lightly." Gemma took a gulp of her tea. "Have you spoken to Liam?"

Sophie groaned. "Yep, I rang to tell him everything and he hates me even more now. I think he's got it into his head that I'm more of a heartless bitch than he gave me credit for."

"Oh, Soph. Is he coming over?"

"Yeah, as soon as he can." Sophie wiped her eyes. "For God's sake talk to me about something else, Gemma, I feel like I've been crying for ever."

"Are you sure you want to just chat? Everything in my life seems a bit insignificant to what you're going through."

"Yes, definitely."

"We – ell," Gemma smiled.

"I know that look, Gemma Philips. It's a man, isn't it?"

Gemma chuckled, "Well, I might've been talking to a guy online…"

Sophie groaned, "Oh no, I thought you weren't going to do that again after that other one. What was his name again?"

"Oh yeah, Steve. I know, I don't think I'll ever forget that one. I mean, there's just not that many people these days with an interest in taxidermy, is there? I still get nightmares when I remember his spare room." Gemma shuddered. "Come to think of it, there really have been a fair few frogs in the last few years, haven't there? Anyway, I know I said I wouldn't do it again and I really wasn't going to bother but then this guy popped up and he was pretty good looking and well, actually he doesn't seem too bad. I mean. I definitely don't think he's a psycho or anything like that. Anyway, I'm considering meeting him, just for a coffee or something."

Sophie noticed the glint in Gemma's eyes as she talked about him.

"Ok, Gem, give me some details then. What's his name and what does he do? You know what we said - something useful this time - builder, joiner, gas engineer… "

"Well, his name's Bob… " Gemma began.

Sophie frowned. He sounded about a hundred years old.

"I know," Gemma agreed, laughing, "not great… but it's obviously short for Robert, so I'm thinking I could call him Rob. Think he'd mind? Hey, get this though, drumroll please… he's an electrician."

"Bingo!"

"Yep. He's also got two kids, owns his own home and looks a little bit like Gerard Butler. Could be a keeper."

For a brief minute, Sophie laughed. Then she remembered what was happening and stopped. How could she be laughing at a time like this? Tears were about to come again. God, hadn't they all been used up by now?

Gemma spotted it immediately. "Oh, Sophie, don't cry, I'll shut up now. You don't want to hear about my life."

The truth was Sophie did. She also wished it was her life, instead of this rubbish one that she was trying to wade through.

"When are you going to see him then?" she asked, blinking the salty drops away.

"In the week, I think, while the kids are at school."

"Well, let me know how it goes. I hope he's nice." Sophie really did. If anyone deserved to be happy it was Gemma.

Dates, normal stuff. Sophie couldn't imagine all that again.

***

When Gemma had gone, with a heavy heart Sophie picked up the phone. She made two appointments to see the homes that Jane had given her the information for.

How the hell was she going to choose where to send Rosie?

9

That evening, just as she was about to put Rosie to bed, a knock at the door brought Liam back into Sophie's life.

Ever since she had received the text from the airport to say that he was on his way, there had been a growing sick feeling in the pit of her stomach. The very last thing she needed was someone else saying all the terrible things to her that she was thinking of herself anyway.

When she opened the door, on the doorstep stood a very different Liam to the one she had last seen. Normally an epitome of the smart, professional surgeon that he was, this evening his hair was unkempt, his clothes dishevelled and it looked like he hadn't slept for a few days. In fact, Sophie thought it was probably like looking in a mirror for both of them.

"Come in," she said quietly.

Liam wandered into the hall and stood awkwardly by the stairs.

"So… er… do you want a cup of tea or something?" Sophie mumbled, not at all sure how to handle this situation.

"No, I don't want anything. I just… I need to… Can I spend some time with Rosie?"

"Of course, Liam, she's your daughter, you don't have to ask. She's upstairs with her books."

Sophie watched as Liam took his coat off quickly and trudged up the stairs to find her while she stayed downstairs clearing up the kitchen. She heard Liam's voice talking softly to Rosie and every now and then she heard them laughing. It was lovely to hear. Sophie felt a pang that things hadn't worked out between them and they hadn't brought the girls up together.

Would she be carrying that particular back pack full of guilt forever?

Eventually Liam reappeared. He walked slowly into the living room where Sophie was sat clutching a mug of tea. He slumped on the chair opposite and put his head in his hands.

"I just can't believe what's going to happen, Sophie." Looking up, he ran his hands through his hair and sighed. "She doesn't seem that bad at the moment. Is she really that difficult that you've got to put her in a home?"

Sophie felt the fury at being judged take hold. "Difficult doesn't even begin to describe it. You don't have the first clue about autism do you, Liam? This isn't how it is all the time. This is a good hour out of a whole day. A day when I'm constantly treading on eggshells, never knowing how she's going to be from one minute to the next. I've lost count of the amount of places that I can't take her to now." Sophie rolled her sleeves up. "This. This is what she's capable of." Sophie watched as Liam's face barely concealed his shock at the multitude of scratches and bruises on her arms. "You don't live with this every day like I do, so you just don't know."

"That wasn't my choice, Sophie, you know that!"

"You didn't have to run all the way to Ireland though, did you? I mean did you really have to put a sea between us?"

"Yes I did. You… you broke my heart, Soph."

"Yes," Sophie was screaming now and spat the words out. "I did! Not Chloe, not Rosie. It was me. Me! So why did you have to abandon them?"

Liam shouted back. "Don't you dare, Sophie. I never abandoned my children."

"Well, what else do you call moving miles away from them? Nothing would have made me leave the girls."

"Oh of course not, because you're a saint aren't you? Except you're not are you? Don't ever blame me for what happened, Sophie, you finished us. You."

Sophie was stung by the venom in his words. Was it all her fault? It hadn't felt like that at the time, so why did she always feel so guilty about the past?

Sophie began to sob. "Things might have been different if you'd been closer. We could have helped Rosie more… or found more help… maybe stopped the meltdowns or… "

She felt herself running out of energy for this stupid argument. It seemed so pointless to be raking over old ground when something so terrible was about to happen. Just then Sophie spotted tears running down Liam's cheeks. It was a sight that shocked her. She hadn't seen him cry like that since that one momentous day years ago.

"I do love them, Sophie. I love Rosie and Chloe so much."

She leaned back against the sofa and felt well and truly empty. "I know you do. Just… why couldn't you have run away somewhere closer? You're so far away and I've been struggling so long on my own."

Sophie closed her eyes and wished that she didn't have to face anything. Nothing. Anymore. She was about to lose her baby. She was having to justify herself to the man she had broken in two. Could she feel anymore guilty than she did right now? She doubted it.

Suddenly, she was aware of Liam's voice.

"Sophie, look, this isn't the time for all this. Let's just… " he sighed, "we need to think about Rosie."

"I know," she agreed quietly. Throwing insults at each other was just going to make everything worse. Sophie took a deep breath. "Look, we've got two homes to look at. Will you come and see them with me, Liam?" As she said the words she felt her face crumple. "I don't think I can't face it on my own."

"Yes."

Sophie noticed that his face was now completely awash with tears too.

10

Finally the worst half term ever was over.

On Monday morning, the girls returned to their respective schools; Chloe to the local secondary school and Rosie to a special school further away. Just as Sophie expected, as always, the first morning back was difficult. It was hard for Rosie to understand that, after a week of no real structure, this morning they were on a time limit and she had to do all the things she hated like getting dressed, brushing teeth and hair in a short space of time. Sophie delayed the process of getting her ready until Chloe had left to get the bus. Knowing it was going to be challenging, she put it off for as long as she could.

Sophie was right.

Rosie definitely didn't want to get dressed and once she heard the word 'school' she flew into an almighty rage.

The curtain pole was pulled down (again), Sophie was spat on (again), a clump of her hair was pulled out (again) and a multitude of heavy objects were thrown with the force of a child much older than Rosie (again). On examination later, Sophie noted a few more dents in an already pockmarked wall. Finally, Sophie was forced to shut Rosie in her room and hold the door while she exorcised the intense fury which she just could not communicate to Sophie in any other way.

Eventually, Rosie calmed down enough for her to be put into the taxi with her chaperone, Linda, who it had to be said these days, was starting to look quite nervous around Rosie. If it wasn't such a dire situation, Sophie would have found it quite comical how Linda would walk a few steps away from Rosie on the way to the car.

She breathed a sigh of relief when the taxi had left, though immediately felt intensely guilty. Wasn't she just passing on

Rosie's problems to someone else? She decided to ring the school and warn them that the morning had been difficult (again). To the school's credit they assured her that Rosie would be fine and they would cope with whatever Rosie threw at them today (literally).

Putting the phone down, Sophie wondered for the thousandth time *why couldn't she cope then?*

Clutching her second cup of tea, she took a moment to sit at the kitchen table and catch her breath after the challenging morning she'd had. Normally she would be rushing out the door soon after the girls, but not today. Sophie wasn't due back at work until the following week, not until after she had been on the visits.

The visits.

And it was the first one today. Sophie was absolutely dreading them. The thought of sending her little girl away was bad enough but what if they were both awful? She knew categorically that if she wasn't happy with them she would struggle on at home rather than send Rosie somewhere she would be miserable or badly treated.

Sophie looked again at the names of the homes on the piece of paper in front of her. Both of them had warm, welcoming names which she decided were obviously designed to make parents like her feel better about what these places actually were. Places for you to send your child to when you could no longer cope at home. When you had failed as a parent. When you had given up. When you had no energy left. Dumping grounds. Sophie couldn't stop the thoughts spiralling around her mind and as the tears fell they blurred the letters on the note so that she could no longer read them. Better that way.

Hearing the beep of a horn outside, Sophie finally heaved herself off the chair. Grabbing her coat and handbag, she slammed the door behind her and made her way to Liam's car which was waiting just in front of the house. Sophie realised that this was the first time she had been in a car with her ex-husband in years. It felt strange and the sense of impending doom of the day ahead didn't make it any easier.

Liam managed a half smile. "Hi."

"Hi." Sophie put her seatbelt on and concentrated on looking straight ahead.

"How were things this morning?" Liam asked as he pulled off.

"Oh the usual, you know, horrendous meltdowns, chaos, normal morning really."

Sophie realised that Liam probably couldn't think of an appropriate reply to that. The rest of the journey was spent in silence which was bearable for them both since they weren't in the car for that long. The first home was only about ten miles away which obviously would be much better for Sophie as she could visit as much as possible and she wouldn't feel that her little girl was too far away from her. She was hoping against hope she preferred this one.

Before long, a beautiful new sign with ornate letters welcomed them to Maple Grove. Sophie sighed as Liam put the handbrake on. "Here we are then."

She was surprised when he reached over and squeezed her hand, "It'll be okay, Sophie." She looked at him and managed a tight smile to show that she appreciated the gesture, though she severely doubted anything would be okay.

They got out and wandered up the driveway, neither quite knowing what to say. At first glance, Sophie was impressed with the setting. Although it was in a busy residential area of the town, the building was set back from the road and surrounded by plenty of grass, bushes and flowers. It really was very pretty. Sophie frowned and wondered what she should be looking at really. Should she have a checklist? The whole thing was just so surreal. She was here viewing a potential home for her daughter who was only twelve years old.

Unbelievable.

Perhaps she should just go for the feel of the place. Somewhere that Rosie could be happy. But she's happy with you a voice screamed inside her head. Sophie took a deep breath, she mustn't cry here.

The man who met them in reception introduced himself as Mr Finlay, manager of the home. By Sophie's calculation, he was probably around the forty years mark and was very smartly dressed in a sleek, grey suit with a silver tie. Clean shaven and emitting a rather pungent smell of after shave, he shook their hands briskly and whisked them off on a tour of the school and residential home.

Clearly, Mr Finlay was efficient and this attitude had fed down to the institution he was in charge of. Sophie noticed that everywhere was clean and tidy; you could almost say it shone like a new pin. In the school the classrooms were organised and busy with obviously very capable teachers.

The residential part of the building was quiet, as the children were obviously all at school, and Sophie was impressed with the layout of the place. The rooms for the children were spacious and brightly painted. It was visibly safe with all the appropriate doors, fire escapes etc. There was plenty to do with lots of toys (neatly stacked of course), technology, play areas etc etc.

All in all, there was nothing really that Sophie could say was actually wrong with the place.

The trouble was there were lots of little things.

It turned out Mr Finlay had a really annoying laugh and he seemed to insert this laugh every five minutes. She tried desperately not to focus on it but it was always there and it was starting to grate on her. She could tell Liam felt the same as they had exchanged a few weary glances during the tour. In addition, he grinned inanely and his voice had quite a patronising quality to it. He seemed to forget that he was not the only expert on autism on this particular tour. Sophie found herself gritting her teeth whenever he started to talk.

Sophie also noticed that the children, while they were obviously happy, seemed different somehow. They didn't appear to have the same needs as Rosie. They were higher functioning and not quite as extreme as her daughter. They all seemed to be co-operating with the staff without too many issues. Sophie was starting to wonder would Rosie really fit in here.

Or was she just finding excuses?

She breathed a sigh of relief when Mr Finlay said his goodbyes (Sophie felt well and truly dismissed) and the visit was finally over. As they got back in the car, she turned to Liam.

"What did you think?"

Liam rested his hands on the steering wheel for a minute. "Well… " he finally said, "… it was certainly clean and… er… well organised."

"That's true but didn't you feel it was a bit… well… a bit… " Looking again at the institution they had just left, Sophie searched for the right words, "a bit… soulless?"

"Now you've said that, yes, I can see what you mean." Liam groaned, "Oh and that Mr Finlay was pretty annoying too. I felt like telling him to shut up half way round."

Sophie thought back to the man's irritating manner. "I know. I really don't want to have to meet him every time I come to see her."

'Come to see her' saying the words suddenly made her feel cold. This was real. Soon Rosie wouldn't be living with her anymore and Sophie would be reduced to just visiting her own daughter. She turned to look at Liam and saw that he was gripping the wheel and staring out of the window with tears coursing down his cheeks. Stifling her own sobs, she reached for his hand. At that moment he turned, pulled Sophie to him and enclosed her in his arms. The closest they had been in years, they simply cried on each other's shoulders. Crying for their loss, for the future that would now be very different.

After a while, Liam silently turned back to the wheel and turned the engine on. No words were necessary. As he drove off, Sophie put her head in her hands. How could anyone bear being this sad?

11

The next morning Sophie woke up with a feeling of dread. She and Liam were going to have to do the whole visit thing all over again and she wasn't sure she could put a brave face on it for yet another day. Life felt relentless at the moment. Why couldn't she have normal problems, like getting the washing dry when it was teeming down with rain or fitting in a coffee with a friend when all the sheets needed to be changed? As she heaved her body out of bed, she hoped against hope that the place they were visiting today was going to be much better or she had no idea what would happen next.

Just as Sophie had dreaded, this morning was virtually a replay of Monday morning. Rosie really wasn't coping with the transition of returning to a routine of school in the morning and she was letting them know in the only way she knew how. The difference this morning was that Liam was here to witness the meltdown. He had wanted to see the girls as he was due to fly back to Ireland later that day and arrived just as Chloe flew out of the door.

As soon as Sophie started to try and get Rosie ready, the meltdown started. Sophie dealt with the fury as best as she could with some attempts from Liam to help. Sophie felt slightly sorry for him, he looked genuinely shocked as Rosie's rage took hold and he probably felt like he'd walked into a warzone.

They both breathed a sigh of relief when their daughter was safely deposited in the taxi.

"Oh my God," was all Liam could say as they both got in the car. "I see what you mean, Sophie. Is it always like that. Is she always that angry during a... a... meltdown?"

"Yes." It was all Sophie could get out of her exhausted body. She leaned back in the car seat, just glad that she wasn't having to drive as her similarly exhausted mind would really struggle to concentrate today.

The journey was a lot longer today and certainly much more difficult. Thorpe Cloud House was much further away at the end of a multitude of winding roads. It was in the heart of the Peak District, hence the name, so would obviously be much more difficult to get to. Sophie was trying to imagine what it would be like to do this drive every week when driving wasn't one of her strong points. She tried to stop her mind doing its usual tour of all the 'what ifs' and concentrate on the scenery, after all she didn't even know if the place would be suitable yet.

Sophie listened to Liam attempt to make more conversation with her today. He was certainly trying hard, so Sophie tried too. They talked mainly about Chloe since neither of them wanted to arrive at the home in tears having discussed what was happening to their beautiful Rosie. Sophie was impressed with how much Liam knew about what was going on in Chloe's life. She realised that they must text each other much more than she had given him credit for.

When they pulled up to the gates of Thorpe Cloud House Sophie saw that whereas the other home was in pretty surroundings, this building had a magnificent backdrop of hills and dry stone walls. Stunning really.

She soon realised that it really was true that you can get a feel for a place as soon as you walk in because that was exactly what happened at Thorpe Cloud House. The manager, Mr Brown, strode towards them with a warm smile and the first thing he said made the decision very easy for Sophie in the end.

"This must be an incredibly difficult day for you today, Mr and Mrs Reilly."

Sophie wanted to hug him immediately.

Throughout the tour, he empathised but didn't patronise. There was no annoying laugh, just a reassuring chuckle at times, intended to lighten the mood.

Sophie felt at home right away and she sensed that Liam did too.

It was friendly, busy and above all happy. Sophie got a sense of order without regimentation. The children she saw in the school were much more similar to Rosie this time; one was even in the middle of a meltdown which she noticed the staff were coping with well. Perhaps she could take some of them home with her? They were so calm, not like Sophie who couldn't help getting upset when Rosie flew into a rage.

Obviously the residential part of the home was quiet since all the children were in school. The rooms were similar in style to the other home but somehow felt different. Maybe it was the homely touches of photos of the children and their families on the walls. They all looked so happy in them.

Sophie couldn't help but comment on this to Mr Brown.

"Well, we try to provide a home from home here. You can bring things to make it like Rosie's room at home and put whatever you like on the walls."

He noticed Sophie's face fall at the thought of Rosie leaving her home and put a reassuring hand on her arm.

"We know that all of this is so hard for parents, so we try to make it as painless as we possibly can. She will be looked after here, you know."

"I know it's just so hard, I… " she felt the tears coming. "God, is everyone a wreck like me?" She tried to laugh but it stuck in her throat. She saw Liam visibly stiffen by the side of her and look down at his feet. Was he trying not to cry?

"Everyone feels the same you know, it's massive. Even the parents who only bring their children for respite care struggle to leave them. That's why I always carry tissues!" With that he produced a packet and handed one to Sophie. She smiled at this kind man.

"You know I don't want to do this don't you?" She desperately wanted him to understand that she wasn't just dumping her daughter when the going got tough. "I can't control her anymore. She's hurt me, she's hurt my other daughter, the house is a wreck, I can't leave her with anyone now, but I've got to work. I just don't know what to do next."

"Honestly, Mrs Reilly, no one here is judging you. We all realise that for you to have made this decision, it must come at the end of a long and extremely rocky road."

What a lovely, kind man.

Sophie also met a few of the staff and, while the ones she had encountered at Maple Grove had been polite but brusque, the people here were more friendly and seemed to understand some of what Sophie might be feeling.

"Do you know what, Sophie, I think this place is so much better than the one yesterday," Liam commented as they walked back to the car.

"I think you're right, Liam, my gut instinct is that this is the place."

He sighed, "I agree."

That was it then. If Rosie couldn't live at home then this was the best alternative possible for her.

And only the best was good enough for her baby.

12

A weird phase began.

It was a waiting period. They were all waiting for a place to be made available in Rosie's new home and, to all intents and purposes, everything was back to the normal routine. Liam went back to Ireland promising to come back as soon as he could, the kids were back at school and, after she had made the decision about the home, craving routine and something to stop the constant whirl of thoughts in her head, Sophie went back to work.

So everything was normal

Although actually nothing really was.

Every morning when Sophie woke up, she felt the weight of the decision she had made pressing down on her so that she could barely breathe. The rest of the day she would wander round thinking about Rosie and how she would soon be leaving her. When Rosie was near, Sophie found herself staring, watching her every movement, committing every feature to memory. What would it be like not seeing her every day?

Every time Rosie smiled or giggled and was back to her lovely Rosie, Sophie was desperate to pick up the phone and tell everyone involved that it had all been a big mistake and that actually Rosie would be staying at home after all.

But.

Every day there seemed to be a report of an incident at the school, either in the taxi on the way or in the classroom. Sophie wondered if everyone was scared of her daughter by now. She couldn't decide whether that thought was horrible or funny. She knew it should have made her feel better, when time and time again Rosie proved that she couldn't be controlled at home, but instead it just made her feel sad.

Every day she felt as if she was just treading water.

Of course while Sophie was barely existing, everyone else seemed to be getting on with their lives. Gemma in particular could hardly conceal the glow which emanated from her at the prospect of her budding relationship. Sophie knew her friend was trying hard to hide it but actually sometimes Sophie just wanted to listen to something normal, no matter how difficult it was to hear anything good at the moment.

After her third successful date, over a coffee one morning, Gemma had literally been bursting with excitement. Her usually so tough friend had dissolved into a teenage-like wreck.

Sophie smiled, "Come on then spill the beans, Gem. Is he the next Mr Gemma?"

Gemma laughed. "Not sure about that, Soph, but he is lovely. He's taken me to some really great restaurants and he, and before you say anything I know this sounds so cheesy, he treats me like a princess you know."

Sophie stuck a finger down her throat as if to be sick which made Gemma grin. "Not in a creepy way, you cow! He just does nice things. Like he holds the door, he says how beautiful I'm looking and he listens to me, you know. He doesn't just talk about himself he actually asks me things too. He's just really sweet and of course he's not too bad to look at either!"

Sophie tried not to feel jealous.

Gemma's face became serious, "Do you know what though? Part of me keeps thinking back to how Joe was and how brilliant it all was with him at the start. I thought he was perfect and we all know what happened there. I really like Bob but part of me can't relax completely. It's like I'm trying to find something wrong with him all the time. What if all men really are shits?"

Sophie grasped her friend's hands and looked at her solemnly. "There is something wrong with him, Gem… he's called Bob!"

They both giggled.

"Seriously though, Gem, try not to think too much about it. He might turn out to be a complete idiot, but why don't you just enjoy it for the moment. Stop looking too far forward. You're always telling me off for worrying too much, aren't you?"

Gemma visibly relaxed. "Yeah you're right. Well, we're going out again at the weekend – he's taking me to a show this time."

"Oooh get you – a show! Aren't you going up in the world? What is it?"

"It's 'Rock of Ages' in Nottingham. He likes rock music which is another tick. Not the crap that Joe used to listen to."

Gemma's eyes shone and Sophie could tell that she was smitten. She hoped against hope that this man was going to be good to her friend because then at least one of them could be happy.

***

Later that day, a phone call at work ended the 'weird waiting' period and sent Sophie into the depths.

It had been a busy shift. As usual, there were no beds to send the patients to, so recovery was starting to get crowded. Sophie and everyone else had been running around until they were ready to drop. Finally, after attaching her last drip, she was able to take a break. Before she escaped into the staff room for a much needed cup of tea, however, she dashed into the changing room to check her phone.

As she reached into the locker, Sophie found herself holding her breath. These days she never knew what message or voicemail would be there. Usually it was a voice detailing the latest terrible thing which Rosie had done. Sophie's heart sank yet again when she saw the symbol for voicemail. She sat down on the nearest seat and listened carefully.

"Hi Sophie, this is Jane. I'm just calling to let you know that there is now a place available at Thorpe Cloud House for Rosie.

If you can ring me back at a convenient time we can discuss a date when she can go."

Go.

Sophie felt her heart start to beat faster and suddenly her breathing became just a bit too quick. Her hands became clammy and she felt pins and needles starting to spread over the left side of her face. She had to get out of here. She stood up and despite waves of dizziness she managed to stumble over to the door. Anna burst in just as she reached for the handle.

"Hi Sophie – hey are you ok… you look a bit –"

Sophie pushed past her. She didn't want to see anyone. She didn't want to speak to anyone. She just wanted to get out. Be on her own. Be anywhere but here. Her baby was going and there was nothing she could do. Now the whole process had been set in motion, Sophie was starting to feel as if she had boarded a rollercoaster and things were moving too quickly. She could almost feel the force on her face as if she was really moving, removing her ability to breathe. She desperately wanted to scream, "Let me off!"

Pushing through the first door she came to, Sophie collapsed on a pile of linen. She drew her knees to her chest and clutched them tightly waiting to be able to breathe again. If she just sat here, in this little room, then nothing would happen; nothing would change. Time would stand still and Rosie would never have to leave her.

Sophie sobbed.

She didn't know how long she had been there when she became aware of a knocking sound, then a familiar voice.

"Hello? Is somebody in there? Are you ok?"

The door opened slowly and Mark's face appeared. When he saw it was her, he knelt down in front of her.

"God Sophie, I didn't realise it was you. I thought a patient had come in here. What's happened? Are you hurt?"

"No I - " She didn't really know what to say. She sighed. "Rosie's going," was all she could get out.

Mark looked confused. "Sorry, is Rosie your... "

"Daughter," Sophie finished slowly getting up and leaning on a shelf full of sheets. She realised how ridiculous she must look sitting on the floor in a crumpled heap. What was she thinking? God she needed to get a grip. "She's my younger daughter, the one with autism and she's... she's going into residential care."

"Oh Sophie, I'm so sorry." Concern replaced his confusion. "Have they... have they taken her away or something?"

"No!" Sophie shrieked and took a step forward hands clenched into fists. How dare he? "Is that what you think of me that I'm someone who's had to have her child taken away?" Would anyone ever understand? Sophie noticed Mark take a step back as if he was worried she was going to hit him or something. She took a deep breath and tried to calm down. "She's been violent... and has meltdowns... it's so hard... so I've asked for her to... oh God... I'm having to put her into a home."

"That's awful. I mean not awful that you're doing it, I mean awful that it's happening to you. Well it's just awful." Mark gave up and leaned against the door. Sophie studied him for a moment and suddenly felt sorry for this poor man who was clearly feeling at a loss as to what to say to her. He was certainly struggling to string sentences together that made any sense.

"Look," he tried again, "I don't know you very well but I'm guessing that you're a pretty good mum and if you've decided to do this then it's probably because you haven't got any other choice."

"But that's the problem, Mark, I have chosen it. I bloody well wish they had just taken her off me because the guilt is killing me." Sophie couldn't say anymore, the words just wouldn't come. The tears flowed easily enough though.

Sophie stood in front of him and let the tears run down her cheeks. It was as if suddenly she couldn't function anymore. She felt as if she had lost the ability to move, use her legs, arms anything. She was just aware of her heart racing and her breath not coming quickly enough. The room was spinning.

Gradually she became aware of arms pulling her forward and those same arms holding her tightly as her body rocked with each sob. The desperation and sadness of the last few weeks poured out of her until she felt as if her body was empty. Completely empty.

Sophie wasn't sure how long they stood like that, but at some point she realised he was gently guiding her out of the cupboard back to real life and into Caroline's office. As she sat in the chair, Mark by her side, one of his arms round her shoulders, she was told to take as much time off as she needed.

Sophie wondered, *how long do you need to say goodbye to your little girl?*

13

With the final date now settled, people had to be told.

Sophie sat down at the phone and worked through a short list as calmly as possible. Everyone was very kind and said all the right things. She tried to keep the conversations short and to the point. The call to Liam was the most difficult though thankfully very brief.

Finally, after much nagging from her mum, Sophie got round to a particular call she had not been looking forward to. Her older brother.

"Hello."

Oh great, Natalie.

That voice.

Sophie gritted her teeth. "Hi, it's Sophie."

"Oh, Sophie, how lovely to hear from you! How *are* things?"

Sophie wondered whether Natalie saved that particularly irritating voice just for her or if she used it with everyone. If that was the case it would explain her lack of friends.

"Fine. Can I speak to Andy?"

"So sorry Sophie, but he's out with the children at the moment."

Why didn't she call them kids like any normal person?

"Andrew always takes them to their swimming lessons on Saturday mornings."

God, it infuriated Sophie when her sister-in-law insisted on calling her brother *Andrew* all the time, he had always been Andy when they were growing up. Sophie absolutely refused to call him anything else and enjoyed the way it wound Natalie up.

Sophie knew she should have called her brother a while ago but as they had such separate lives now, he didn't immediately spring to mind when she was giving out information about her life. She loved him and she would always help him out if he needed her – he was her brother after all – but they had certainly never been close. Sophie had always felt that he had been the golden boy and it was so difficult having an older flawless sibling. After all, he was the one who had done well at school bagging a huge collection of GCSEs and A levels before moving on to triumph at a top university. Meanwhile, Sophie had felt barely average in comparison achieving just enough grades to get into nursing college. He'd simply never put a foot wrong as a teenager as opposed to Sophie's countless drunken episodes often resulting in her creeping in in the early hours of the morning. Since he had been married to Natalie, the gulf had widened considerably.

With the awful Natalie, Andy had embarked on the perfect life. They owned the perfect detached house with double driveway; they had perfect jobs, he a solicitor, she a legal clerk. Though of course when the children came along she had given it up so that she could *be there* for the *children*; and obviously they also had the perfect two children (of course one boy and one girl) with absolutely no sign of a disability. Gemma had nicknamed them 'The Smugs' after the one and only time she had met them at Sophie's house for Chloe's thirteenth birthday celebration.

Natalie had looked uncomfortable in Sophie's ex-council house. She had voiced her surprise that an ex-wife of a surgeon was living on the local estate but Sophie couldn't be bothered to explain how pride and guilt wouldn't allow her to take any more money from Liam than was strictly necessary. In fact, Natalie had looked down her nose at everything; the state of the local park, complete with fruity graffiti; the neighbours' untidy gardens; the local school which had only been deemed 'requires improvement' in the latest OFSTED. In particular, the lack of a husband in both Sophie and Gemma's lives seemed to be too much for her to comprehend in her textbook middle-class existence. Gemma's tales of online dating hadn't met with many laughs from Sophie's uptight sister-in-law. As Sophie remembered, Natalie and Andy had left well before the end of the party and hadn't come to the house since.

The last time they had all got together though, was when the frostiness had well and truly set in. About a year ago, Sophie had taken the girls over for Saskia's ninth birthday party, which of course was an all singing, all dancing affair. The downstairs was decorated fully with silver and gold balloons and banners, an entertainer had been booked and a civilised glass of wine was on offer to any parents who might be staying. Everything had been thought of.

Everything apart from an autistic child in the house.

Sophie tried to keep Rosie occupied and away from anything that could get damaged in this beautiful home. She wasn't interested in the magic tricks the entertainer was amazing the children with so, as it was a lovely day, Sophie managed to coax her out into the garden for a while. She could run around to her heart's content. After all, a few trampled flowers was preferable to a few broken expensive ornaments.

Everything had been fine however until Rosie had spotted the huge chocolate birthday cake. It had been made professionally (of course) and was proudly displayed in the middle of the buffet table for all to see, but no one to touch, until it was time for the candles.

The trouble was Rosie just could not understand why she couldn't have it there and then. And Natalie couldn't understand why Rosie couldn't understand. Sophie had tried not to laugh when she saw that every time Rosie had hovered near the cake, Natalie would sidle over and hiss a 'no' in her slightly hysterical hushed tone.

Unfortunately, Sophie didn't realise until too late exactly how wound up Natalie's constant nos were making Rosie. When their backs were turned for a moment, Rosie just simply decided to dive right in and help herself to a large chunk. Not only that, as she stuffed the cake as fast as she could into her mouth while running around the room, she dropped big pieces all over Natalie's pristine cream shag pile carpet. This had then promptly been trodden in by a multitude of nine year old feet which came running in from the garden when they spotted that Rosie had started the buffet. Excitedly, the other children tucked straight in too.

To her absolute horror, Natalie watched as her carefully constructed birthday celebration fell apart and her lounge floor resembled something you might see on an advert about specialist carpet cleaning detergent.

Sophie had never got the girls out of a house so fast.

Andy had tried to make her feel better, saying it didn't matter over and over. However, Sophie caught Natalie's death stare as they were going out of the door and knew it wouldn't be forgotten any time soon.

Ever since then Sophie had kept her distance and avoided Natalie productions like the plague.

Sophie realised that Natalie was still talking. "They're doing so well you know; Saskia has moved up to the higher swimmers session and Nathaniel has been asked to try out for the club!"

Sophie managed to stop herself from actually groaning. Instead she took a deep breath, the quicker she could say all this the better.

"That's great. Right, well the reason I'm calling is to let you know some bad news. I don't know how much Mum has told you about Rosie but well she's (deep breath) got to go into residential care and well… we've got a date now. So, anyway, I was thinking of having sort of a leaving party for her so that everyone can say goodbye. I mean we can go and visit her in the home but it's quite a way and I thought it would be nice if everyone could at least get together before she goes, especially her cousins. So, do you think you could tell Andy?"

"Of course I will, Sophie! Your mum did explain a little about the situation and we are all so sorry for you."

Sophie winced.

"I'll let Andrew know about your little gathering for Rosie and we'd definitely all like to come and see her. She's a very special girl."

Sophie was surprised. That was actually quite a thoughtful comment, maybe she had misjudged her sister-in-law.

"It must be awful for you all. Try to remember though, Sophie that at least now Rosie will be in a place with others like her and it means that you'll be able to have a normal life now. You'll be able to go out and enjoy yourself again. It'll be much better for you."

Feeling like someone had just poured ice-cold water all over her, Sophie very carefully and very definitely put the phone down.

14

"Shall I start taking the cling film off the food now, Mum?"

Sophie looked up as Chloe wandered into the kitchen. It was the day before Rosie was due to leave and even though she actually felt like crawling into her bed and staying there for ever, Sophie had thrown herself into organising the special get together. If nothing else it had stopped her thinking about what was happening tomorrow.

"I'd leave it for a bit, love. The sausage rolls are still cooking and everyone seems happy enough chatting at the moment."

"Ok. Oh by the way we put some music on for Rosie and she's jumping around to it with Nathaniel and Saskia!"

Sophie laughed. "I know, I can feel the floor shaking in here!"

The small house was loud and full. Sophie had invited everyone that she thought would want to see Rosie before she went. Gemma was in the lounge with her kids, Alex and Jess trying to keep Rosie amused. Her mum was bustling between rooms making sure that everyone had drinks. Anna and her husband, Paul, had popped in with a beautiful bunch of flowers for Sophie and chocolate for Rosie. Nicola, the lovely teaching assistant who had worked with Rosie for a few years when she had been at the local infant school, had kept in touch with Sophie and had asked to come as soon as Sophie had told her she was going away. Unfortunately for her though, she had been cornered by Natalie.

As usual, Natalie and Andy had been very prompt and turned up at the exact time Sophie had mentioned, with their beautifully presented children in tow. Sophie had been startled when Andy had given her a big hug and told her how sorry he was. He wasn't usually the hugging type so it had actually meant quite a lot. Natalie had done her European kissing on both cheeks and told her that she was thinking about her. Sophie managed to stop herself telling her to get lost or something worse.

After sitting uncomfortably for a while trying to make small talk, her generally quite brusque dad had disappeared into the garden where he felt more at home. Sophie knew he tried but her dad didn't really understand Rosie's condition. Ian was ex-army and dealt in black and white, right and wrong. Autism, she guessed, with all its shades of grey, was a little bit beyond his experience and he obviously didn't know what to say to Sophie these days. Instead he threw himself into helping with practical problems which he felt much more comfortable with.

"Well, let me know when you want me to tell everyone to get food," Chloe called as she ran back into the lounge.

"I will." Sophie was relieved that Chloe was being a bit more like her old self today. She seemed to be enjoying having everyone here. It had certainly lightened the mood in the house.

Just then Rosie bolted into the kitchen and made a dash for the garden. Obviously she had had her fill of crowds and was craving some space now. At least she was in a good mood, Sophie wouldn't be able to bear it if her leaving party descended into chaos. She didn't want everyone to remember Rosie like that.

Cradling her lukewarm tea, Sophie watched as Rosie trotted outside. As usual she had dispensed with her socks and was barefoot. She flapped her hands wildly as she made her way to her favourite place, the trampoline. It was probably a huge relief for her to be away from people for a few minutes. Her senses had clearly been completely overloaded.

"Oh my God!" hissed a familiar voice behind her. Gemma had a pained expression on her face. "No wonder you don't invite that awful woman round here very often. I think I may have to hide in here for a while!"

"Let me guess… Natalie?" laughed Sophie as she finally lifted the sausage rolls out of the oven.

"Yep! I could probably give you the full itinerary of their FABULOUS holiday to the South of France. If, that is, you were at all interested!! You should have seen my face, Soph, I had to plaster a smile and think of something else! Poor Nicola's with her now, I just couldn't stand anymore. Why, why, oh why did your brother marry her?"

"Hmm not really sure. To be fair, I don't remember her being that bad in the beginning. I think the more money my brother earns the worse she gets!"

"Who?" asked a breathless Chloe, appearing at the door.

"Oh, no one you know," Sophie shot a grin at Gemma. "Why are you so out of breath, love?"

"I've been dancing with the kids. Rosie's run off now though. I think it was 'cos Natalie tried to give her hug and she didn't like it."

Gemma stifled a giggle with a gulp of tea.

There was a knock at the door. Sophie idly wondered who that could be since everyone she had invited was already here.

"Just get that Gem, would you?" She said as she carefully put the hot sausage rolls on to a plate.

Sophie half listened to voices in the hall and the front door shutting. She couldn't have been more surprised by the figure that stood in the kitchen doorway seconds later.

"Liam!"

"Dad, you're here!"

Chloe ran over and threw her arms around his neck.

Feeling awkward, Sophie tried to smile. "I thought you couldn't get here until tomorrow, Liam."

He shrugged, "I know…I managed to rearrange things. It was an impulse thing. I just woke up yesterday morning, thought about what was happening and I just felt like I needed to see her. I managed to get an earlier flight so here I am. I didn't realise you were having a party."

Sophie felt her anger rising. Was he criticising her? "It's not a party or a celebration if that what's you think. We're not bloody happy that she's going." Sophie couldn't stop her voice becoming louder and sharper, "I just wanted to give everyone an opportunity to say goodbye!"

"Mum, stop it!" Chloe snapped. "I'm glad Dad's here!" Sophie looked in surprise at her normally so calm daughter.

Liam sighed, "Hey, it's ok, Sophie. I'm not getting at you – I know why you've done it. I'm sorry, I don't want us to argue today. This is Rosie's day."

"Right," Sophie took a deep breath, knowing he was right. "Well, she's in the garden at the moment. Why don't you go and play with her for a bit. I'll make a cup of tea when you come back in."

"I'll go with you, Dad."

Chloe tucked her arm in his and took him outside. Sophie watched as Liam and Chloe walked over to Rosie. She saw her dad look up in surprise when he spotted his ex-son-in-law and heard them exchange frosty pleasantries. Always completely on her side, her dad just couldn't forgive the ex-husband who had left his daughter and galloped off to Ireland, though of course he didn't know the whole story.

Rosie was happily sitting in the middle of the trampoline making her sounds and examining her hands. So far she had been fine, no outbursts and no meltdowns. Sophie had made sure that everything was about Rosie today to try and keep her calm. She could eat what she wanted, put her DVDs on, put her music on, go where she wanted. Anything to ensure that her last day with them was without any trauma.

Liam and Chloe climbed on and sat next to her. Rosie grinned and cocked her head when she saw them but then wriggled away when Liam tried to hug her. He settled for simply sitting next to her with Chloe on the other side. Sophie realised with a shock that it had been years since she had seen her husband and daughters in the same place all sitting together like that.

Her family.

For a few minutes Rosie was happy to let them invade her space and sat there tapping the side of the trampoline with a plastic cup she had found in the garden. Then, in true autistic style, she had had enough. She got up suddenly and ran on to the lawn; Chloe ran after her. It soon turned into a simple game where Chloe would run to Rosie, Rosie would giggle and run away shouting "No!"

After watching for a while, Liam came back in and sat down at the kitchen table.

"She seems happy today." He commented taking the tea which Sophie handed him.

"She does doesn't she?" Sophie smiled. "I'm just hoping it lasts. I think we're all holding our breaths in case she kicks off." She looked straight at her husband's green eyes. "Do you know I don't know which would be worst? For her to be in a great mood all day, so that I will then convince myself that I am doing totally the wrong thing and that after all I can cope with her at home. Or for her to have a huge meltdown in front of everyone. But then at least they would all understand why I've made this terrible decision." Sophie sighed, "Including you."

Liam frowned, his dark eyes fixed on her.

"I do understand, Sophie. And for what it's worth, even though it's way too late to say it, I am sorry I went so far away. I shouldn't have left you to cope on your own especially after the diagnosis." He studied the table. "I just couldn't be near you. I couldn't see you every day knowing that we wouldn't be together anymore."

"I know." Sophie said quietly.

"And," Liam leaned forward. "I know you're a brilliant mum and I'm damn sure you wouldn't have done this if there was any other way."

"Thank you," Sophie whispered.

"Didn't you ever feel like running away, Soph?" Liam asked," All these years you've managed Rosie on your own?"

"Only about a hundred times a day. And if it makes you feel better, I still do. Especially recently."

They sat in silence. Sophie looked at the man across from her and found it hard to believe they were ever married and shared a life. So much had happened it felt like a million years ago.

Liam smiled. Sophie remembered that in another life her heart used to race when he looked at her like that. Indeed he had been the catch of the hospital. With his heroic status as a dynamic young surgeon and slow, charming smile, he had always been half way there before he even opened his mouth. That smile had melted her heart. Now it just made her feel sad.

"It wasn't supposed to be like this was it?" he said sadly, reaching for her hand.

"Nope," she agreed, letting him take it for a minute, then slowly withdrawing it. She didn't want him to hold her hand now. It just didn't feel right anymore.

"Are you okay, Soph? You look so pale."

"Not really." She tried to stop herself crying in front of him. "I'm just so tired and I don't know, just so sad I suppose. I can't believe it's come to this really. I thought I could keep her at home safe with me for ever. It doesn't matter what you or anyone else says, I feel like a complete failure, if you must know."

"I'd better go," he whispered, slowly getting up.

"No, don't," Sophie urged him. "Stay for a while and be with your girls, especially Chloe. She's finding this tough you know. She never had a sister she could play with and now she's not even going to be living with her. She's trying not to show it but I know she's struggling."

"Okay."

"Oh and your mum might call in too. She'd probably like to see you." Sophie saw Liam wince. "Don't look like that. She's done her best to stay in contact with us all these years, despite everything."

Liam and his mum weren't close. As a pillar of the local Catholic Church, Mary had always been more interested in the lives of her fellow parishioners and her charities than her own family. It was true though, after their marriage had finished, Mary had made an effort to keep in touch with Sophie and the girls, even though she had never really forgiven Sophie for her only son fleeing to Ireland. Although she knew none of the details, she had made up her mind it was obviously all Sophie's fault. Sophie privately thought the rot had probably set in way before the divorce when she had put her foot down and refused to christen the children. Sophie wasn't Catholic herself and Liam was so lapsed he was almost horizontal, so she had argued that it made no sense at all to make them part of a church they would never go to. Mary, of course, had thought otherwise and had been quite vocal in her disapproval.

For the sake of the girls, though, Mary remained civil whenever they saw each other, which wasn't often. She didn't have the slightest clue about autism and often looked baffled at Rosie's often extreme behaviour. It would certainly never occur to her to offer to look after Rosie. Mary never forgot a birthday, though, and would always arrive armed with presents.

Liam got up with a sigh. "I'll go and find the girls."

The rest of the afternoon passed quite smoothly. Sophie was pleased to see that Rosie appeared to be having a good time. She certainly enjoyed the food which was everything that she liked. Lots of chocolate-based goodies and not too much healthy looking food – certainly no fruit or vegetables – which usually sent Rosie into a frenzy.

Sophie tried her best to stay in the moment and not let tomorrow enter her head. She moved from room to room, talking to different people; trying to keep busy. The only person she tried to avoid was Liam since there was always the danger that they may start arguing or crying if they talked too long. In fact, he spent most of the time either chatting to Chloe, who was thrilled to have her dad around for once, or talking to Paul, Anna's husband who, it turned out, was a fellow Derby fan.

Mary did call in. She arrived with a new outfit for Rosie and a large, obviously expensive, bouquet for Sophie. Although considerate, Sophie had to admit that she was starting to wonder why everyone seemed to think flowers were going to make everything better. Still, they were beautiful and the thought had been there. An extremely well turned out though uncomfortable looking Mary didn't stay for long. After a cup of tea, exchanging a few pleasantries with Diana, though in truth, there had never been much love lost between the two mums, an attempt at a one-sided conversation with Rosie and a short chat with her son, Mary left.

Ian stayed outside for most of the afternoon, just appearing for the odd cup of tea or sausage roll. Diana bustled about, doing most of the clearing up. Her mum was always happiest being busy. A few times, Sophie caught her gazing at Rosie, eyes glistening, a stark reminder that Sophie was not the only one who was going to feel the loss.

All the kids were getting on well. Gemma's son, Alex, and Sophie's nephew, Nathaniel, were similar ages and had played on the Wii for a while. Chloe had been like a mother hen to the younger girls, Jess, and Saskia, creating new hairstyles for the pair of them who, in turn, thought that it was wonderful that a cool sixteen year old was spending time with them. All the kids enjoyed being with Rosie and were as usual amazing with her. Sophie was always impressed at the amount of patience and empathy children showed to special needs kids if they were brought up with it like Chloe, Jess and Alex had been. Even Nathaniel and Saskia, who hadn't spent much time with their cousin in the past, were happy to play and dance with her. Rosie, for her part, glided in and out, joining in when she wanted to and disappearing when she had had enough. *If only life could be like that all the time*, Sophie thought sadly.

Sophie was sitting at the table, putting the latest bunch of flowers into a vase, when Liam wandered into the kitchen.

"Right, Sophie, I'm going to get going. Text me when you set off for the home tomorrow and I'll meet you there. Okay?"

Since Liam needed to leave earlier than Sophie tomorrow in order to catch the flight back to Ireland, they had arranged to travel separately to the home, Liam in his hire car and Sophie with Rosie and also Diana for moral support. Sophie didn't want to be rushed into leaving Rosie the same time as Liam, she needed to spend the whole day with her and make sure she was alright before she left. If in fact she was able to leave. Thinking about it now she wasn't sure how she was going to say goodbye.

"Okay," Sophie muttered, still busy with the flowers in front of her. Then to her complete surprise, Liam leaned down and kissed her cheek. She smelt the familiar after shave and the touch of his lips brought back a multitude of memories.

With that he was gone.

Sophie stayed at the kitchen table for a few minutes thinking. Even though they had been apart for years and hardly exchanged words during most of them, part of her still felt a connection with him. After all, he was the father of her beautiful children and nothing would ever change that. It felt right that they were getting on better at the moment as she knew he was feeling the loss of Rosie too.

All of a sudden, there was another knock at the front door. Sophie picked herself up and wandered past the still noisy lounge, to open it. Just when she didn't think this day could get any more surprising, there stood Mark at the door brandishing a big bunch of beautiful flowers.

Where the hell was she going to put all these damn flowers?

"Hi Sophie."

"Hi," was all she could get out. She hadn't seen him or spoken to him since the day in the cupboard. Not just because she was a little mortified that he witnessed her at probably her lowest moment, but also because the only thing she could focus on at the moment was Rosie going. Anyone or anything else just didn't come into the equation.

After a few seconds, she recovered from her shock. "Sorry... er... do you want to come in?"

"Ok, great, but don't worry I'm not stopping." He stepped into the hall and handed over the flowers.

"Wow, I'm going to be able to open a florist after this afternoon," Sophie smiled.

Catching sight of the many full vases, Mark laughed. "Oh, seems like everyone had the same idea then."

"No worries, a girl can't have too many flowers. It was really thoughtful of you."

"Anna told me you were having a sort of ... um... send off for... er..."

"Rosie," Sophie helped him.

"Yes, sorry, never been any good at names. Well, anyway, I just wanted you to know that I was thinking of you and how hard it must be for you. I mean I haven't got any children, so I suppose I can't really know how you're feeling. Just... I don't know... It's just so sad for you. And when you were upset in the cupboard... "

"God, I'm so sorry about that. I must have looked a complete mess," Sophie blushed. "Everything, you know, just... "

"Please, no don't say sorry, you didn't look a mess at all, you just looked so sad...I didn't really know what to say to you, to be honest. Anyway, I wanted to pop in today just to let you know, I'm here if you ever need a chat or a shoulder to cry on or anything."

Sophie opened her mouth to speak.

"*As friends!*" Mark added smiling.

Sophie smiled. "Thank you, you've been really kind and I appreciate your offer. Yep, definitely, next time I'm in a linen cupboard upset, you'll be the first person I call."

Mark grinned.

Sophie noticed for the first time what a lovely smile he had. In fact she studied his face and that wasn't the only nice thing about him. Her mind started to wander and she found herself studying his features. Sophie audibly gasped. What was she doing? Her daughter was going away tomorrow and she was thinking about a bloke she hardly knew. What was she doing? She found herself becoming furious with herself.

At that moment, Rosie ran down the stairs. Sophie gasped when she saw that Chloe, who had started to use it for her spots, had obviously left the top of the tub of Sudocrem and Rosie had found it. Her face, hands and hair were plastered with the white stuff.

"Oh no, Rosie!" Sophie abandoned a bewildered looking Mark, and followed a speeding Rosie who was now jumping all over the settee, leaving a white trail wherever she went. Sophie had to stifle a smile when she saw an extremely nervous looking Natalie back away, obviously terrified that her expensive clothes were about to take a battering.

Sophie managed to grab Rosie in a giggling bear hug trying to pretend it was a game so that she wouldn't kick off, just as Mark appeared in the room with a handful of kitchen roll.

"Will this help?

"Brilliant!" she cried. "Quick wipe her hands, but try and make it fast 'cos she won't like it!"

Sophie was very impressed when an efficient Mark managed to clean Rosie's hands in a few seconds, while Sophie sang to her and Chloe tried to make her laugh with silly faces.

Finally, when she didn't pose any further threat to the furniture or people around her, Sophie let an excited, though thankfully happy Rosie go. Glad to be free she ran back into the garden.

"Chloe, go and find the cream and put it away will you, hon?" Sophie sighed.

A sheepish Chloe trotted upstairs.

"Thanks, Mark," Sophie said gratefully.

Mark clumped the tissues together and put them in the bin. "Hey, no worries – knew that nursing training would come in handy sometime."

Sophie suddenly realised that she and Anna were the only ones who knew who this stranger was. "Sorry everyone, this is Mark from work. He just came by to save the day!"

Lots of hellos from the room followed. Sophie turned to a self-conscious looking Mark.

"Look, would you like a cup of tea or something?"

"No really, it's fine," he smiled and turned to go. "I've got to be somewhere, so I'll get off now."

"Okay, well, if you're sure. Thanks for stopping by and thanks so much for the lovely flowers." Sophie followed him to the door.

"You're welcome. I hope tomorrow isn't too bad and well… like I said… you know where I am."

"Yep, appreciate that, Mark, bye then,"

"Bye, Sophie."

As she closed the door, Sophie found herself wondering where he was going.

At the end of the afternoon, just like most gatherings, everyone seemed to collect in the kitchen. The lovely Natalie was now hovering by the stove describing her new extension to anyone who would listen to her. Poor Nicola seemed to be bearing the brunt of it again. Gemma, who was busy making tea, kept catching Sophie's eye and grimacing. Sophie couldn't work out if Natalie really wasn't aware how inappropriate it was to go on about her dreadful problems with builders on the day before Sophie was about to hand her daughter over to the care system, or if she just didn't care. She hoped it wasn't the latter because that would make her sister-in-law incredibly nasty. The only reason she didn't tell the woman to get out was that her children were having a lovely time with their cousins. Probably one of the few times they were allowed some unstructured play time.

Hearing a bang from the garden, Sophie looked out of the window and spotted her dad still furiously hammering. "Is Dad ok out there? He must be freezing! You know, he didn't have to fix it right now."

Sophie had only had to mention in passing that her gate wasn't shutting properly and her dad had gone straight out there to mend it.

Taking a break from the washing up, Diana joined her at the window. "He'll be fine, darling. Anyway you know what he's like, he can't sit still, he's happier doing. He just wanted to make sure that it was sorted ready for the winter. You need to be able to lock your gate at night or who knows what might happen."

Sophie privately thought that, as the worst thing had already happened to her, she was happy to take her chances. She said nothing though.

Just then Alex and Nathaniel came charging into the room.

"Is it ok if Nat and me go for a kick around in the garden, Sophie?" Alex asked busy putting his old, muddy trainers on.

"It's Nathaniel actually," Natalie cut in.

"Oh Mum, everyone at school calls me Nat now." Nathaniel looked embarrassed and once he'd pulled his immaculate trainers on, he couldn't get out of the door quickly enough.

"Great idea, lads. Have fun!" Sophie called after them.

"And be careful with those jeans, they were new last week. Don't get them too muddy!" Natalie called after them.

"Does your lad play much footie then?" Gemma asked Natalie, trying to be sociable.

"Oh yes, he's really sporty actually. Well they both are I suppose. Of course we make sure it doesn't distract them from their schoolwork though. Saskia's year five now and she'll be taking her SATs next year, so obviously we're trying to make sure she comes out with level fives and sixes. The trouble is I don't think she has the best teacher really. I mean we've had to go in a few times about homework and reading books. Do you know they didn't even have her on the right reading level?"

That was it. Sophie spun round and couldn't help shouting. "OH. MY. GOD!"

Gemma and Natalie both looked shocked at Sophie's outburst.

"Do you realise what today is? Do you have any idea whatsoever what we are all going through? There you are talking about sodding reading levels and SATs and bloody builders and God knows what other complete crap and my little girl is leaving home tomorrow! Not to go to university at eighteen like most kids, like your kids will. At twelve! Twelve years old! I've got to hand her over to people I don't know. Never mind sodding reading levels, I'd just like my little girl to be able to stay at home and talk to me! Tell me that she knows who I am…that she loves me…just…God…just tell me anything." With that Sophie collapsed on to the chair and tried to breathe.

Gemma put her arm round a shaking Sophie and a shocked Diana sat down in the chair next to her and grasped her daughter's hands.

"Sophie, sweetheart, are you okay love? Can I get you something?"

Natalie started getting her things together. "I think we'd better go. Sophie, I can see you're upset, but I'm not sure I deserved to be spoken to like that," she snapped. "Diana, do you know where Andrew is?"

Diana turned to her daughter-in-law, who if she were honest she'd always struggled to warm to, and tried to contain the anger she felt at Natalie's complete thoughtlessness.

"I think he's in the living room with Saskia and Jess on the Wii, Natalie. Look, love, it's been a very difficult day for Sophie. Don't rush off. Why don't you just go and find Andy and I'll make us all a cup of tea."

Muttering under her breath, Natalie disappeared out of the room. Sophie started to cry.

"Doesn't she realise how bloody lucky she is? I can't stand it, Mum, I can't stand it."

Diana, took her daughter in her arms, just like when she was a little girl and hugged her tightly. "I know, I know," she soothed as the sobs rocked her daughter's body. "Let's get cleared up and have a cup of tea, eh?"

For the next half an hour, with a cup of tea going cold in front of her, Sophie sat still and was dimly aware of people leaving and saying goodbye. She responded as best she could. As she heard the door click for the final time, she sighed with relief and looked out of the window.

Sophie rested her head in her hands and noticed that her dad had stopped working. Ian was now sitting on the bench near to the house and perched next to him was Rosie, who was busy shaking a play tambourine next to her ear. Sophie watched as Rosie looked closely into her grandpa's face and giggled. Smiling back at her, he ruffled her hair, not seeming to mind that it was covered in Sudocrem which was consequently all over his hands now.

Sophie watched as his smile slowly disappeared and a tear made its way down his cheek.

15

It was here, the morning she had been dreading. Sophie woke early, though she had tossed and turned so much during the night she felt like she hadn't slept at all. Rosie's last day…

Sophie was worried about the drive today. She wasn't sure she was in any condition to do it really so she was very glad that her mum had agreed to go with her. However, she knew the worst bit was going to be the journey back when Rosie wouldn't be with them. Leaving her there was going to be the most difficult thing Sophie had ever done.

She found Chloe sitting in the quiet kitchen on her own, with a piece of toast in front of her. Sophie had been surprised when she had decided not to go with them and go to school as usual. But then she had been very quiet since last night. As usual her organised daughter had got herself up early for school and was already dressed with her bag packed. Rosie, meanwhile, was still in her room looking at her books. Sophie made the usual cup of tea which would give her time to prepare herself for the onslaught of getting Rosie, fed, dressed, teeth brushed and ready to leave the house. At least Diana had agreed to come round to help, just in case there were any difficulties. Just in case I collapse in a heap of tears, Sophie privately thought.

She stood at the sink with her cup and looked out at the trampoline in the garden, Rosie's place, wondering who would use it now.

"You okay, Mum?"

She turned to Chloe who was still sitting with her toast, not touched. "I'm okay. Now are you sure you don't want to come today? It's not too late for me to ring the school. They said it was absolutely fine if you wanted to take the day off."

Chloe shook her head. "No, I... I... think it's better if I go to school Mum. I'll see her next week when we go and visit her."

"Okay," Sophie kissed the top of her head and watched as she went to brush her teeth, before she headed off for the bus. What was Chloe thinking? What if she hated Sophie? What if she never forgave her for sending her only sister away? Was it possible for your heart to ache like this and still be alive?

Ironically, considering the situation, Rosie was fairly easy all morning. She got dressed, washed and ate her breakfast without the usual fury. She even made a valiant effort to brush her teeth. *Well, that was autism for you*, thought Sophie, *you just never knew what you were going to get.*

All morning Diana was being extra jolly. Sophie knew she was trying to keep the atmosphere light, but she had to stop herself snapping a few times. Where was the joy today?

Just as they were about to go out of the door, the phone rang.

"Hi, is this Mrs Reilly?" a soft voice asked.

"Speaking."

"Hi, this is Jenny Barnes, Chloe's head of year. Look I've got Chloe in my office at the moment. She became quite upset in her form room, so her teacher sent her here. We're aware of the situation and I've told her it's absolutely fine if she wants to go home. Do you want to have a word with her?"

"God, yes, please put her on."

"Mum," Chloe sobbed down the phone, "I'm really sorry... I... is it too late to change my mind... I'm really sorry... it's just... Can you pick me up, Mum?"

"Of course I can, baby, I'll be there as soon as I can, okay?"

"Okay, Mum... Love you."

"Love you too, honey." More than she would ever know.

The easy morning with Rosie was at an end when Sophie and Diana attempted to put her in the car. Whether it was sixth sense or just a new dislike of the car, which had always been a favourite of hers, Rosie decided she didn't want her seatbelt on. She became quite agitated and started to claw at Diana when she tried to put it around her. Sophie, trying to avoid her mum getting hurt again, took over and between them they finally managed to secure her in the car.

Feeling way too frazzled to drive, but knowing she had no choice, Sophie went to pick up her other distressed little girl. When Sophie met Chloe at the school ten minutes later, she was shocked at the force with which her oldest daughter hugged her.

"Sorry, Mum."

Sophie kissed her soft cheek, which still smelt of baby to her, "You have absolutely nothing to say sorry for. Now, do you want to keep Rosie company in the back?"

"Course." Chloe shoved her bag in and jumped in next to her little sister. "Hi Rosie, Posie, you okay?"

Her question was met with a broad smile, "Choc choc," Rosie asked hopefully, pulling at her seatbelt which was obviously annoying her.

"Right, time to go!" Sophie said, jumping back into the driving seat.

The journey was far from easy. Rosie became agitated on quite a few occasions. She pulled her seatbelt so much, Sophie thought that she was going to take it off. Thoughts of her child jumping around in the car without restraint, causing an accident and becoming hurt herself, raced through her mind. In her fury, Rosie kept kicking Sophie's seat while she was driving, which considering it was a new route for Sophie and she was having to concentrate quite hard, was disturbing. Chloe and Diana did their best to distract Rosie, however she seemed determined that she wanted to get out of the car. Sophie couldn't work out why she was getting so upset. She had always settled down on a car journey before. At times her crying and yelling was almost like she was in physical pain. After years of living with autism, Sophie knew there was no pattern, no certainty; one day an autistic child could love something, the next it could drive them into a frenzy.

Sophie was exhausted by the time they pulled up to the gates of Thorpe Cloud House. A contrast of emotions welled up in her. Relief that the journey was over but terrified at what lay ahead today.

As she wound the window down to press the button on the control panel at the gate, Sophie noticed that the sky had turned a dark shade of grey too, perfectly matching the atmosphere in the car.

"Hello," called a cheery voice from the speaker.

Sophie leaned out of the window, "Hello, it's Rosie Reilly and her family."

"Come on in!"

As the gate slowly opened, Sophie tried not to think of a prison camp. *This isn't her home* kept whirling around in her head.

When they parked up in front of the residential building, Sophie spotted Liam's hire car. She could see he was simply sitting in the front seat staring out of the window. Sophie knew just how he felt.

Rosie was more than happy to be let out of the car. Sophie, Diana and Chloe, though, all got out slowly and stood for a minute by the side of the car. They were joined a minute later by Liam.

"Hi everyone. Hiya Rosie," He gave her a big hug which lasted a few seconds before as usual Rosie pulled away.

Diana, glanced at Sophie.

"Are you ready?" she asked softly.

"Nope," snapped Sophie. She would never be ready for this.

They all made their way into the reception area, Rosie virtually bouncing off the walls tapping their arms and asking for food all the way. Sophie guessed that she was completely confused as to where she was and what she was doing here. So, food was the comfort she craved.

"Good morning, everyone."

A smiling Mr Brown had come down to meet them and was extending his hand.

Tears already forming in her eyes, Sophie made herself shake his hand. "Hello Mr Brown, well we're here," was all she could get out.

"It's Geoff, we don't stand on ceremony here. Look, I'll tell you what, why don't we have a cup of tea and let Rosie calm down for a while, then we can see about meeting Rosie's key workers and getting her settled in."

Sophie nodded. When she looked back, months later, Sophie would realise just how wonderful Mr Brown or *Geoff* was that morning. His calm voice definitely made her feel less panicky and more ready to face the events of the day.

First of all, Sophie had to deal with the meetings, which took up most of the morning. There were a multitude of people she had to see and where lots of things were discussed. Jane, the social worker with her beautiful accent was there, the doctor, and various people from the home. The discussions went by in a bit of blur, care plans, strategies, all sorts of important phrases were bandied about. Phrases which, she thought bitterly, not many people would have to think about in relation to their child. Weren't they the lucky ones? Sophie just signed the various documents which were handed to her.

Geoff had noticed her hand shaking when she was signing the first form and put a hand reassuringly on her arm.

"I want you to remember, no one has taken Rosie off you, Sophie. All you've done is asked us to take care of her for you. At any time, if you changed your mind, you could come and get her and take her home."

Sophie looked into his kind eyes and wondered if he really understood how this was for her or was he just really well trained.

After all the legalities had been completed and yet another cup of tea, it was time for Liam to leave. After he had hugged Rosie and Chloe, he stood in front of Sophie.

"I'll be in touch soon, Sophie, about visiting Rosie. Are you going to be okay?"

Sophie looked up at him. "Truthfully? No. You?"

"No," Liam answered. United in grief, they hugged each other. Then he was gone.

Sophie decided it was time to start sorting out Rosie's room. Emily, who was Rosie's key worker today, led Sophie out of Mr Brown's office to Rosie's new room. She was a friendly, pretty girl who could only be in her early twenties, Sophie decided.

"Have you seen all the rooms on your other visits?" she asked.

"Yes," Sophie managed to smile. "Geoff showed us everything. I think Rosie's room's down here isn't it?"

"Yes," Emily smiled warmly, "just follow me."

"It's a lovely place, isn't it?" offered Diana hopefully. "You were impressed when you first came, weren't you, Sophie?"

Sophie wasn't stupid. As she made her way, with the others, to Rosie's room where she could hear her daughter was already making herself at home, she realised that the layout of the home was so much better for her autistic daughter. From her previous visit, she already knew that everything had been thought out and planned with autism in mind. Not like your conventional house. Not like Sophie's house.

Rosie would be living with one other girl in this part of the home. The central area which was full of bright pictures and photos of the activities which the children did, had many different rooms leading off it. There was a music room, with a vast array of instruments; a room with a ball pool where loud music could be played in the background; a computer room with a huge screen, even an indoor hydro pool. The spacious, bright living room had a large television in and lots of toys.

Sophie was impressed with all the safety features which had been put in place. The television had a safety cover which meant that no amount of throwing toys during a meltdown would damage it. In all the rooms, the curtains were simply stuck up with velcro which meant Rosie couldn't do her usual trick of pulling the curtain pole down. The kitchen was to the side of the living room and every cupboard had safety locks on. Outside in the extensive grounds was a trampoline, play equipment and swings, all enclosed with high fences. Plenty of things to keep Rosie occupied. A dream home really.

Except Sophie wouldn't be there to take care of her.

Rosie's bedroom was across from the other girl's, who Sophie would soon learn was a sparky and wilful sixteen year old called Carly. The room itself was large and had a big bathroom attached. Although, decorated in light colours and certainly in no way depressing, the room was missing the homely touches which would make it more 'Rosie's' room. Sophie was determined to change that.

While Rosie alternated between running into the living room and skipping a DVD to her favourite part, and sitting on her new bed flicking through one of her well-worn books whilst making her repetitive noises, Sophie, Diana and Chloe set to work.

They unpacked her clothes, tidied away her favourite toys into the cupboards and put her special duvet cover and pillowcase on. Sophie had also brought up some colourful posters for the wall, characters from films that she knew Rosie liked. As a final touch, Sophie placed a photo of her, Chloe and Rosie next to the bed. By the time they had finished it looked much more homely and more like a young girl's bedroom.

Emily came in to see how they were getting on.

"Oh, this is lovely! I just came to see if you would like some lunch. You could sit and eat it with Rosie."

"Oh that would be smashing, wouldn't it Sophie?" Diana said softly.

"What like the last supper?" Sophie said a little more sharply than she intended. Seeing Chloe's sad face she added, "Sorry, yes that would be great, but only if it's no trouble catering for all of us?"

"No not at all, I'll let the kitchen know."

Chloe sat down on the bed next to Rosie who had wandered in again. She stroked her hair. "Do you like your room, Rosie, Posie?" Rosie looked at her sister intently as if she was trying to work out what she meant. She flicked her book to a picture of paddling pool and began to tap it, trying to say "I want…"

Despite the sadness of the day, Sophie, Diana and Chloe burst out laughing. "A paddling pool? In November? You're bonkers!" giggled Chloe.

The rest of the afternoon was turned over completely to Rosie. Sophie wanted to spend as much time as she could with her daughter before she had to leave her. It would be another week before she would see her again. As usual with Rosie there were funny parts, anxious parts and furious parts of the afternoon. A typical afternoon with autism. Sophie took every opportunity just to sit and hug her daughter.

The time came to leave. Having flitted from room to room, Rosie had finally settled happily in the computer room. She was busy repeating the same song over and over again. Chloe and Diana said a tearful goodbye to her and waited for Sophie in reception.

Sophie held Rosie's face in her hands and kissed her cheek, while as usual Rosie tried to twist back to the screen which was holding her attention.

"I'm going now sweetheart, but Mummy will be back at the weekend to see you."

Rosie grunted, not taking her eyes off the screen. She giggled again at the same part of the video which had been played over and over for the last few minutes. Sophie sighed. She wondered for the millionth time if Rosie had any idea what was going on. She hugged her tightly, not really wanting to let go.

"I love you, Rosie. Mummy loves you so much."

Rosie's hand moved the mouse again. Another giggle.

At least she was happy while Sophie was leaving. Wouldn't it be harder if she was wailing and thrashing about wanting her mum? Sophie got up to go. Immediately she felt the familiar anxiety rising. Other people were going to take care of Rosie tonight. They were going to give her tea, play with her, bath her, and get her ready for bed. People Sophie hardly knew. What sort of mother was she, doing this? Her chest felt tight and, for a moment, she thought she wouldn't be able to take another breath. Somehow she made it out of the room into the reception area to join Diana and Chloe who were standing with Emily.

Emily tried to be kind, with a promise to call later to let Sophie know how Rosie was. So this was how it was going to be then? In the future, other people were going to let her know if her daughter was all right. She was twelve years old for God's sake.

It was all so wrong.

Her breath was coming too quickly now. Her heart was racing and she gripped the doorframe. She felt her legs shaking and her hands were becoming clammy. Everyone's voices seemed far away. Was this it, was she going to die?

Suddenly, she was vaguely aware of Geoff's voice. His calm tone floated inside her head and she was slowly being put into a chair. It took a few minutes but eventually the panic subsided and Sophie was back in the land of the living.

"Are you feeling better, Sophie," Geoff asked gently.

"Yes... yes... I think so... I... just everything... everything was... "

"Too much?" he finished softly.

"Yes," Sophie smiled up at him gratefully. He really did seem to understand.

A concerned Diana crouched down in front of her, "Sophie, do you want me to drive home?"

"No, it's fine, I just need a few minutes of fresh air, Mum. Get yourselves in the car, I'll be there in a bit."

While Chloe and Diana walked over to the car, Sophie dug her hands in her pocket and walked along the grounds for a few minutes until she reached a low wall. She sat down pulling her coat around her to protect her from the chilly November wind. Tears began to fall and sobs wracked her tired body.

A few minutes later, Sophie was aware that she wasn't alone.

"Is there anything I can do?"

She looked up to see where this concerned voice was coming from. A tall figure stood awkwardly to the side of her. Casually dressed in a thick coat and woollen hat, the sort usually favoured by walkers, his head was cocked on one side in sympathy.

"Well, unless you've developed a cure for autism in the last few minutes, probably not!" Sophie snapped.

"Unfortunately not," he laughed quietly. "But, I have got a tissue." He handed her a small packet of tissues, which she took, a little more abruptly than was probably polite.

"Thanks."

"Is it the first day?" he asked, starting to sit down next to her.

Sophie was beginning to feel irritated now. Why couldn't she just be on her own?

"Look, I appreciate your concern, but this has been a hell of a day and actually I would just like to be on my own, if you don't mind… Sorry," Sophie added with an attempt at some manners.

"No, that's fine. I understand absolutely," he smiled kindly, standing up again. "I've been there too." He walked away.

Sophie sighed. She realised he was only trying to help, but she just couldn't listen to one more well-meaning comment today. She just wanted to dwell in her misery and rage at the world at how bloody unfair everything was.

Bloody, bloody unfair.

16

The next morning Sophie woke up and wondered how on earth she had managed to drive home last night. In fact, if anyone asked her about the journey she wouldn't be able to tell them anything about it.

She lay there for a minute. The house was so quiet.

So, so quiet.

All the usual sounds from the house had disappeared. Rosie's noises. Books flicking, DVDs being repeated, feet up and down the stairs, loud music – same song over and over – and Sophie wanted them all back. She turned to her side and gripped the duvet, driving her face into the pillow. Sobbing, groaning, heart breaking.

What had she done?

Hearing her mum weeping, Chloe ran in to her. Sophie clasped her older daughter tightly and they seemed to stay like that for ages.

"Shall I make you a cup of tea, Mum?"

Sophie looked into her daughter's tear stained face. What would she do without her?

"Thanks, Chloe, I'll be down in a minute. Listen, I'll take you to school today."

"You don't have to you know, I can get the bus,"

Sophie thought she might cry again looking at her daughter's concerned face.

"No, it's fine, I want to. Anyway, I'm not at work at the moment so what else will I be doing?" Certainly not looking after my other child, her mind screamed.

Sophie had arranged to take more time off from the hospital. Initially, she had thought she could go back to keep herself busy, but after last night it had been obvious that she was nowhere near ready. She just knew she would never be able to concentrate and with her job there was no hiding in the corner of an office if things got difficult. Caroline had been a little bit put out and did her usual sigh when presented with a problem. She had been expecting Sophie back once everything was sorted, probably wondering what the problem was since Rosie had gone now. Like most people, Sophie decided, she had absolutely no idea. Sophie didn't care though, work was way down on her list of priorities at the moment.

On her way downstairs, she hovered at Rosie's door. Everything was tidy for once. There were no toys strewn over the floor, no pile of books on the bed. The curtains were still up at the window, not pulled down in a rage. The duvet wasn't in a crumpled heap. It was as if Rosie hadn't ever lived here.

It was like she was dead.

17

The next couple of days merged together. Sophie felt as if she was simply going through the motions until she could see Rosie again. Everyone she knew seemed to be ringing or popping in all the time to check that she was okay. However, she just didn't want to see anyone so she dealt with every caller with a sharp "I'm fine". The truth was she just wanted to hide away.

Even Mark had rung to see how she was. She had simply told him, politely though firmly, that she couldn't speak at the moment. He could make of that what he wanted, Sophie didn't care.

For the last few nights, she had sought solace in a couple of large glasses of wine, anything to take the pain away. Sophie knew it was absolutely the wrong thing to do but she was past caring. Unfortunately, Liam had chosen one of the nights when she had had a particularly huge amount to call. The irritation at his sympathetic voice was felt even more keenly after half a bottle of Merlot.

"Why have you even bothered to ring?" she had shrieked with a notable slur down the phone at him.

He'd tried to tell her that he was feeling sad too, but at that she had rounded on him.

"Go to hell! How dare you tell me you have the right to feel sad? You've had hardly anything to do with her for years. You left me… " She'd sobbed hysterically. "You left me to cope on my own you shit! I hate you!"

When he had tried to say some nice things, despite her insults, it had wound her up even more and she had ended up slamming the phone down.

"Just go away and leave us alone!"

Everything felt wrong.

The house was quiet and calm all the time. Wasn't this what she had always wanted? To be living in this other world where she wasn't constantly terrified what Rosie was going to do next? Where she could just go to the shop when she needed to? Where her house wasn't a constant warzone?

The dismal November mornings seemed to mirror the mood of her house. Everyday Sophie would wake up in this dark, silent house and remember with a dull ache in her heart that Rosie wasn't here. She would drag herself out of bed to get Chloe up for school, but as soon as Chloe had gone, Sophie would either go back to bed for a while and lie there, her body feeling like a dead weight, fighting back the tears, or she would go and lie in Rosie's room. She found herself putting on sad songs all the time and joining in with the tortured souls clearly in agony because of some awful loss. They were the only people who seemed to have any idea how she was feeling.

Every day she rang the home constantly to check how Rosie was doing. Sophie wondered whether they were getting fed up of her phone calls but they didn't show it if they were. A patient voice would come on the line to reassure her that everything was fine and Rosie was settling in well. They were honest when Rosie had had a meltdown but they always made it clear that it was nothing that they hadn't seen before and that they would cope with it.

They might be coping but Sophie didn't think she was.

Finally Friday arrived.

At long last she could go and see Rosie.

She had arranged to drive up and see her in the morning. Even though Diana had offered to come with her - she knew her mum was missing her too - Sophie felt completely selfish and wanted it to be just her. She would see Chloe off to school and set off straight away.

"Are you sure you're alright to go on your own, Mum? Chloe asked, packing her bag in the hall. "I could call in sick, nobody'll check. Anyway, I'd like to see her too."

"No, Chloe, I'll go on my own this time and see that she's okay. You can come next time when she's a bit more settled. Is that alright, honey?" Sophie hugged her tightly. "If I'm not back by the time you get back from school, just get yourself a snack, there's plenty in the fridge. Your nan keeps buying us food, I think she's worried we won't eat or something."

"Okay," Chloe hugged her back. "Love you, Mum."

"Love you too." Sophie called after her disappearing daughter.

The journey to the home was awful.

All the way Sophie was a bag of nerves worrying how Rosie would be when she got there. Would she still want her anywhere near her? Would she prefer the people at the home now? Could she have forgotten her? Nobody knew everything about autism. It was such a confusing condition. Would she be happy? What if the home turned out to be totally wrong for Rosie? What would she do then? So many worries spun around Sophie's head, she could hardly concentrate on her driving. And boy was it a long drive. It was an hour and a half before she was finally buzzed in through the tall gates in front of the home. By that time she felt as if she had done the journey to London and back.

She was met in reception by the lovely, smiling Emily, who had been Rosie's key worker the day she had left her. Sophie knew it wouldn't always be Emily but she was glad it was the same person today.

"Hiya," she beamed. "How was the journey?"

"Oh it was okay, I suppose." Sophie lied. "How's Rosie?"

"She's absolutely fine. She seems to be settling in well and getting used to the routine. She's in her room at the moment, do you want to go through? I'll make a cup of tea in a bit."

"That would be lovely," smiled Sophie gratefully, just about managing to stop herself running to Rosie's room.

Sophie heard her before she saw her. The familiar sounds which Rosie made while flicking through her books were making their way down the corridor. When she peered into her room, there she was, her precious Rosie sitting with the duvet over her knees surrounded by all her favourite books. Sophie was impressed that she had been dressed with matching clothes and her hair had been brushed. She looked really quite smart. Sophie had imagined (and been terrified) that Rosie might be left to run around in any old clothes covered in the food which she might have dropped down her with her face dirty and hair unkempt. In short, she couldn't ever imagine anyone looking after her daughter as carefully as she would.

"Hi Rosie." Sophie called softly, "How's my lovely girl?" She sat next to her and hugged her tightly despite the valiant effort Rosie made to get away. "Oh, I've missed you so much, my beautiful girl. Mummy's here now!"

"Choc-choc?" asked Rosie hopefully, pointing to a picture of a huge bar of chocolate in one of her books.

Sophie sighed. Autism.

***

Sophie spent the next few hours of her visit following Rosie round. She didn't care though, it was just wonderful being close to her again, hearing her making noises, attempts at language, and all the sounds which used to be in her house.

The home really was a great place for Rosie. Although, she had always been able to flit from room to room in her own house, in her new home there was so many more places she could take herself to. She loved the computer room and sat happily for quite a long time working her way through 'YouTube' videos of 'The Tweenies' and 'Teletubbies'. Each time she would giggle at certain points then repeat the video again. It was like they were on a permanent loop. It was enough to drive most people who had no experience of autism completely mad. It never failed to amaze Sophie just how adept with computers Rosie was. She might not be able to say many words, but she could find the most obscure teletubby videos in the world.

In the music room, Rosie perched on a large bean bag and spent a few minutes tapping a tambourine. When Sophie tried to join in though, Rosie just upped and left. "I'll try not to take that personally," she laughed with Emily, who'd poked her head round to check everything was fine.

"Cup of tea now?" Emily offered.

Sophie managed to drink her tea while Rosie flicked through 'Shrek' in the living room, again winding it backwards and forwards to her favourite parts. Although Sophie was never sure how much Rosie understood, she seemed to be content that Sophie was here. Every now and then she would put her face on one side and peer into Sophie's face as if she were examining her mum's features in detail.

Had Rosie missed her? Sophie wondered. Did she wonder why she had been sent here? God, she wished she could just talk to her and explain. Tell her that she loved her more than anything else and how she never wanted this to happen. When she was like this Sophie was questioning herself. Should she bring her home again? She was fine like this. Surely she had overreacted?

Lunchtime however was a short sharp reminder why the home had been her only option. Everything was fine at first. Rosie sat at the table quite happily picking apart her sandwiches eating the ham inside, then a little of the bread. She seemed quite happy to have Sophie sit next to her. That was until Sophie tried to persuade Rosie to eat some cucumber - something healthy at least. Rosie had other ideas. With a loud 'no' she clawed at Sophie's face, gripped her hair and tried to bite her shoulder. Fortunately, Emily was there to shepherd Rosie into her room until she calmed down.

"Hey, don't worry," Emily reassured her when she came back, "it's nothing we haven't seen before."

"Has it happened a lot over the last few days?"

"A few times, like I said on the phone. But you know I'd expect it really. I mean she's getting used to a new place, new people, new routines. She'll settle down."

Sophie winced at the 'new' and felt the familiar tears arriving. It was all her fault. What had she done to her daughter? Hadn't she been the cruellest mother in the world sending her child here and putting her through all this?

Emily seemed to read Sophie's mind.

"Come on, I'm sure you've done absolutely the right thing, Sophie. I don't think any parent we've ever seen has found this easy."

"Thanks, Emily. I just feel so rubbish at the moment. I can't stop feeling guilty and nothing feels right."

"I know." Emily gave her a hug. "Would you like another cuppa or a coffee?"

The answer to everything, Sophie sighed.

They left Rosie to take her anger out on her safe room – very different to the room at home – and had a coffee. Emily told Sophie a little more about Rosie's week and the activities they had done and what they had planned in the next few weeks. Sophie was amazed at the range of things which would be on offer. Much more than she would ever be able to do at home.

Breathing a sigh of relief when her angry daughter was finally playing happily again, Sophie sat down and thankfully managed to have a calm hour with Rosie before it was time for her to leave. She hugged and kissed her and, even though she wasn't ever sure she understood, she told Rosie she loved her over and over again.

Sophie just didn't want to go.

Rosie was here.

Chloe was at home.

Which daughter should she be with?

Life was so bloody cruel.

Autism was so bloody cruel.

Sophie looked at Rosie who was busy flicking through the videos again. Emily, and the other key worker that she had just met, Angie, were very nice and friendly, but she still didn't know them well. Sophie thought of all the horror stories you heard. She was basically entrusting the care of her special daughter to strangers. The worry seemed to loom larger in her head. Her heart started to beat extremely fast and she found herself having to get her breathing under control before she could talk again.

"Are you okay, Sophie" a concerned Emily placed her hand on Sophie's shoulder as they both stood in the doorway. Emily's voice seemed to be far away and for a moment Sophie felt dizzy.

"Look, why don't you sit down for a minute?" asked Emily.

"No… I… think I'd better go… I need to get back for Chloe… I'll just get a bit of fresh air before I drive." Sophie picked up her bag and made her way to the front door.

"Alright, well take care, Sophie, and drive carefully. Look, you can come and see her whenever you want, you know. It can be the weekend, or in the week after school. Geoff's always happy for family to be here. There's no restrictions. You're still her mum."

"I know," Sophie answered quietly. "I'll ring later to check she's got to bed okay, is that alright?"

"Of course, absolutely," Emily answered. The door closed behind her.

Sophie sat on the wall outside. This was becoming her wall.

It was getting dark now and she knew that she really should head back. She just didn't want to leave. As she stared out into the gloomy car park, lost in her thoughts, she gradually became aware of a tall person walking slowly towards her. When he was standing in front of her, she recognised it as the man who had talked to her last time.

"Hi again!" he said brightly, "we really must stop meeting like this."

Sophie managed a weak smile. Jokes? Really?

"I don't know if you remember me but I talked to you a few days ago when you'd dropped your child off."

"Yes, I remember."

She was surprised at his well-spoken voice, it was normally a very strong Derbyshire accent in these parts.

"Can I sit down for a second?"

Sophie shrugged. "Help yourself." She really didn't want to talk to anyone but she'd been quite rude before and she was starting to worry that that was all she could be these days to people she had just met.

The stranger looked down at his hands and seemed to be thinking intently about what he was going to say. He turned to look at her and held out a hand.

"My name's Greg."

He paused. He seemed to be requiring a name in return.

Sophie shook his waiting hand.

"I'm Sophie."

"Well it's good to meet you." He laughed nervously and let go of her hand. "Look, I just wanted you to know that I completely understand what you're going through, you know. My son, Robbie's in the boy's home on the other side. For about a year now. I... well... I'd like to say it gets easier... and well it sort of does. I mean... " He was twisting his hands now. "You get sort of used to the new routine and the fact that they are not at home anymore... but I mean obviously you never stop feeling sad that you had to do it. Does that make any sense at all?" He smiled. "I just thought you looked so miserable last time I saw you and I think it's important for us all to know we're not alone, isn't it?"

Sophie wiped away the tears which had started to run down her cheeks. Who knew there were such a lot of sad people in this world? "Thank you, you're very kind, Greg. I appreciate you're trying to help. I'm sorry, I'm going to have to get off now." She got up. "I've got to get home for my other daughter."

"Of course. Yes, yes you must go." He stood too and took something out of his pocket sheepishly. "Look, I'm going to give you my card. Please don't think it's a stupid go at trying to get a date or something." Another nervous laugh. "I just want you to know that if you ever want to talk to someone who's been through it all, you can ring me anytime. Or you could just throw it away if you think I'm a nutter or something," he smiled. "Okay?"

Sophie looked at the card in her hand for a moment. She could just about make it out in the early evening gloom. Greg Summers-architect. Impressive. Looks like no profession was spared heartbreak then. She tucked it away in the pocket of her jeans.

"Thanks, I'll… er… keep it and… er… I do appreciate the thought." Sophie managed a smile. "How old is your lad? Robbie, isn't it?"

"He's fourteen, fifteen in a couple of months. What about your daughter?"

"Rosie's twelve, just twelve." Sophie walked away. She just couldn't talk anymore.

18

Liam

Liam sat at the table in his silent flat cradling his coffee. The light was fading so fast, he was aware he would soon be sitting in the dark. He just couldn't summon the energy to get up, though, and put the light on. It had been a difficult day at work not least because he had found it so hard to stop thinking about Rosie.

He'd struggled to go back to normal life since his return to Ireland. The job he loved had always proved to be a good distraction from difficult times but not from this. He couldn't believe his Rosie was in a residential home now, away from her mum, sister, all of her family. Every time he pictured her in that room, lovely as it was, he felt his heart lurch. It was just all wrong handing over the care of his child to a bunch of strangers no matter how well trained they were.

Liam sighed. He knew he'd been really sharp with everyone today. Most of them probably couldn't understand why this usually so mild-mannered guy had suddenly turned into an ogre. After all, he'd only told a handful of people what was going on in his private life. He'd been short with patients, snapped at one of his colleagues and almost bitten off that new nurse's head today. What was her name Siobhan or something? He'd definitely have to apologise tomorrow.

Liam thought autism was probably one of the cruellest things which could hit a family. All of a sudden the child you thought you had was never going to happen. He'd struggled to take it in when Sophie had told him the diagnosis all those years ago.

Although he'd noticed Rosie frequently flapping her hands before he'd left and wondered at her lack of speech, he had simply put it down to all children being different. It had never occurred to him that it could be autism. It had been a massive shock and it had certainly taken a while for him to truly accept it. Despite her condition though, Rosie was still his little girl and even with the distance he had fought to keep a connection with her. He knew deep down that Rosie knew he was her dad. Didn't she?

A slight rumbling in his stomach, reminded Liam that he hadn't eaten for a while. He still didn't move though. Lost in his memories, he wanted to stay where he was and just let them wash over him like a comforting gentle breeze on a hot day. It was true what they said, life really did pass you by so fast. Everything had seemed so simple when Chloe and Rosie were young, when he and Sophie had still loved each other.

He'd never considered himself much of a romantic, but he could still picture the exact moment all those years ago, when he knew Sophie was the one. She had been looking after one of his patients and the moment she'd smiled at him, he knew that he wanted that smile all the time. The man who had always been so sure he would never settle for one woman had fallen completely and utterly in love.

Everything moved so fast after that, a true whirlwind romance. He couldn't wait to marry her and after they had moved into a beautiful home, starting a family had seemed like the natural progression. Liam had thought they were happy. Even with the addition of the girls, he'd thought they'd been alright. Granted life was stressful with two young children and both of them working but he thought that they would get through it. Perhaps things might have been different if Sophie hadn't carried on working. After all, he'd always told her she didn't need to, he earned enough money for her to give up, but she was adamant she wanted to keep some independence.

It had broken his heart when their marriage had ended. It had broken him.

After that, it had just been too painful to stay. A job had come up at the hospital here and with his links to Ireland, it had seemed like the ideal solution. Liam had grabbed the opportunity to start all over again. He knew what Sophie thought of him. He knew she was angry with him for running away, but at the time he had been desperate to get away. Being so far away, he reasoned, he wouldn't have to watch Sophie moving on from him. He realised now, though, that he'd been so selfish, so wrapped up in how he was feeling at the time all those years ago that he hadn't thought about what he was doing. Leaving his girls, leaving them all.

In place of the anger he had felt towards Sophie for so long, Liam had started to feel guilty. Had he abandoned them? Was she right; could things have been different for Rosie if he'd stayed?

Liam thought back to the meltdown he'd seen. It had shocked him just how wild and furious Rosie had been. Of course, he'd seen her have outbursts before when he'd visited but never like that, on that scale. Contrary to what Sophie thought of him, Liam had read quite a few books on autism in an attempt to educate himself about his daughter's condition. He certainly knew that autistic children were prone to terrible rages but it was different to witness it first-hand. Watching his daughter in the midst of a dreadful rage, Liam had felt helpless. There he was, a capable, skilled surgeon, who regularly saved lives, completely unable to make it all better for his little girl.

Sophie wasn't the only one who thought she'd failed.

He'd left that day with a new respect for his ex-wife. Despite the tears of sadness and frustration that he'd seen rolling down her cheeks, Sophie had known what to do and had managed to prevent Rosie hurting herself or anyone else for that matter. It must have been exhausting, though, dealing with that daily, in fact, he couldn't believe she had coped for so long on her own. In that moment, he had completely understood Sophie's decision.

It had been strange spending time with his ex-wife again. There had been moments when they almost talked like normal people once more. She was still beautiful. Even with the pain and tiredness etched on her face, she still had that spark that he'd fallen in love with. There hadn't been anyone since Sophie, not any kind of real relationship anyway. Despite the odd fling, after all Liam had never claimed to be a saint, there hadn't been anyone who'd consumed him the way Sophie had.

Liam slowly got up. He picked up the phone and dialled Sophie's number. He just needed to speak to her. Speak to someone else in this world who was feeling like him at this precise moment.

19

Diana

Diana plunged her hands into the bowl of hot soapy water. She gazed out of the window as she so often did when she was washing up. She'd often thought the person who built this house had a real understanding of how boring washing up could be and having a window here was the ideal thing to take your mind off it.

She certainly felt like she had the weight of the world on her shoulders at the moment. In fact, she didn't think she had ever felt so low, which was unusual for her as she had always been such a positive person. She just couldn't stand seeing her daughter going through all of this. It didn't matter how old they got, your children were always your children and the intense need to look after them and make everything right just never went away.

Except she couldn't make this right.

Diana had loved becoming a grandma. She had wondered how she was going to feel, but as soon as she had seen Chloe in the hospital she had fallen in love just like she had done with Sophie and Andy. The same had been true of Rosie. Diana had jumped at the chance of looking after them when Sophie went back to work and it had been wonderful to be so involved with their upbringing. She had taken them to local toddler groups, played all the games that she hadn't had time for when she had had her own children. But wasn't that the beauty of being a grandparent? All the fun and none of the boring bits.

It had broken her heart when Rosie had been diagnosed, even though in her heart of hearts she had suspected something wasn't quite right. She would watch her at the toddler group and notice how she just wouldn't play with the other children. She simply jumped around, tapped toys and flapped her hands. How do you tell your daughter that you think something isn't quite right with their child? How do you even broach the subject? She couldn't. When it had all been made official though, she had been determined to support Sophie as much as she could.

Of course in her day no one had really known about autism so it had been an even steeper learning curve for her than Sophie. But learn she had. She had read the books that Sophie had given her, watched the documentaries Sophie had recommended, gone to specialist appointments with Sophie and listened intently to all the advice. And despite how difficult it got, she had been determined to help Sophie with childcare as long as she possibly could.

Over the last few years, Diana had watched her daughter cope with the increasingly changing and challenging world she had been thrown into, with a huge sense of pride. Sophie had carried on working, she had made time for Chloe and importantly, she never gave up on Rosie.

However, everything had become much more difficult in the last few months that Rosie was home. It had got harder and harder to look after her and Diana hadn't wanted to admit to Sophie that, despite the incredible love she felt for Rosie, she had grown increasingly nervous of her granddaughter and what she might do next. It was no wonder then that things had come to a head like they had. How on earth could things continue as they had been going? Anyone could see that Sophie had made the right decision, Diana knew she just couldn't accept it and it was terrible to see her daughter wracked with guilt like she was. She tried to imagine what she'd have done if it had been Andy or Sophie and she really couldn't say. But it was only when she put herself in Sophie's place that she could get a taste of what she was going through and it was horrible. To hand over your child into the care of others. Unthinkable.

Upstairs she could hear Ian, banging away putting more loft boards down. She knew he didn't know what to say and so he just didn't say anything at all. He just *did*.

It was exactly the same with Andy. Sophie's brother was so like his dad, neither of them was demonstrative, even though Diana knew they cared. She had finally managed to persuade him to ring his sister after the debacle with Natalie. It was awful the way that woman had upset poor Sophie on what had probably been one of the worst days of her life. If it wasn't for the fact that Diana didn't want to upset her other grandchildren, she would certainly have given Natalie a large piece of her mind. Diana had never really taken to her and it looked like her instincts had been right.

Anyway, what was important now was to try and get Sophie through this difficult time as best she could. Wasn't that what a mother had to do? Diana made sure she rang her or saw her as much as she could, even though she knew that Sophie didn't really want to see anyone. Diana had also decided to go and see Rosie as much as she could. She wasn't going to let her become detached up there on her own. Anyway, it made her heart soar when she got a smile or a 'nan'. It always had. Anyone who said autistic children couldn't show love were wrong, she had seen it.

Diana washed the last plate with a sigh and a heavy heart.

20

Ian

Ian tapped another nail in. He'd been meaning to finish boarding this loft for a while now but he'd had jobs to do at Andy's house – his son had never been one for DIY – and various jobs to do for Sophie.

Sophie. His lovely daughter.

Ian found himself hammering harder. If he wasn't careful he would be going through the ceiling soon.

He was feeling every one of his sixty-eight years at the moment.

Nothing felt quite right. Everything was so chaotic at the moment with the family and he found it hard to cope without order. That's why the army had been a perfect fit for him. Every day was structured. Everyone knew what they had to do and nothing was left to chance. He followed orders and then when he had become a sergeant he had issued the orders.

Perfect.

His years in the forces had been among the happiest of his life. They had travelled, made lots of friends and he had had order. The trouble was life hadn't been like that when he'd come out and now, well now he was completely out of his depth.

It was supposed to be easier with grandchildren wasn't it? That's what everyone had told him. It was certainly a truly amazing thing to see your children become parents and becoming a grandad had certainly been enjoyable. He and Diana had looked after them and taken them out to all the sorts of places they couldn't afford when Sophie and Andy were little. He had thoroughly enjoyed taking them for long walks in Derbyshire and teaching them all about the local area, just like his own grandad had done. Ian and Diana had soon found that as grandparents, they got all the good parts without the worry. Well, of course that's what it was supposed to be like in an ideal world. Unfortunately that hadn't been the case for long.

He had to admit that he'd been utterly bewildered when Rosie was diagnosed. He hadn't known anything about autism. He couldn't remember knowing anyone with autism when he was growing up or since. He'd always felt it was one of those made up conditions to explain bad behaviour these days. Until Rosie that is.

Now he knew it was anything but made up.

He loved Rosie of course. As a baby her laugh had been infectious and she had been a rough and tumble toddler – just the sort of toddler he could relate to. But then everything changed and she failed to develop like Chloe had. With no speech and difficult behaviour, he found himself feeling awkward around her, he just couldn't communicate with Rosie like Diana could. Diana was, and always had been, so much better at that sort of touchy feely thing anyway. She just seemed to know what to do. He'd tried to do the right thing and spend time with Rosie but usually she would just run off from him. So he'd decided long ago to wait for her to come to him, which he was glad to note, she had started to do occasionally.

Until she had gone away of course.

In the last few months, he had hated seeing Sophie getting hurt physically. She was his daughter after all and his first instinct was to protect her. So, although it was desperately upsetting to see his grandchild leave, part of him was glad that Rosie was safe somewhere else now. Not that he could ever voice this of course, not when everyone was so miserable and least of all to Sophie who was simply devastated.

Ian couldn't bear seeing her so distraught. He just didn't know what to do or say to help her. Frankly, he never had been one for words anyway and besides, all the talking in the world wasn't going to solve Sophie's problems. No, the best thing he could do was help her with the practical things. And if he was doing, he wasn't thinking.

A trickle of sweat ran down Ian's red face as he pounded another nail in. In the absence of any solutions to his family's current unhappiness, he would simply get this job done and see if Sophie wanted any decorating doing. He'd noticed that Rosie's room was in desperate need of sprucing up after all the times she had lost her temper in there and pulled various things down. Perhaps he could offer to make it ready for when she came home. She would be coming home sometime wouldn't she?

He reached for the last nail.

21

Chloe

Chloe got off the bus and quickly put her brolly up to keep off the worst of the rain. If her mum was here she would probably laugh and make some comment about Chloe being obsessed with her precious hair. Chloe missed her mum's laugh. It had certainly been a while since she'd heard it.

She walked up the road slowly, dodging the puddles which were rapidly forming. She dreaded going home at the moment as she never knew how her mum would be. She might be trying to put a brave face on it with fake smiles or she could be weeping uncontrollably. Chloe tried desperately to think of something she could do to make her feel better. She was so worried about her. She wasn't eating much and she was drinking wine every night. She just wasn't like her mum anymore. It was as if Rosie had died. Chloe kept catching her mum sitting in Rosie's room looking at old photos and crying. All the sad songs she kept playing weren't helping either.

It wasn't fair, they'd never hurt anyone. Why should all this happen to them?

Chloe missed her sister too. So much. Oh, she knew they hadn't had the normal relationship that sisters had, sharing clothes, chatting about boys, arguments and everything else, but she loved her just the same. Rosie was part of her life.

Chloe missed the noise and the chaos that Rosie created. She missed that chocolate covered face that would suddenly appear running from the kitchen. She missed her giggling over unexplained things. She missed the same bit of a song played again and again. She missed the same part of a film being played over and over. Chloe missed everything. The house was simply too quiet now. It was just her mum and her now and it didn't feel right.

There was no one she could talk to about it either. She didn't want to upset her mum and nan with yet more pain. Grandpa wasn't the sort of person you talked to about feelings and stuff. She never saw her Uncle Andy and as for Auntie Natalie, well she didn't even want to talk to her when she was happy, never mind sad.

She wished she could see her dad more often. Perhaps if he lived nearer it might be easier, though, as her mum didn't have much time for him. She guessed he would never really be welcome at the house. She just wished that Mum understood that, even though *she* didn't get on with him, he *was* still her dad and Chloe loved him.

Her friends knew all about Rosie and what had happened but they didn't really understand. How could they? None of them had an autistic sister or brother. When she was younger Chloe remembered feeling jealous of some of her friends who had 'normal' brothers and sisters. Her best friend Megan had a younger sister and even though she moaned about her a lot, at least when they went on holiday they had each other that they could go and do stuff with. They didn't have to make friends like Chloe did so that she would have someone to play with in the pool. They always had a readymade best friend.

Chloe looked at other people's families and saw how different they were to hers. She tried not to wish she had their lives but it was hard sometimes.

As she trudged nearer to the house, she sighed. Everything was rubbish really. She had all this going on at home and then her teachers kept banging on about her GCSEs and how everyone should be revising hard for their mocks now. The problem was that she just couldn't seem to focus. There was too much in her head already at the moment without adding more.

When would it all get easier?

22

Sophie woke up to a hammering noise. It took a minute for her to adjust to where she was. She opened her eyes slowly and realised that she had fallen asleep on the sofa. The telly was still blaring out and there it was in front of her, the reason for the blur in her brain. Yet another empty wine bottle on the coffee table.

Sophie looked at the clock and saw that it was nearly eleven o'clock. Her stomach was rumbling. She couldn't actually remember the last time she had eaten. It didn't matter really since she'd seemed to have completely lost her appetite at the moment anyway. Everything made her feel sick. All she knew was that as soon as Chloe had gone to her friend's house tonight, unable to stand the silence and emptiness in the house, Sophie had reached for the wine.

The hammering continued with more urgency. Sophie heaved herself off the sofa. She realised she had better see who it was before they woke up everyone in the street or battered the door down. Or both.

Moving as fast as she could despite the effects of way too much wine. She finally reached the door and unlocked it. She was shocked to find her parents on the step. They both wore the worried look which seemed to have taken up permanent residence on their faces these days.

"Oh, thank God," her mum breathed, her face immediately relaxing slightly.

"For God's sake, Sophie. Why didn't you answer the door? Didn't you hear us?" Her dad asked, his anxiety now replaced with anger.

"I'm sorry, I was asleep," Sophie muttered.

"What about your phone? We've been ringing for ages." Her dad continued, his voice rising to the sort of volume he had used when she was a child and had done something wrong, which was usually quite often. Andy and Sophie had used to call it his sergeant's voice.

Sophie picked up her phone which she had left by the door in the hall and saw with a start that there was a huge amount of text messages and missed calls.

"Sorry, I didn't hear it," Sophie sighed. "Look come in, we don't want to wake up the whole street."

They followed her in to the living room and hovered awkwardly by the door. "We were just so worried about you, love." Her mum started to cry.

"Mum, what did you think had happened?" Sophie was puzzled by their extreme concern. She couldn't remember a time they had ever turned up on her doorstep at this time of night unannounced, even when she was going through her divorce. They both fell silent and she saw them look at each other, obviously unsure of what to say to her next. The penny dropped.

"Oh, I see." Sophie groaned. "You thought I'd topped myself, didn't you?"

Her mum moved forward to put her arms round Sophie. "We just know how depressed you've been and we wanted to check that you were okay, darling."

"How could you think that?" Sophie felt herself growing cross and pulled away from her mum. "I would never leave my kids for God's sake!"

"We know that, but –" Her Mum tried to explain.

"But nothing." Sophie shook her head appalled. "How could you think that?"

Look," her dad chipped in, "Your mum just wanted to check everything was okay, that's all."

"Whatever," Sophie mumbled, aware that her mouth was extremely dry and desperately craving a cold drink. She also felt incredibly tired and just wanted to lie down.

Sophie saw her mum looking at the empty bottle. "Shall I make you a coffee, love?"

"No thanks. Look, I appreciate your concern, but I'm fine. I just need to go to bed, alright?"

Diana took Sophie's face in her hands and spoke softly. "Sophie, you will ring us if you're feeling really miserable, won't you?"

Sophie looked at her mum. Her soft, kind mummy who had always made everything better. "Why? What will you do?"

Silence.

Sophie smiled sadly. "See, there just isn't anything you can do, is there?"

23

Sophie slumped at the kitchen table with her head resting on her folded arms. Sleep just hadn't come so she'd ended up coming downstairs in the early hours for a drink and simply stayed there. Eyes fixed on the grain of the wood in the half light, Sophie decided that these last few weeks had been absolutely the worst time in her whole life. Every day she seemed to limp through just waiting for her next visit with Rosie.

Sophie had been a few times now and Rosie had seemed fine each time. Everyone said how well she was settling down and enjoying the routine, something Sophie could never give her. She desperately hoped that Rosie was missing her even just a little bit and was actually pleased to see her. It was true that she would immediately smile when she saw Sophie, but the reality was you just never knew what was going on in an autistic child's head. Did they love you or did they just see you as some sort of facilitator for their needs?

Sophie was trying desperately to encourage other people to go and see Rosie because she hated the thought of her stuck in a home forgotten about – out of sight, out of mind. Her mum had been of course, though she hadn't managed to drag her dad there yet, and Chloe had certainly come with her a few times. Rosie had loved seeing her big sister again. It had been wonderful to see the two of them sitting together on the bed sharing a book. Spending time together, just like sisters were supposed to.

Then too quickly every visit would end and Sophie would have to leave her again. Off she would return to her much too quiet and now fairly untidy house.

Sophie who had always prided herself on a clean, neat house just couldn't be bothered anymore. She couldn't seem to summon the energy to do all the meaningless jobs. The hoover was only dragged out when Sophie thought that they might be in danger of getting cockroaches moving in if she left the crumbs on the floor any longer. The dust on all the surfaces was starting to get quite thick. The kitchen and bathroom were beginning to look like rooms from a student house with the bins overflowing and lingering smells. Sophie tried to care but what was the point?

She was still off work as she simply couldn't face it and she wasn't entirely sure when she would ever be able to again. How could she look after other people when all she could think about was Rosie? What was she doing? Who was giving her breakfast? Who would make sure she hadn't wet herself? Would her hair be done the way Sophie did it? Was she eating enough? So many questions, her brain felt exhausted.

Of course everyone she had met at the home was fine. She had actually encountered quite a few of the key workers now, though her favourite remained the smiley Emily, and certainly nobody seemed mean or unfriendly. Nobody had given her any indication that they wouldn't be patient with her demanding Rosie and treat her with anything but kindness. It was just that they weren't Sophie. They weren't her mum. They were paid to be there and they would never ever love her like she did.

So, Sophie drifted through the days and every day was the same. When she got up she was sad, when she went to bed she was sad. Her body felt heavy all the time. In fact, a permanent black cloud really did seem to be following her around.

The trouble was the run up to Christmas was in full swing. Everyone seemed to be talking about it and making plans. Except Sophie. The cheerful voices she heard just grated on her, making her feel as if she could cheerfully slap the source of them. She switched channels whenever she saw the usual lively adverts, which now seemed to be continuously on the telly. The heavily decorated shops simply irritated her. Sophie just couldn't bring herself to care. How could she even think about any kind of celebration when her baby wasn't home to share it all with them? Everything felt gloomy, dark and dismal.

It wasn't as if Sophie had a lack of visitors and people checking in on her. It was just that she didn't want any of them there. They all said the right things and she knew they meant well, the simple fact was no one could make it better. Nothing anyone said or did could take this huge ache away from her. It wasn't just the sadness, it was this vast ball of anger that seemed to be knotted up inside her. Nobody else she knew would have to send their child away. She couldn't help it, she felt angry with everyone.

And tired of it all.

Sophie must have drifted off again as the next thing she was aware of was Chloe's frantic voice and her feet stomping down the stairs.

"Mum! You didn't get me up."

"What… " Sophie was confused. Chloe usually got herself up. She'd always been brilliant at organising herself and getting out to school on time. Much better than Sophie had ever been at her age.

"I asked you last night to get me up early cos I've got my presentation this morning and me and Megan said we'd get the earlier bus." Chloe pulled open the fridge and poured herself a glass of orange juice in such a rush she managed to splatter most of it on the side.

Sophie lifted her head and tried to remember. She had a vague recollection of Chloe saying something about the morning but everything was a bit hazy. She looked at the empty glass by the sink, with its tell-tale red ring, and suspected that might be the reason for her lapse in memory.

"Well, shall I get you some breakfast?" Sophie started to get up.

"Oh for God's sake, I haven't got time now!" Chloe snapped. After a few gulps, she slammed the glass on the table and ran back upstairs.

Sophie pulled her dressing gown tighter around her. The house had a real chill this morning. Looks like she had forgotten to put the timer on for the heating too. Her body felt sluggish as she moved around the kitchen. When had she ever felt this tired? She suddenly realised that Chloe was shouting to her from upstairs.

"Have you washed me anymore school tops, Mum, I haven't got any left in my wardrobe?"

Fortunately she had. They were certainly clean but extremely creased and now sitting in a mountain of washing which had been dumped on the dining room floor. Sophie had meant to do some ironing last night, but hadn't seemed to have enough energy.

Retrieving one, she called back, "I have, but they're not ironed yet. I'll do it quickly now." As she began to pull out the ironing board from the chaotic cupboard under the stairs, Chloe's face appeared over the banister.

"No, don't, Mum, I haven't got time. Just throw it up. No one'll see it under my jumper." Chloe caught it quickly and disappeared again. Sophie was mortified. When the girls were little she had taken huge pride in dressing them smartly and making sure that they had all the right uniform. Never in her wildest dreams would she have sent either of them to school wearing creased clothes. Everything seemed to be unravelling before her weary eyes.

Accepting defeat, she wandered back into the kitchen and decided she needed a cup of tea to wake her up. Just as she had finished making one, a now fully dressed Chloe ran back in to the kitchen hurriedly opening and closing doors obviously looking for something. "Have we got any snacks or anything?" she asked irritably

"Yep, try the bottom cupboard. What's your presentation about, love?" Sophie asked. She couldn't remember if Chloe had mentioned it or not.

Chloe carried on rooting around in the cupboard impatiently, pulling out crisps and a cereal bar. "It's for history. I told you about it last week. I knew you weren't listening."

Sophie couldn't remember Chloe ever being this irritated with her before. "I'm so sorry. Look if you wait, love, I'll take you. Just let me throw some clothes on. I'll only be a few minutes."

"No, it's fine." Chloe darted to the door. "Megan's already at the stop and it'll only take me a minute if I run. See you tonight, Mum."

"Well, good luck with your… "

Too late, the door had slammed and Chloe was gone.

"… presentation."

Great. Yet more guilt.

24

By Friday that week, everything suddenly became much worse. Gemma was the first to feel Sophie's pent up fury at what life had done to her and her family.

Sophie had been to see Rosie and it was fairly late by the time she arrived home. On a weekday visit she would try and get there for the end of school, spend a few hours with her and bath her. It was usually lovely getting to snuggle up with her, smelling that bubble bath smell, just like when she was a baby. Then before she left she would tuck her up in bed, making sure that she was surrounded by all her favourite things, and more importantly kiss her goodnight telling her that she loved her over and over. Just like Sophie used to do every night.

This visit, however, Rosie had been agitated and had kept asking for chocolate. Nothing Sophie did would divert her and it had ended with a meltdown where the staff had had to restrain her. Sophie had left feeling sad, emotionally drained and like a complete and utter failure.

Chloe was already out with her friends when Sophie got back, so she sat alone on the sofa clutching a glass of wine, staring at yet another bland TV programme, as usual trying to avoid any Christmas adverts. She drank her wine much too quickly, feeling as usual, cross with the entire world. It was only just after ten and she was already on her third, when there was a soft knock at the door.

Sophie answered it, hoping whoever it was didn't intend to stay for too long. She breathed a sigh of relief when she saw it was Gemma, she at least wouldn't need her to be too welcoming.

As usual, Gemma enveloped her in a big hug. "Hi love, are you okay? Thought I'd just pop by and see how things are."

"Well, I'm drinking alone so as you can see things are just fab. Come on in." Sophie was aware she sounded a bit sharp.

Gemma followed her into the living room.

"Want a glass?" Sophie raised hers and smiled.

"Yeah, go on then. It is Friday after all! You sit still, I know where the glasses are."

Watching her disappear into the kitchen, Sophie called after her.

"So, seeing as it's Friday, why aren't you out with the wonderful Bob then?"

Gemma reappeared with a glass and poured herself some wine. She chuckled when she managed to finish the bottle with only half a glass.

"Wow, Soph, you're putting it away tonight, aren't you?"

"Well it's not a crime is it? Not much else to do anyway, 'cos if you notice," she held her glass up to the room, "I've got no kids tonight. One's out and oh yes if you remember one's in a home."

Lost for words for a moment, Gemma put her head down and studied her wine, taking a small sip.

"So, go on then," Sophie asked again, "why aren't you being whisked out tonight, my oh so lucky friend?"

"He's got his kids tonight, so I won't see him until tomorrow night. He's taking me out for a meal. We're going to try that new Italian in town."

"Oh, very nice," Sophie muttered taking an extra-large gulp of her wine. She couldn't remember the last time anyone had taken her out for a meal. "Still going well then I take it?"

Gemma smiled. "Aww yeah, he's really lovely. He spoils me and a man hasn't done that in such a long time. I was starting to worry there weren't any decent ones left out there."

"Well in my experience… " Sophie felt herself slurring a little, "… there actually aren't!"

"You know what, Soph, I'd love you to meet him. Do you fancy coming out one night with us for a drink?"

"What? Play gooseberry? No thanks, hon." Sophie reached for the bottle. Had she really finished it? Oh well, she thought, there was always another in the cupboard. She got up but felt herself swaying a little bit. "Whoops," she laughed, "probably had a bit too much! Still never mind, everything's gone to shit anyway, so I might as well send my liver that way too."

Gemma watched as Sophie regained her balance and made her way to fetch another bottle. She called after her, "Soph, do you think you should have anymore, love? You don't usually drink like this."

Sophie sighed as she unscrewed the cap while on her way back to the sofa. "Gemma," she frowned at her friend, "I haven't had nearly enough!"

"Okay, whatever you say. Are you sure you don't want to meet Bob? It won't be awkward or anything – we're not teenagers all over each other in public displays of affection. Come on, Soph, it would do you good to get out for a bit."

"Oh really?" Sophie felt her anger mounting. "You might be my friend, Gem, but who the hell gave you the right to tell me what's good for me?"

"Hey, hey Soph. calm down. I'm only trying to help, you know."

"Well don't." Sophie started to shout. "I thought you, at least, understood. I'm getting sick of everyone trying to help when there's absolutely nothing they can do. I mean are you going to go and get Rosie? Are you going to stop her being autistic? No? Well then… just leave me alone."

"Whoa, Sophie, I know things are tough –"

"Tough? Tough? You have absolutely no idea. Tough doesn't even come close."

"Hang on a minute, mate, I haven't exactly lived a charmed life either you know. Don't you remember –"

"I hope you aren't going to try and compare your crap husband walking out to my beautiful daughter being sent away?"

"No, of course not but –"

"Because it doesn't come close. Not even a little bit. I should know that since I've had both happen to me. Lucky me, eh? And let me tell you, I would take the pain of breaking up with Liam a hundred times over if it meant I could keep Rosie at home."

"I know that, Sophie… "

Sophie banged her glass on the coffee table.

"Do you? Do you really? It's alright for you isn't it? There you are with your lovely new bloke who *treats you like a princess* and both of your children at home with you. No one's going to come and get your Jess are they? You're not going to have to put her in a home miles away from you with God knows who. You're never going to have to make arrangements to visit your daughter? Are you?!" Sophie felt the rising fury take a complete hold of her now. "Oh no, your daughter will probably go to university, get married and have children. All the normal things. I'm sick of people saying they understand. NONE OF YOU DO, SO JUST GO AWAY!" Sophie collapsed on the sofa.

"Okay, I'll go." Gemma said softly placing her virtually untouched glass down.

"Fine. And do you know what? Don't bother coming back. I just want to be left alone!"

Through bleary eyes, Sophie saw that Gemma had tears running down her cheek as she walked out. The door slammed and the house was quiet again. Sophie reached for her glass again managing to make short work of its contents. She leaned back and realised the room was starting to spin. Sophie closed her eyes. *Great*, she thought, *I've drunk too much and been vile to my best friend.* Tears began to roll down her cheek and Sophie felt in her pocket for the tissue which she made sure she permanently had to hand these days. As she pulled it out, she noticed a card came with it and dropped on the floor. Reaching to pick it up she immediately remembered that bloke from the home had given it to her.

She toyed with it for a while, rolling it and twisting it in her fingers, before she made an impulsive decision fuelled by too much alcohol. Maybe he would understand, she thought, as she did what she had never done before and rang a man she hardly knew. *Well, he did say anytime, didn't he?* She reasoned.

It didn't ring too long before it was picked up.

"Hello?" a soft voice came on the line and already Sophie felt calmer.

"Hello… " Sophie was well aware she was still slurring a little. "I'm so sorry for ringing at this time… well what is the time actually… I've lost track… I… "

"Who is this please?" the voice was a little more insistent now.

"It's er… Sophie… um… I don't know if you remember me from the home… we talked… and… er… well you gave me your card… and I'm ringing to… er… actually I don't know why I'm ringing really… "

"Oh yes. Sophie. I remember you. It's good to hear from you. How are you doing?"

Sophie couldn't stand it – he was just too nice. That serene tone hitting her ears was as if suddenly someone had opened a gate and all the grief of the last few weeks came pouring out.

She began to sob. "Not very well… I… I can't stop crying. I can't stand it… I just want her home with me. Where she belongs… It's just not fair. Why did this have to happen to me? I've never hurt anyone, you know… I think my heart actually hurts with it all. Is that possible? Do you think I could die from a broken heart? Cos I really think I could." Sophie was vaguely aware that she wasn't making a lot of sense now. She was in that drunken state where it was as if she was watching what she was doing from a distance. He probably thought she was a lunatic ringing up at this time but she ploughed on anyway. "I'm sorry for ringing up this late… is it late? I've no idea, you see… I've had a bit of wine… well more than a bit actually… I don't normally drink this much honestly… I… well… I… just felt so sad and … and… I… I've just been horrible to my best friend and I didn't mean it, it's just that I'm so jealous that I'm not her." Sophie ran out of steam at last.

"Oh Sophie, I'm so sorry. It's such a hard time isn't it? Look, I can hear you've got yourself in a bit of a state. Do you want to meet up for a coffee tomorrow afternoon? We can meet at a café, you can come here or I could come to you? Whatever you want."

"Thank you," she breathed, starting to worry that if she talked much longer that she was actually in danger of being sick, "You… you… can come here if you want… " Sophie gave him her address.

"I'll come early afternoon, Sophie, and look, in the meantime, why don't you get yourself off to bed, you sound really tired."

"I will," Sophie mumbled.

"And Sophie… "

"Mmm?"

"Hang in there."

Sophie put the phone down.

Hang in there. What else could she possibly do?

25

"Mum?"

Sophie opened an eye slowly and wondered for a minute where she was. Then she remembered.

She was lying in Rosie's room, fully dressed on top of the covers. She had a distant memory of stumbling up the stairs, wanting only to sleep in Rosie's room near to her smell and next to her things. Chloe was kneeling down by the bed, frowning. Sophie slowly propped herself up on one elbow.

"I'm so sorry, Chloe. What time did you come in? I don't even remember hearing you come up the stairs."

"Yeah, I know. I was in about half eleven. Vicki's dad dropped me off. I poked my head round the door but you were snoring for England so I left you in here."

"Oh God." As she struggled to sit up, like pieces of a very difficult jigsaw, the events of the night started to fall into place.

Gemma.

How could she have been so nasty to her? Sophie couldn't believe that she had fallen out with her very best friend in the world. Mortified, she screwed her eyes up in when she remembered the whole sorry scene.

Greg.

What had she arranged? She was dimly aware that he might be coming here at some point. What on earth had she been thinking arranging to meet a man she hardly knew in her own home? She must have truly lost the plot. She fell back on the pillow and groaned, it really hurt too much to sit up.

"What's up?" Chloe asked, now sitting and leaning on the wall.

Sophie closed her eyes tightly. Maybe if she lay here for a bit the events of the previous night might disappear. "Nothing much, honey. Just managed to fall out with Gemma and make arrangements to meet a stranger. Just a normal night with too much wine."

Chloe grunted. "Well, I did notice a few empty bottles downstairs. What did you manage to fall out with Gemma about? Did she do or say something?"

"Not really, I think it was mostly me. Everything's just a bit rubbish at the moment and I lost my temper at something she said."

Chloe narrowed her eyes, "Well, I don't think the amount of wine you're drinking is helping, Mum. You never used to drink every night like this."

"Well, I never used to have my daughter living in another place either!" Sophie retorted sharply.

"Don't get cross at me, Mum!" Chloe snapped and got up to leave. "I'm only trying to help. And try to remember you've still got me you know. Oh and by the way I feel quite sad too, you know, if you just bothered to notice!" She slammed the door.

Sophie turned over and sunk her face into the pillow. Oh my God, she thought, it could be that she might actually end up falling out with everyone she loved if she wasn't careful.

***

A shower, an enormous brunch and quite a lot of coffee later, Sophie was beginning to feel less like an alcoholic, just in time really for the knock at the door which came early in the afternoon.

After a silent meal together, Chloe, clearly still seething judging by the deep frown on her face, had disappeared into her room. Slamming the door behind her, she had made it quite clear that she wanted to be alone. Sophie had decided to let her cool off for a while, but when she had tapped softly at the door a little later determined to smooth things over, she had been greeted with an angry "Leave me alone!"

It wasn't like Chloe to hold a grudge for long; like her dad she was normally quite laid back, however nothing was normal these days. Pressing her ear to the door, she could hear the rustle of paper from inside the room and assumed that her angry daughter had finally settled down to some GCSE revision. Sophie would try again later.

So here she was alone downstairs about to let a stranger into her home. How life had changed. Feeling just a little bit embarrassed about her emotional call the previous night, Sophie opened the door slowly. She was met however with a warm friendly smile that immediately seemed to understand everything. Standing there on her doorstep, Greg looked very different to how she remembered him. When she had met him before at the home, he had been wrapped up against the cold winds of Derbyshire. Now, however, obviously having only just got out of the car, he was dressed casually in just T-shirt and jeans, hands in his pockets and therefore seemed younger, barely mid- forties she reckoned. She noticed that his short blonde hair was greying at the temples which gave him a stylish look but not so sophisticated that he couldn't be approached. His bright blue eyes were by far his best feature and were accompanied with attractive wrinkles when he smiled.

"Hi Sophie."

Sophie felt herself redden a little and felt flustered before eventually remembering her manners. "Hi Greg, please come on in."

He followed her into the living room and sat a little awkwardly on the sofa. "I wasn't entirely sure that you'd remember you'd rung me." He smiled.

Sophie lingered by the door. "Well, to be honest our conversation is a little bit hazy…er… coffee or tea?" she offered. "Or wine?" Her attempt at humour to break the ice was met with a deep laugh.

"I'll stick with coffee, thanks."

What should she say to him? While making the coffee, Sophie tried, for the umpteenth time that day, to remember exactly what she talked about last night on the phone. Only a few little snippets had come back. She knew she had cried. Oh God the shame. She didn't even feel comfortable crying in front of people she had known for years. What on earth did he think of her? He probably thought she had a drink problem. Maybe she had?

Finally, she could avoid it no longer, the coffee was ready and she had to go back in.

"Here you are," she tried to sound brighter than she felt as she handed him the better of the two mugs and sat opposite him on the other chair.

"Look, I'm so sorry… " she began.

"Now, wait if you are about to apologise, Sophie, let me stop you there. Honestly, there really is no need. You were obviously very upset and to be honest I feel quite honoured that you felt you could ring me to ask for help."

"I just want you to know that I'm not in the habit of getting quite that drunk and ringing strange men."

"Oh I'm sure you're not. But it's an odd time isn't it and I bet you're all over the place, aren't you? I know I definitely was."

"How long ago did your son go to the home?" Sophie asked tentatively.

"Robbie got a place just over a year ago." He looked down at his mug. "Feels like yesterday though. It was terrible. Just terrible. I understand everything you feel you know."

"What about Robbie's mum? How did she cope?"

Greg laughed drily. "Quite well I believe!" Spotting Sophie's confused face he stopped. "Sorry I should explain. Robbie's mum left years ago, soon after the diagnosis actually. She couldn't really accept it. Not surprising really, I suppose, Nikki was always a perfectionist, in her work, in everything and she couldn't really accept that Robbie wasn't like all the other children. You know, that he was never going to go to university, have a family etc etc. So she threw herself more and more into her work."

"What did she do?"

"She was an architect like me, though much more talented," he laughed. "Anyway, she eventually found someone else and left. Cut us out of her life."

"Oh no, that's awful." Sophie couldn't imagine ever abandoning her child. Or was that what she was doing now? Her mouth went dry and she shuddered. Maybe she was.

"Anyway, I don't have anything to do with her now. She's got her own life and a few years back, I heard on the grapevine that she got married again."

"Doesn't she see Robbie at all? Aren't you furious with her?"

"No and no." Greg's face hardened. "She said it's too painful for her and that he's happy with me anyway. I actually feel sorry for her that she never really saw how special Robbie was. He was a beautiful toddler you know and just so funny." Sophie recognised the look that floated across Greg's suddenly still face for a fleeting moment, a longing to be back in happier times. He shrugged. "So, well there you are, I'm a single dad."

"God, I'm so sorry, Greg."

"Why? It's not your fault!" He laughed.

"I know but it's what we all say isn't it." Sophie smiled wryly. "I mean, when we don't know what else to say. I've had quite a lot of it recently."

"Yeah, I bet. But why is it any harder for me being a single dad than someone being a single mum? Anyway, I'm sure you've got enough grief of your own to cope with without taking on mine." Greg's face softened again. "So what about you, Sophie, what's your story?"

She soon found herself pouring out her heart to this kind stranger. All the anguish of the last few years and the agony of the last few months came flooding out. Greg listened without interruptions, without platitudes, without clichés. Just his face focussed on her.

When she had finished she felt exhausted. This was what it must be like going to a therapist.

"So there you are, you now know everything about my nightmare of a life," She sighed. Everything except about what a terrible wife she was.

"I don't know, it doesn't sound so bad. It sounds like you have a lovely family, great friends, a job you like and your two daughters – not too shabby really." He looked thoughtful for a moment, "I do sometimes wonder if maybe me and Nikki had had another child, if things might have been different."

Sophie put her head in her hands. "How did you get through it though? How do you bear it, having to put your child, your baby into a home?"

"I don't really know. Just like you in the first few months, I cried a lot and felt so, so angry. I remember shouting and screaming at the wall a lot. The neighbours probably thought I was going nuts. Actually, I think I probably did for a bit. I felt like I'd gone from being a dad with a teenage son, to just a man who visits his son somewhere else. I also felt like a fraud calling myself a parent. Still do if I'm honest. There's no easy solution. I'm not pretending that things will suddenly be okay because we both know they won't. After all, our children will never not be autistic. The thing is, I hold on to the fact that I did it for him. It makes me feel less guilty. I didn't do it because I wanted the single life and wanted to go out all the time. It was nothing like that. His violence was getting worse and worse and I couldn't control him. I couldn't leave him on his own and I certainly couldn't leave him with anyone, so how was I meant to work? If I didn't work how was I meant to keep a roof over our heads? He needed things I couldn't give him – things you couldn't give your daughter either – routine, specialist help, a tailored environment."

"You make it sound so reasonable. So why do I feel so bad?"

"Because it's awful that's why. No reasonable explanation will ever take away the hurt." Sophie could see tears forming in this kind man's eyes.

"I know." she said quietly. "It's like she's… she's… "

"Dead?" he finished.

"Yes," The floodgates had opened and Sophie began to sob. "It's like she's dead. Everything is still here. Her room is exactly the same. It's just that she isn't with us."

"Yeah I get that. I used to spend hours just sitting in Rob's room." Greg leaned forward. "But you know what? I've noticed that Robbie is actually really happy. More settled and calm than he ever was with me. He loves it at the home. He's certainly not sitting there pining for me. It's just me who's sad."

Sophie smiled wryly. "Just us, the crazy parents, who can't cope then?"

"Probably." he laughed.

"I just can't stop feeling angry though. I mean, last night I just flew at Gemma and she's my closest friend. I know she didn't mean to upset me but I just feel… "

"Furious? With absolutely everyone?"

"Yes." Sophie looked at him. Greg just knew.

"Look, if I were you, I'd go over and talk to your friend. She sounds like she's been pretty good and just because things are going well for her doesn't mean she deserves the wrath of the parent with autism," he laughed. "To be honest, I think she'll probably be feeling a hundred times worse that you are. I mean doesn't every friend of people like us feel guilty that it's not them? And they never quite know what to say to us do they?"

"You're right, she does deserve an apology."

Just then, Sophie heard the front door slam.

"Damn it," she whispered.

"Everything alright?"

"Yeah, sorry, I just heard the door and it must have been my older daughter going out. Well, actually storming out is more like it. We had words earlier and I wanted to speak to her and sort it out before she could go anywhere. But it looks like she's beaten me to it."

"You're not going to argue with me if I stay much longer are you?" Greg looked intently at her for a few seconds but, when his face broke into a smile, Sophie soon realised he was joking.

"No of course not, I'm only nasty to people that I've known for ages." Sophie retorted with a grin.

"Nah," Greg got up, "I can't imagine you being nasty to anyone, Sophie. Anyway, listen, I'm going to go now and let you build some bridges." Greg started to rise.

"Please, don't feel you've got to go."

"It's okay, I've got a meeting with a client this afternoon so I've got to get going anyway. A huge new extension, I believe."

"Sounds expensive."

"Probably," he chuckled. "More money than sense some people. But then I would be out of a job if they didn't spend it!"

Sophie smiled sadly, "I wish an extension was all I had to worry about. Don't you?"

"Sometimes." Greg looked serious for a moment. "But I think we both know what's really important in life, don't we? And I guess some people will never have a clue."

***

After she had watched Greg drive off, Sophie sat down in the quiet of the living room and thought about what he had said. It was good to have talked to someone who knew exactly how she was feeling. It had made her feel less like she was alone.

Greg had given her a hug before he had got into his car. Normally, Sophie would have been annoyed at a man being presuming he could do that when they had only just met but she knew he hadn't meant it like that. It had been a 'I understand, I feel your pain and I'm here for you' kind of a hug. He had promised to ring her soon.

Now to face Gemma.

26

Sophie stood at the front door and felt quite nervous. She had racked her brains to think of a time when she'd fallen out with Gemma before and realised they actually hadn't ever had cross words. It had always been Sophie and Gemma against the cruel and nasty world which always seemed to have it in for them.

Gemma opened the door.

"Hi Gem, can I come in?" Sophie asked quietly

To Sophie's surprise, Gemma pulled her into an immediate hug. "Don't be a numpty, of course you can come in!"

Relief washing over her, Sophie hugged her friend back tightly and began to cry.

"I'm so sorry, Gem, I don't know what happened to me."

"I do," she laughed, "lots and lots of wine!"

Through her tears, Sophie managed to laugh. Gemma took her face in her hands. "Sophie, I will always be your friend. Understand? I know what a shit time you're having and if it makes you feel better you have my full permission to shout at me anytime you like."

"Okay," Sophie smiled. Gemma put her arm around Sophie. "Anyway, come into the kitchen there's someone I want you to meet."

"Oh no, do I look a sight?" Sophie smoothed her hair down.

"Nah, no more than usual, hon," Gemma chuckled and guided her into the next room. There, sitting at the table, was a man that Sophie could only guess was Bob.

First impressions were certainly favourable. A friendly face, with the odd wrinkle or two and a pair of bright green eyes, turned to look at Sophie as she came in. Clutching a cup of something and leaning against the back of the chair with his legs crossed, Gemma's new man was dressed casually in jeans and jumper with a leather jacket draped over the back of his chair. He had short, jet-black hair and Sophie spotted a small gold sleeper in his right ear. He had the dark, brooding look of a rocker, rather than an electrician called Bob.

"Bob, this is Sophie, Sophie this is Bob," Gemma waved her hands dramatically between them.

Bob sprang up and stretched out his hand.

"Hey, Sophie, lovely to meet you at last. I've heard a lot about you already."

Sophie winced. "Well, I hope it was from before last night or I'm in trouble!"

"Yeah," he chuckled, "I heard you had a falling out. Don't worry, I've got three sisters and they're always arguing about something or other. I've given up trying to referee them!"

Gemma draped her arm around Sophie. "Aww… she knows I love her."

Sophie spent a few hours with Gemma and Bob. It was relaxed and easy and the conversation just flowed. Not for one moment did she feel in the way – just with friends who wanted her there. She was especially impressed that Bob asked about Rosie. Like so many people, he knew someone who knew someone with autism, however he didn't try and sound like an expert or try to offer all the usual platitudes. He simply asked questions and actually seemed genuinely interested in the answers.

It was very clear from the start that Bob absolutely adored Gemma and was completely smitten. She watched as he gazed adoringly at her friend whenever she spoke. Although thrilled that Gemma had this new totally deserved happiness, it was tinged with just a little, tiny bit of jealousy. Would anyone ever look at her in that way again? As soon as the thought entered her head, Sophie immediately felt guilty that she could be wondering such a thing, given everything that was going on at the moment.

Finally, realising that Bob and Gemma were patiently waiting to go out for a meal, Sophie got up to go.

"Listen, I'd better get back to Chloe, so I'll love you and leave you. Have a fabulous time tonight both of you."

Bob got to his feet and smiled.

"Thanks, Sophie, it's been brilliant meeting you at last. Always good to put a face to the name. Perhaps we could all get together again soon, maybe for a drink or something?"

Sophie smiled back. "That would be nice." Though privately she wondered when she would ever be ready to go out and do the normal stuff again.

Gemma followed her to the front door.

"So?" Gemma smiled, "what do you think?"

Sophie grinned. "Lovely, Gem, just lovely. He's definitely a keeper."

Gemma nodded. "I think so too." She hugged Sophie tightly. "Will you be okay, hon?"

Sophie sighed. "Dunno Gem, everything's just so hard, mate. Just… just bear with me?"

"Always," Gemma took Sophie's face in her hands. "Always."

***

Sophie had been sure that Chloe would have been back by the time she left Gemma's but when she walked into the house, it was still silent.

She ran up to check Chloe's room but there was no sign of her. Where on earth had she gone? It just wasn't like her to leave the house without telling her mum where she was going. Gazing round, Sophie was shocked by the state of Chloe's room too. On the bed and floor were strewn countless pieces of A4 paper, some typewritten, some handwritten, some screwed up into a tight ball. Dotted here and there were dog-eared text books. On her desk it looked like her pencil case had literally just been tipped out as pens, pencils and various felt tips were all over the place. A heap of clothes had been dumped by the side of the bed and some of her posters had been torn down. This wasn't like Chloe at all. She was usually so tidy, always so pristine. Even when she was working, everything was stacked neatly into piles.

The room looked nothing like her daughter's bedroom anymore

Her heart lurched. She felt so sad about the argument they'd had this morning, it just wasn't them. They had always been a team, her and Chloe, together with Rosie, sticking together no matter what.

Sophie ran back downstairs and grabbed her phone. She tried Chloe's number but it went straight to voicemail. She called her mum to see if Chloe had turned up there but neither of her parents had seen her for a few days. Sophie was starting to worry. What next? She didn't have any of her friends' numbers. It wasn't like when they were little and you arranged everything by talking to your children's friends' parents. Now Chloe had her own phone and arranged her own social life.

She slumped on the sofa and put her head in her hands. It was early evening, it was starting to get dark and her sixteen year old daughter was out there somewhere and she hadn't a clue where.

Some mother she was.

27

For the next hour or so Sophie sat rigid. Panic slowly seeped through her entire body, as each time she tried Chloe's phone, there was no answer. She lost count of the number of messages she left. All the terrible scenarios, every terrible news report that she'd ever watched about teenagers being found dead in a ditch crept into her mind. Sophie simply sat clutching her stomach fearing the worst, waiting for a knock at the door and a policeman standing there ready to deliver the worst news a parent could ever get.

Finally, when she was actually starting to consider ringing the police herself, the front door opened and she heard footsteps in the hall. Breathing a huge sigh of relief, Sophie dashed out to see Chloe clumsily stumbling up the stairs.

"Chloe!" she shouted.

"Go away, I don't want to talk." Chloe's words were slow and slurred and Sophie realised that her daughter had obviously been drinking.

She shouted up the stairs after her. "Where have you been? I've been really worried about you!"

Her cries were simply answered with the loud bang of Chloe's bedroom door. Sophie was stunned. She'd always congratulated herself on having such a non-rebellious teenager who was easy and uncomplicated. While other people at work had moaned that their kids were off doing God knows what, Sophie had been relieved that in contrast she could always rely on her dependable Chloe to make the right choices. Well, that would teach her to be so smug.

Sophie decided that this just couldn't go on. Racing up the stairs, she opened Chloe's door and marched in.

Chloe was lying on her bed staring at the ceiling.

"I asked you a question, Chloe, where have you been?"

Chloe turned to face the wall. "Just at a friend's."

Sophie sat on the bed. "Which friend? Was it Megan? And where on earth did you get the alcohol?"

"How do you know I've had anything to drink?"

"Are you kidding? It's bloody obvious!"

Chloe turned to face Sophie. "Well, it works for you doesn't it? I mean just how many have you had tonight?" The words were spat out. "So anyway, I thought I'd give it a try and see if it helped me to feel better."

Sophie felt as if she'd been slapped and the familiar tears arrived. "Oh, Chloe... I... I'm sorry... " She realised that she had completely taken her eye off the ball. She hadn't seen how much Chloe must also be feeling the loss of Rosie in their lives. As a mum, how could she have been so thoughtless?

"Never mind, Mum," Chloe muttered. She turned again, pulled the duvet over her and sighed, "I just need to go to sleep."

Shaken to the core, Sophie stood for a moment and watched as her daughter, who suddenly seemed so much smaller in her bed, drifted into a deep alcohol induced sleep.

28

The sound of soft footsteps in her room, woke Sophie from the light sleep she had finally managed to fall into after leaving Chloe. It had taken her until the early hours of the morning to drift off because her mind kept replaying the last few weeks and wondering what she could have done differently.

Sophie lifted her aching head from the pillow and saw Chloe standing by her bed weeping. "Mum," was all she managed to get out before her body shook with a huge sob and she threw her arms around Sophie's neck.

"I'm sorry, Mum. I was so mean to you."

"Oh Chloe," Sophie started to cry. "My beautiful, beautiful girl, I'm sorry too."

They stayed there for a few minutes, crying together until Sophie put Chloe's face in her hands. "Please, please don't worry me like that, love. I just couldn't stand to lose you too."

"You won't lose me, Mum." Chloe whispered quietly.

"Where did you go, honey? You were gone for hours."

"Just to Jake's. It was a last minute party thing. His parents are away and he had kind of an afternoon gathering."

Boys? Parties? With parents away? Sophie wasn't ready for all this and she doubted Chloe was either. "Who's Jake?"

"He's a lad in the sixth form, a friend of Leah's brother. Leah messaged me and said she was going so I decided to go too. I know I should have told you, but I was just feeling so…so angry with everything. I just needed to get out for a bit."

Sophie understood that feeling. "But Chloe, alcohol?"

"I know, I know," She looked down at her hands. "I was only going to have one but Jake kept filling my glass up and in the end I lost count. But then I started to feel sick and a bit dizzy so I thought I'd better come home."

"How on earth did you get home? Did someone drop you off?"

"No... I... I got the bus."

Sophie groaned. "Oh my God, Chloe, anything could have happened to you. A drunk sixteen year old on her own at night? Promise me, you will never do anything like that again."

Chloe nodded. "I promise. I think lager's horrible anyway. I don't understand the big deal about drinking, it makes you feel rubbish. My head hurts and right now I feel really sick."

Sophie laughed, "Well I'm going to remind you of this when you're eighteen, love."

"And I'm sorry about the mess in my room, Mum, I'll clear it all up. I did try and revise but I just couldn't concentrate. I got so mad that I ended up throwing everything around."

"I guessed that. Aww, Chloe, you didn't even have tantrums like that when you were a toddler." Sophie tried to make her daughter smile.

"It felt good though," Chloe tried to laugh, then her face became serious again. "It's just that everything's so bad. You're sad, Nana's sad. Everything's different and... and... I just miss her, Mum. It's weird without Rosie. I know it was hard work for you, and she hurt us and... well... I know you didn't want to send her away... I just miss my sister."

A tidal wave of guilt washed over Sophie as she listened to Chloe's words and she fought back a fresh bout of tears. How had she been so absorbed in how she was feeling that she had forgotten about her child?

Chloe sighed, "And I've had an argument with Megan."

"Oh no, why?"

"Well, everyone keeps going on about Christmas and what they're doing and it's not going to be the same for us this year, though is it, Mum? I mean I know we'll see her and everything, but she won't be here and it...just...well...it just won't be the same. So, Megan was going on and on about the phone she's getting and how she's going out for a special Christmas dinner with all her family and all that crap. Well, I just couldn't stand it anymore so I told her to shut up and now she won't talk to me."

Like mother, like daughter, thought Sophie wryly. She looked at her daughter's miserable face. Poor Chloe.

"Look, Megan will be fine. Just apologise to her and tell her how you're feeling. She's a nice girl I think she'll understand once you explain."

"S'pose."

"And as for Christmas, we'll talk about that. It'll be fine, I promise." Sophie squeezed Chloe's shoulders. "Now, I tell you what, why don't we go and see Rosie together next weekend? We can have the whole day with her, take some of her favourite sweets, watch her favourite DVDs, have lunch with her. What do you think?"

Chloe smiled weakly. "That sounds good, Mum."

"Right, that's a plan. Now, why don't we have a cup of tea and a bit of breakfast then go and sort your room out. We could even live dangerously and have a takeaway tonight? It is still the weekend after all and we haven't done that –"

Since Rosie went away.

Neither wanted to say it. Neither wanted to remember how Rosie loved to wolf down the entire bag of prawn crackers rather than any of the actual takeaway which had suspicious looking things like vegetables in.

Maybe it was time though, Sophie decided, time to start doing some of the things that they used to do, before they both drowned in their misery.

Chloe rested her head on Sophie's shoulder. "Love you, Mum."

29

After sorting out Chloe's room, Sophie spent the rest of the day trying to make some sense of the house which she had neglected for so long. It wasn't fair to Chloe to live like this and actually Sophie was surprised to find it quite therapeutic getting stuck in to some physical labour. She tackled jobs she had left for a while, changing the sheets, washing the kitchen floor, damp dusting and the pile of ironing that had almost obliterated the dining room floor.

By the time she had got her house back into some semblance of normality, it was early evening. Chloe was just finishing off her work upstairs. She had made a few appearances during the day and seemed a bit calmer now

Sophie reached for the new bottle of wine on the shelf. Almost automatically. Her hands closed around the bottle neck and she stopped with a sharp intake of breath. Sophie realised that she might well be at the start of a very slippery slope. She carefully put it back. This wasn't the answer. Sophie had no idea what was but she was sure this wasn't it.

Sophie filled the kettle and shouted up to Chloe.

"Cup of tea, love?"

30

There was no escaping it. The Christmas period was definitely here. Privately, Sophie could not have cared less. Left up to her she would cheerfully crawl under the duvet covers, hide away for the entire season and make an appearance when it was all over. However, for Chloe's sake she tried to muster some enthusiasm. She dragged the Christmas tree down from the loft, she made some present lists, she bought some Christmas food, and she even wrote a batch of Christmas cards and sent them in time.

On a few occasions, Sophie had braved the trip into town to begin buying presents for everyone. The trouble was every time she ventured out, the smug families that she encountered irritated her beyond reason. Especially those that had small children. Of course, Sophie knew that they probably weren't smug at all and doubtless most of them had their own difficult cargo to carry, it was just how she was feeling. It physically hurt to see the young children with eyes bright and excitement written all over their faces. It reminded her too much of Christmases when Chloe and Rosie were small.

Sophie had loved all of it. Choosing toys for the girls, making Christmas cards, wrapping everything beautifully in front of Christmas films, mince pie and carrot left out on the fireplace. Chloe's excitement had been infectious. Although, once Rosie was diagnosed, Christmas celebrations had changed a little they had all still been together. Mum and Dad's busy, crowded house, where everyone congregated at Christmas, could be stressful but they had always got through it, let Rosie go where she felt comfortable and have time out upstairs in the quiet when necessary. Sophie had always made sure everyone in her little family had had a good time. And actually Rosie had seemed to like Christmas. Of course with autism you could never be sure but she had always torn the wrapping paper off happily to get to the presents. Surely that meant she was excited? Rosie had certainly loved the food. It was the one time of the year when Sophie didn't have to say no and Rosie could have all the sweets and chocolate she desired. It was always a source of amusement that the chocolates off the tree were always the first to go. One day they would be there, the next there would just be a pile of silver and gold wrappers on the floor.

It just didn't feel right that this year, she wouldn't be part of the preparations and celebrations at home. She would simply be visited.

Everything had been organised though. Diana had arranged to go and see Rosie on Christmas Eve to take all her presents from various relatives. Although glad, Sophie was also secretly amused that her dad was being dragged along this time and wasn't quite sure what he would do cooped up for a couple of hours with nowhere to escape to or jobs to do. Sophie had decided to drive up to the home on Christmas morning with Chloe and spend the day with Rosie. Apparently, they would all be provided with a Christmas dinner which, although probably not a patch on her mum's, was a lovely gesture by the home.

On Christmas Day, Greg would also be with Robbie at the home, so they had arranged to get together in a communal room with the kids to have a coffee and a catch up. Since his knight in shining armour visit, the nickname Gemma had given it when she'd heard, Greg had been regularly texting to check how she was. Sometimes he would text funny anecdotes about his day, maybe if Robbie had got up to something outrageous. Things that probably only another parent of an autistic child would appreciate and find funny. Greg was proving to be a good friend.

Diana was frantically worried that she wouldn't see Sophie or Chloe on Christmas Day so she had asked them to call in on the way home. Aware that Andy, Natalie and the kids would be there and knowing that Chloe would love to see her cousins, Sophie had reassured her mum that they would both be there.

She hadn't spoken to Natalie since Rosie's leaving party and had no wish to. Andy, of course had rung to see how Sophie was after Rosie had gone, but as usual the conversation had been stilted and didn't last long. She understood that he didn't really know what to say to her and felt a bit awkward after her argument with Natalie. She tried to be polite, after all he was her brother, but got off the phone as soon as he could.

It was about a week before Christmas when Sophie received some rather unexpected news. She had gone up to see Rosie midweek again, making the most of it while she was off work and had the opportunity. Going in the evening after school meant that she could do all the normal bedtime routines which made her feel like a proper mummy again. It had also fitted in nicely as Chloe was off to the school Christmas disco with Megan and then stopping at her house for the night – since they had finally made up.

Sophie had had a lovely evening with Rosie. She had been in a great mood and cooperated easily with all the teeth brushing, hair brushing and every other bedtime ritual which more often than not send her into a meltdown. Rosie had laughed lots and seemed to enjoy Sophie being with her. When she was like this it was so difficult to remember why she had put her here. It almost made it worse when she was in a good mood.

As usual, it was tough to leave her baby tucked up in a bed so far from home. Would she ever get used to this? Feeling like a visitor?

Before she left, Sophie poked her head into the office to sort out the time she was arriving for the Christmas Day visit. Emily was Rosie's key worker tonight and as always was full of smiles.

"You off then, Sophie?"

"Yep, she's all tucked up surrounded by her books. Not sure she'll be asleep for a while as she's too full of giggles tonight!"

"Ah, I know she's been in a great mood all week. We haven't had too many problems getting her to school in the mornings either. It's a really good phase at the moment. Let's hope it lasts eh?"

"Yep, definitely. It's been a long time coming. Listen, I think we'll be getting here about eleven on Christmas Day, is that ok?"

"That's fine, Sophie. It's not me on but I'll let whoever it is know. Rosie's dad said he'll be arriving about the same time on Boxing Day."

"What?" Sophie thought she had misheard. "Liam's coming?"

"Oh, did you not know? He rang a couple of days ago to arrange to visit. He said he was going to sort it with you."

"Right." Sophie was stunned. Why hadn't he told her?

Sophie said goodbye and walked to the car. How did she feel about this? It was a bit of a shock as he hadn't been in touch since she ranted down the phone at him. Sophie had just thought that he'd done his usual trick of running away when the going got tough. She knew Chloe and he had been texting, but Chloe hadn't mentioned anything about him coming up.

Sitting at the steering wheel, Sophie dialled Liam's number. He probably wouldn't even be there.

"Hi."

"Hi, Liam, it's Sophie. So, I was just wondering when you were going to tell me that you were coming to see Rosie?"

"Oh, right. Look, I was going to phone you but to be honest, I wasn't sure how you would react. The last time we spoke you were so angry and I didn't really feel like another rant down the phone. I thought I'd wait a bit."

"Wait until what exactly?"

"I don't know… er… until I felt braver I suppose. Sophie, I hate to tell you this but you are quite scary, you know."

Sophie couldn't help it. She giggled. Sometimes it was nice to be reminded of what had attracted you to someone in the first place. Liam always did have a fairly dry sense of humour.

They were both quiet for a moment.

"Soph, are you still there?"

"Yes."

"I've been trying to come for ages but we've been snowed under at work. It is okay, isn't it? That I come and see Rosie? I just wanted to make sure she had lots of visitors at Christmas. I don't like to think of her on her own."

"Yes," she sighed finally, "of course it's alright, she is your daughter. I've never stopped you seeing her, Liam."

"I know. How have you been?"

"Terrible. I honestly don't think I'll ever get used to Rosie not being at home."

"Oh, Sophie it must be awful. If it helps, I can't stop thinking about it all either."

"It doesn't." Sophie felt she needed to be honest.

"Right, okay then… so… I'll be there Boxing Day. You never know she might like having another visitor for a change."

They said goodbye.

Sophie blinked back tears. It *would* be good for Rosie to have someone else to come and visit. At the moment, she, Diana and Chloe were her only link to home. Rosie needed to have other visitors to remind her she was loved.

It *was* a good thing.

Sophie drove home feeling just a little bit lighter that night.

31

"Happy Christmas, Mum!" Chloe jumped on Sophie's bed. Despite how she had felt over the last few weeks, Sophie allowed herself to feel a little bit happy that it was Christmas, she had her Chloe and she was going to see Rosie soon.

"Happy Christmas, my lovely girl." Sophie hugged Chloe tightly. She knew they both felt strange not having Rosie here with them. "So, I wonder if Santa's been then." She winked at Chloe and they both wandered downstairs.

Even though Rosie would have her presents at the home later on, Sophie had piled both hers and Chloe's presents under the tree as usual. It looked too sad to just have Chloe's there. She would put Rosie's in a bag before they went.

"Thanks, Mum, there's loads!"

Sophie knew she had gone a bit mad this year but once she had started buying, she hadn't been able to stop. After the last few months they'd had, she'd decided that they all deserved a treat. She would face the credit card at a later date.

"Shall I get us a cup of tea before we open them?" Sophie suggested.

"Okay, Mum." Chloe looked at her and smiled. They both knew it all felt a bit forced this morning. Where was the chaos of Rosie? The excitement? The tearing of wrapping paper? Everything was too quiet and tidy.

As usual, Chloe seemed to read Sophie's mind.

"Don't worry, we'll see her soon," she said quietly.

"I know, love," Sophie tried to smile and wiped away a stray tear. "Right, tea!" She strode into the kitchen. She would hold it together for Chloe's sake.

A little while later the living room resembled much more Christmases of the past. Chloe had opened and loved all of her presents and Sophie had just watched pleased that she could still choose presents that she liked, even though she was a teenager.

After she had finished, Chloe disappeared upstairs. A few minutes later she came back into the room with her hands behind her back. Beaming proudly, she handed Sophie a large, beautifully wrapped present. "This is for you, Mum, from me and Rosie."

Sophie took the gift and gazed at Chloe's shining face, thanking the powers that be once again for giving her this child. She gently opened it and was speechless when she saw what it was. It was a large canvas of a photo of Chloe and Rosie. Unlike in a lot of photos where Rosie avoided eye contact and was usually looking off to the side or at the ground, in this one the photographer had managed to catch Rosie looking into the lens and smiling. It was simply beautiful.

"Chloe, it's… it's… wonderful. Oh, thank you so much. How did you get this done?"

"I asked Emily at the home to take it when you were in the toilet on one of our visits," she giggled. "I guess Emily's used to getting photos done quickly there. Anyway, she emailed it to me and I had it made up for you"

At that moment, Sophie thought it might be impossible to love her older daughter any more than she did right then. She sat for a few minutes just gazing at the beautiful picture realising that she would treasure it always.

A knock at the door brought her next Christmas surprise.

Pulling her dressing gown tightly round her, Sophie answered the door to a flustered looking woman who stood brandishing a huge bouquet of colourful flowers.

"Oh." was all Sophie could get out.

"Merry Christmas!" the woman said quickly, thrusting the flowers at her, obviously desperate to be on her way with other Christmas deliveries.

"Er, thanks," Sophie muttered, perplexed as to who would be sending her flowers on Christmas Day. Liam?

At that moment Chloe wandered out to the hall.

"Ooh, Mum," she squealed, "who's been buying you flowers then?"

"Well, when I look at the card I'll tell you."

Sophie was shocked when she saw who they were from. The card read, 'Hope you have a lovely Christmas day with your girls, love Mark.'

Mark. Mark? Sophie hadn't heard from him in weeks, not since a snatched phone call just as she was about to leave the house to see Rosie. He had rung periodically to check on her but to be honest Sophie had thought he had given up now as she always seemed to be short with him on the phone.

"Is that the bloke from work who came to Rosie's leaving party?" Chloe asked with a smile.

"Yes, but don't get the wrong idea. We're just friends. He's been very kind since Rosie went to the home."

"Are you sure he thinks you're *just friends*?" giggled Chloe. "I mean *I* don't send my friends flowers!"

"Don't be daft! He's just being thoughtful, that's all!" Sophie retorted.

"Hmmmm… " Chloe grinned. "Can I jump in the shower then I've got time to dry my hair before we go? It'll give you time to arrange your *flowers!*"

Chloe leapt upstairs while Sophie walked into the kitchen still surprised by her delivery.

***

They arrived at the home just after 10.30 and were greeted with festive cheer by another smiling key worker. Sophie recognised her as Lucy whom she'd seen a few times before.

"Hey, Merry Christmas! Rosie's in a great mood so you should have a super visit."

Sophie winced. It was that word 'visit' again.

"Thanks, Lucy. We'll go and find her."

Sophie and Chloe carried all the presents in to an excited Rosie who was leaping up and down to some Christmas music in the lounge. She had always loved Christmas music at any time of the year. There was something about the sound of it - maybe the high pitch and energy - that appealed to her. It had often made Sophie laugh when she'd go into Rosie's room in the height of summer and hear 'I wish it could be Christmas' blaring out from her CD player

"Happy Christmas, Rosie!" Sophie and Chloe shouted dashing in.

Sophie gathered Rosie up in her arms where she stayed for a minute before she struggled free to carry on jumping around the room. At first, she wasn't too bothered about opening her presents. They tried to get her interested by opening a few in front of her and showing her what was inside. Eventually, she cottoned on to the fact that they were all for her and there might be things inside that she would like.

Instead of one big gift, Sophie had picked out lots of little presents which would appeal to her. There was chocolate, DVDs, CDs, sweets and also sensory toys; things which lit up, things which made noises, things which felt different. By the end of the unwrapping session, Rosie was immersed in a wonderland of sensory madness.

Chloe and Sophie spent a relaxed few hours following Rosie from room to room, going at her pace. They played with her when she wanted, left her on her own when she felt crowded, sat and watched some Christmas cartoons for a while and showed her a new toy every now and then.

By the time dinner arrived, they were worn out but happy. Instead of trying to persuade her to eat her vegetables, Sophie let Rosie eat whatever she liked today. Sophie was pleasantly surprised by the dinner which was actually quite tasty and could certainly give her mum's dinner a run for its money.

In the afternoon they headed for the communal room where they had agreed to meet Greg and Robbie. Chloe had thought it highly amusing that, after the flowers arriving this morning, they were off to meet another of Sophie's men.

"So, come on then Mum, just how many men have you got on the go, then!" she laughed.

"Chloe!" Sophie exclaimed. "Don't say things like that. Greg's just a friend."

"Oh relax, Mum, I'm only joking." She slung her arm around Sophie. "Love you."

When they reached the room, Greg and Robbie were already there.

"Sophie, hi!" Greg came over and gave her a hug. "Merry Christmas!"

"You too Greg. This is Chloe, my elder, and of course this is Rosie." Rosie bounded into the room completely ignoring Greg and headed to where the snacks were on the table. Knowing autism inside out like he did, Greg wasn't fazed by her complete lack of interest and just gave a wave "Hi, Rosie."

"Well, this is my Robbie," Greg gestured over to the armchair in the corner where a large teenage boy was busy playing on a phone. Just like with most autistic children, at first glance you would never know anything was wrong. Sophie had long ago decided that was one of the biggest problems. Unlike conditions such as Down's syndrome, where it was clear from the outset that there was a disorder, with autism, because they didn't look any different, it led to impatience and a lack of understanding when they demonstrated difficult behaviour.

Sophie walked over to Robbie and knelt down by the seat.

"Happy Christmas, Robbie!" He looked up briefly from his game and replied with a cursory "Hi."

Sophie could already hear that his speech was much more coherent than Rosie's often mumbled half-formed words. "Robbie, we've got a present for you."

"Present?" he looked up and grinned.

167

Sophie handed him the selection box which she had wrapped. Robbie tore off the wrapping paper excitedly and beamed when he saw what it was. "Chocolate!" he cried to Greg. "Chocolate, Dad!"

"Hey that's great, Rob!" Greg smiled. "Hey guess what I've got Rosie?" He handed Sophie an identical selection box. "We certainly know autism, don't we? Chocolate is the way forward." Greg laughed.

Greg had brought a CD player into the room, so they put some music on for Rosie and Robbie to enjoy. For a while the five of them had a lovely time. Greg and Sophie chatted for a while comparing notes on their various workplaces. Greg was interested in Chloe's exams and offered some advice on revising. Sophie thought Chloe had probably heard it all before but in true Chloe style, she smiled and thanked him politely.

Robbie and Rosie moved around the room. Sometimes walking, sometimes jumping, sometimes just to sit in a different spot. When the mood took them they would start to sway to a particular song. Never together or seemingly aware of each other. Just side by side. That was autism, thought Sophie, watching them. Always in their own world.

All of a sudden, Robbie started banging his head with his hand. "Don't like. Don't like!"

"Hey it's alright, Rob." Greg went over and stretched his arms round his boy. Robbie allowed him to hold him for a moment, just whimpering. But Sophie could see it was escalating. He was starting to try and tear Greg's arms away from him. "No! No! No! Don't like! Don't like!" He was alternating between banging his head with both hands and trying to hit Greg and anyone else who was near him now. Rosie, apparently unaware of the drama in the room, continued tapping her toy on the window she was gazing out of.

"I think I'd better get him back now," Greg gasped while avoiding Robbie's punches. "Something's obviously upset him."

"What was it?" asked Sophie. "Is it us being here?"

168

"Who knows? Could have been anything. That's autism for you. I'll text you, Sophie, okay?" He managed a weak smile, "It's been lovely up to now."

"Will you be alright, Greg? Do you want me to get someone?" Sophie was concerned with how loud and violent Robbie was getting.

"No, no it's fine. I'll just get him to his room to calm down." Greg replied. "When things are going well, you just forget sometimes don't you? You know, why you brought them here in the first place."

Looking at her beautifully behaved Rosie, Sophie knew just what he meant.

After Greg and Robbie left, Sophie and Chloe stayed in the room for a little longer treasuring Rosie's happy mood. When the light faded outside, Sophie decided it was getting late and it was probably time they should leave. In previous Christmases this would be the time when they would all sit down full from dinner and snacks and chill out. Instead Sophie had to say goodbye to her little girl and leave other people to care for her.

As she and Chloe pulled their coats on, Sophie tried to sound jolly, though part of her was dying inside. "Right, Chloe off to Nanny's then!"

***

The celebrations at her parents were in full swing by the time Sophie and Chloe arrived. Diana hugged her daughter and granddaughter tightly and ushered them in. Although obviously it was good to see her mum and dad, Sophie could have done without this tonight. She really felt like just going home now and crawling under the duvet. She had survived Christmas which had been her goal this morning, but to ask her to be sociable as well seemed just too much. Still, she *had* promised and she didn't want Chloe to miss seeing her cousins. Sophie was glad that she'd made the effort when Chloe was greeted with hugs and excitement by Nathaniel and Saskia. The two of them shared a hero worship of their older cousin. They soon dragged her off to see their presents, some high tech, no doubt expensive, gaming equipment.

On entry into the festivities, Sophie managed to exchange pleasantries with everyone. They all swapped gifts and Sophie started a mental countdown of how long it would be before she could leave. The only saving grace was that as it was walking distance back to her house, Sophie could leave the car here overnight and finally have a glass of wine.

Diana, had as usual, put on a lovely Christmas tea buffet which they would all probably be eating for the next few days, since everyone was still full from dinner. Christmas music was playing softly in the background so that everyone could talk. Sophie knew the telly would have been turned off after the Queen's speech, since her parents had always considered Christmas a family occasion and not just about sitting in front of a film. Something Sophie wished she was doing right now.

Andy was sitting next to their dad having an animated discussion on the state of the country. The two of them were at opposite ends of the political spectrum which sometimes made for heated debates especially when fuelled by alcohol. However, tonight Sophie noticed that her brother was nursing a cup of tea since he was probably the designated car driver again, while Natalie was delicately holding a glass of what looked like Prosecco. Ever since Sophie had arrived, her sister-in-law had been boring the pants off Sophie's Auntie Pat and cousin, Jenny, who only made an appearance around this time of year.

Sophie picked at the buffet and chatted to her cousin who wandered over. Although they had spent a lot of time together when they were children, she didn't see much of her these days and had little in common with the high flying career woman now. Sophie was starting to wonder if she had anything at all in common with anyone, anymore. Certainly not Natalie whose glares she was currently trying to avoid.

Natalie had given Sophie a very wide berth all evening. They had exchanged a cursory 'Merry Christmas' but that was it. Sophie sensed that her sister-in-law had finally washed her hands of her since their conversation on the phone on Christmas Eve.

To say that Sophie had been extremely surprised to hear from Natalie, was an understatement. In truth, she hadn't expected to have any contact with her ever again after Rosie's leaving party. In true Natalie style though, she had phoned just as Sophie was wrapping the last of her presents, and acted as if nothing of any consequence had ever happened.

"Hello, Sophie. How *are* you?"

"Fine, Natalie."

"Look, I'm ringing as it's, you know, the season of goodwill and so on. I know last time we met it was a difficult time for you so I fully understand why you were a little abrupt with me and I'm prepared to let that go. After all, we *are* family, aren't we?"

Silence. Sophie was determined that she would not apologise.

"Well, anyway, water under the bridge." A horrible tinkling laugh resonated down the line. "So, I was wondering if you and Chloe would like to come to ours on Boxing Day for a little Christmas get together. Your mum and dad will be there and some of my family."

Oh no, more people like Natalie.

"There'll obviously be food as always… "

It suddenly struck Sophie that was the first time in years that she had been invited to Natalie and Andy's for Boxing Day. Sophie had made an excuse many years ago when Rosie was small and after that Natalie simply hadn't asked her. Sophie thought she knew why.

"Why are you asking me this year?" Sophie cut in.

"Well, you could have come before. I thought you knew you were always welcome."

"No, you've never even mentioned it for years, so why invite me now?"

"Well, I… "

"I'll tell you why. It's because Rosie's not here this year, isn't it?"

"Sophie, I don't… "

"It is isn't it?! Rosie's not here so you won't have to worry about your precious house and all its expensive soft furnishings. That's right isn't it?"

"Well, obviously it will be easier for you this year, Sophie. You won't have to worry about what Rosie's doing and you'll be able to relax a little more. To be brutally honest it did take a long time to sort the house out after she was here the last time for Saskia's party."

Sophie took a deep breath.

"NO."

"Sorry?"

"No, Chloe and I have absolutely no interest in going anywhere where Rosie is not welcome. Do you understand that?"

"It's not that we don't care about Rosie… "

"You definitely don't care about Rosie. You just see her as a nuisance. You're probably glad she's been put away aren't you? Makes your family dos a lot easier in future eh?"

"Sophie, I think you're being a little unfair!"

"Really? Well, actually I have no interest in what you think so I *think* that's us done. Goodbye – have a lovely little perfect life won't you!"

With that Sophie had slammed the phone down. Of course, Andy had rung again in the evening to try and smooth things over and although Sophie wasn't angry with her brother, she was sometimes disappointed with his lack of loyalty. She listened to his apologies and explanations patiently, she still wasn't going on Boxing Day though.

So it was no surprise then that Natalie kept throwing her dirty looks now. Sophie tried to ignore her. She'd decided that life was much better if you just pretended that the people you disliked weren't actually there. Having decided that she really couldn't fit any more food in, she sat herself down on the sofa next to her dad and Andy.

"Hi Sophie," her brother smiled, "how's Rosie?"

Her Auntie Pat looked over from where she was sitting with Diana.

"Oh yes, how is Rosie. Has she settled in?"

"Yes," Sophie sighed, "I think so."

"I often wonder how she's getting on, you know." Auntie Pat's face crumpled in concern.

"Really?" Sophie was sceptical.

"Yes, of course, we all worry about her."

"Well if you're that worried why don't you go and see her?"

Her Aunty Pat looked as if she had been caught stealing. "Well, it's a long way and I… "

"I mean there she is on her own up there and only Mum and Dad have been to see her." She turned to Andy. "Even my own brother hasn't been up!"

"Soph, I'm sorry, work's been manic and the kids…"

"Yes, yes, I'm sure you all have a good excuse, but the point is you've all forgotten her. Out of sight out of mind eh? And you," she rounded on Natalie, "you're glad she's gone!"

"Well, honestly –"

"Sophie, please… " Andy began

While a mass of voices began to argue. Sophie put her head in her hands. *God*, she thought, *why did she feel so angry all of the time? If she carried on like this she wouldn't be talking to anyone soon.*

To her surprise, it was her dad who suddenly told everyone to be quiet in an authoritative voice reminiscent of his days on the parade ground. She was further shocked when, despite never having been a tactile kind of dad, he wrapped his arms round her.

"Sophie, love, we all love and miss her."

"Not like me, Dad," she whispered into his shoulder.

"No, not like you, Sophie. Of course not. None of us can imagine what you're going through. But we're not the enemy, we want to help. Just give everyone a chance, eh?"

After she calmed down, Sophie made her excuses and left with Chloe. That was enough family gatherings for the foreseeable future.

***

It was quite late into the evening when she realised that she hadn't thanked Mark for the flowers. She decided to give him a ring as she could do with hearing a friendly voice. Chloe had gone to bed so Sophie was sitting alone in front of some rubbish Christmas telly and missing Rosie terribly.

He answered after a few rings. His voice was warm when he heard it was her.

"Hey Sophie, it's lovely to hear from you. How was Christmas?"

"It's been okay, thanks, different but okay. Glad it's over now though." It was true, it had been a very different Christmas day but it hadn't been as terrible as Sophie had feared it would be. Despite the episode at her parents' there had been good parts. "But hey the reason I'm ringing is to say thanks for the flowers. They're absolutely beautiful and it really was a wonderful thought."

"Aww you're very welcome. I just thought it might be a nice start to the day."

"Well it was. How was your day then?" Sophie realised that she knew very little about Mark and his life.

"Good, yeah. Me and Dad went to my sister's for dinner. She's got three boys so as you can imagine it wasn't quiet, actually really noisy, but, you know, it was fun."

174

"Oh good, well, Christmas is all about kids isn't it? Anyway, I won't keep you I just wanted to say thanks… "

"Sophie… "

"Yes… "

"Are you doing anything tomorrow?"

"Well, no. Chloe's going to see Rosie with her dad and I think I'll just curl up with a box set."

"Because… if you're at a loose end… "

"Thanks, Mark, I appreciate the thought, but to be honest, it's been quite an emotional day and I think I need a quiet day tomorrow on my own. I hope you understand."

"Yes," Mark replied quickly, was that disappointment in his voice? "Of course, well I'll probably see you at work then, you're back soon aren't you?"

"Yes, in the new year all being well."

"Well then, take care, Sophie."

"Thanks, Mark. See you soon."

Sophie put the phone down. He was a nice bloke. Had she made a mistake?

32

Boxing Day began late. Sophie emerged from underneath her duvet dimly aware of someone moving around her room.

"Sorry, Mum, I tried not to wake you but I just needed to borrow the hairdryer."

"That's ok, babe. What time is it?"

"It's ten. Dad'll be here in about half an hour."

"Okay, I'd better get up and get sorted then." There was no way, Sophie wanted to greet Liam in her dressing gown.

Sophie felt jealous that it would be Liam seeing Rosie today and not her. Boxing Day had traditionally been a relaxed day full of cuddles for her little family and she was really going to feel it today without even Chloe around to keep her company.

She'd just finished clearing up the breakfast dishes when she heard a knock at the door.

"I'll get it, Mum!" An excited Chloe called, running down the stairs.

Sophie wandered out into the hall just in time to see Chloe throw her arms round Liam standing in the doorway.

"Dad!"

"Hey, baby, Merry Christmas!" He hugged her tightly then caught sight of Sophie behind her. "Hiya Sophie, Merry Christmas to you too."

"Hi Liam," she managed to smile, "good journey?"

"Yep, not much on the roads really. You ready to go, Chlo?"

"Yeah, I'll just grab my bag." Chloe dashed upstairs again.

"Thought I'd take Chloe round to my Mum's for a few hours before I head back, if that's okay? She's having a family thing and she's been nagging at me to see her over Christmas. She'd love to see Chloe too."

"Yep, course, she'd like that." Great, she thought, more time on my own then. How could she say no though? At least these days Sophie wasn't forced to spend time with Liam's extended family. She'd always felt a little overwhelmed by the huge clan anyway.

"How's Rosie been?" Liam asked.

"Good, mostly calm. The staff are brilliant with her, probably better than me," she gave a hollow laugh.

"Sophie… "

"No it's okay, don't say anything to make me feel better. It won't work anyway. So, have you got some nice pressies for her then?" she asked, trying to change the subject.

"Yep, got her some sweets and stuff. Oh, and I managed to get her some disco lights. I thought she'd like them. She's always loved bright colours and things like that."

Sophie was impressed that he'd obviously put a lot of thought into it.

"Speaking of presents… " Liam continued, "um… I know we don't do that anymore, but I… well... I know it's been really hard for you over the last few months, so I wanted to get you something." He handed her a small package, beautifully wrapped.

"Right," To say she was surprised was an understatement. "Thanks… I haven't got anything for you… sorry."

He laughed. "I don't want anything. I just hope you like it."

"Oh right… " he was waiting for her to open it then.

Feeling very awkward, Sophie tore off the wrapping paper quickly. Inside she was astonished to find a beautiful pair of earrings. She remembered that Liam had certainly always had good taste. Presents had never been the problem, presence had. "They're lovely," she muttered. "Thanks."

"You're welcome, like I said, you deserve a treat or two."

My children's father in the same country might have been enough, Sophie wanted to say, but didn't.

"Well, I'll… I'll put them in today." She put them in her pocket. "I'm glad you're going to see Rosie."

"Me too."

At that moment Chloe leapt downstairs. "Right, I'm ready, Dad!"

"Great! Well, I'll text you later, Soph, and let you know how it went. I'll drop Chloe off tonight."

Sophie kissed Chloe. "Have a great day with your dad and Rosie, love you."

"Thanks, Mum," she smiled eyes shining, "Love you too."

And with that they were off.

The house was suddenly quiet.

Sophie sat down in the living room and leaned back. She realised suddenly that this is what it would be like when Chloe went. Rosie had already gone and when Chloe went she would not only be husbandless but childless too. She'd be rattling around in this house on her own with nothing but her thoughts for company. It was so unfair. If things had been normal, she would have had Rosie for much longer. She wasn't ready to be on her own yet.

Sophie wasn't sure how long she had sat there when she heard a soft knock at the door followed by a cheerful 'hello.' There was only one person in Sophie's life who let herself in without asking.

"Gem, come in." she called. "I'm sorry I'm in my chair and I can't be bothered to get up."

Gemma wandered in. "Charming and a very Merry Christmas to you too! So how's you?"

"Fine, just wondering whether to go and get myself a few cats since I am clearly going to end up on my own soon."

"Ha! Funny you should say that. Chloe's just texted me to come and check on you at some point as she's worried about you being on your own today."

Lovely, caring Chloe. Sophie wanted to cry.

"Oh, I'm fine. I'll just put some telly on, curl up on the sofa and feel sorry for myself, I think."

"Bugger that, madam! Right, well Jess and Alex have gone to their dad and supermodel Helen's today. Apparently she's making some fantastic Jamie Oliver recipe for the kids. They're dreading it."

Sophie began to laugh.

"That's better… a smile. Anyway honey, Bob hasn't got his kids either so why don't me and him come over with a few bottles later. As long as you promise not to shout at me when you've finished the first one." Gemma winked wickedly.

Could Sophie be bothered? She knew her friend was only being kind but actually all she wanted to do today was sit and feel sorry for herself about all the shit that life had thrown at her.

"It's a nice thought, Gem, but… "

"Absolutely no buts! Chloe will never forgive me if I leave you on your own. Anyway, you need to see Bob when he's had a few drinks. He's hilarious. His impression of Mick Jagger is like nothing you've ever seen before, believe me."

Sophie knew when she was beaten. "Oh, alright then," she sighed.

"Good. We'll be over this afternoon. See you later."

Sophie watched Gemma go. Her friend had been so happy since she'd met Bob and it was so typical of her not to be selfish with her happiness, but to come and make sure Sophie was okay too.

She spent the morning flicking between channels, feeling restless. Her mind kept wandering to Rosie. She wondered how she was getting on with Liam being there. After all, she really hardly knew him these days. She hoped against hope that she wouldn't have a meltdown. Just fleetingly, the evil part of her thought that maybe it would be a good thing as it might give Liam more of an idea of what she had been coping with on her own all these years.

Actually, it had been on the tip of her tongue to ask to go with him this morning. She missed her baby so much. However, each time she felt the words slipping from her mouth she reminded herself just how weird it would be spending Boxing Day with her ex-husband.

Sophie realised that she must have dropped off for a while when she was woken by a tapping at the door. She dragged herself to the door and was soon shaken out of her drowsiness when she saw who was there.

"Greg… hi, I wasn't expecting to see you today."

A very different looking Greg stood there in the doorway. His hands were dug deep into his pockets and his face was pale and drawn. His whole being looked just so weary and haunted.

"Sorry Sophie, I hope you don't mind, I know it's Boxing Day. I called in on the off chance. I've been driving around for ages. I wondered if you had time for a chat… I didn't really know what to do with myself today."

"Of course I don't mind, come in." Sophie put her fingers through her hair as she led Greg into the living room. Since she had just woken up, she was well aware she probably looked a sight

Greg slumped on the sofa. "I'm actually supposed to be at my mum's today but I got up this morning and I just couldn't face it."

Sophie smiled in agreement. "I know what you mean. My sister-in-law invited me to a get together. Mind you, the fact that she and I *do not* see eye to see had more to do with me refusing."

"Families eh?" Greg rolled his eyes. "Sometimes it's too hard to be around all those normal people with their normal lives. They haven't got a clue what it's like for us, have they?"

"Definitely not." Sophie agreed emphatically. "Would you like a drink?"

"Just a coffee would be great." Greg gave a half-smile, "I know it's not very festive but I'm driving."

"Coming up." Sophie quickly made them both one. When she walked back in with them, Greg was sitting, head in his hands. Sophie was concerned at seeing him look so beaten. "You okay, Greg?"

"Not really. I had a terrible day yesterday. Robbie didn't calm down after we left you. He trashed his room and managed to get me with one of his punches, right in the ribs. I… just… I thought that I'd become immune to it all by now, turns out I was wrong." Sophie noticed a tear make its way down his cheek. From the state of his red-rimmed eyes it clearly wasn't the first today. He wiped it away quickly. "Sorry, this isn't very masculine is it? And to think I was supposed to be helping you. You know, the old hand at this residential stuff."

Sophie just smiled. "Well, from a purely selfish point of view, I suppose it's good to know I'm not the only one in the world struggling because it certainly feels like it sometimes. The last few months it's been like I've been watching everyone else getting on with their lives feeling so jealous because here I am stuck, just sad all the time."

Greg raised his eyebrows. "No, Sophie, you're definitely not the only one."

"It's such a shame though, that Robbie kicked off Christmas Day." Sophie frowned. "Do you think perhaps it was all of us getting together that set him off? If it was, I'm so sorry."

Greg took a sip of his drink and leaned back. "Don't worry, Sophie. To be honest it could have been anything, we both know that."

"So are you going to see him again over Christmas?"

Greg replied with a sigh. "Yep, I'm going tomorrow, taking my mum and dad."

"Well, that's good. I'm sure he'll be better tomorrow."

"Hope so." He grimaced. "I haven't told my parents what he was like yesterday. In fact, I always play down his meltdowns. I just don't want people looking at him like he's some sort of monster. When they look at him, I want them to see what I see, my beautiful, clever, funny son."

Sophie knew just what he meant.

"They're quite a lot older anyway and I think their generation don't really get autism do they?"

Sophie nodded sadly. She'd lost count of the amount of stares and glares she'd had from the older generation who simply thought that she had an uncontrollable child.

"So, what about you? How was the rest of your day yesterday then?" Greg asked, forcing a smile.

Sophie recounted her evening at her parents' including her outburst. Greg listened closely, his eyes only leaving her face to take sips of his coffee. Sophie decided that it felt good to unload to someone who really understood why she was so angry.

When she had finished, Greg reached over to put his coffee cup on the table and Sophie saw him wince.

"Is that where your bruise is?"

"Yep it's a good one. In the history of Robbie injuries, it's certainly one of his most impressive."

"Let me just check it, Greg, you're obviously in pain and I am a nurse you know."

"Okay, but I want you to know that I'm not in the habit of getting my kit off for just anyone!" He smiled and for a moment his bright blue eyes looked less miserable.

Sophie moved over to sit next to him. Out of nowhere, the thought popped into her head that it had been quite a while since she had been this close to a man in her living room. Suddenly, she was all too aware of how near they were and struggled to keep her breathing regular. She tried not to think about how good he smelt and how he was quite muscular for a man in his forties. What was she doing thinking like this?

Very carefully and slowly she lifted his shirt. Although her eyes were looking down, she could feel those piercing blue eyes on her, studying her. Sophie was all too aware of her fingers brushing his skin. When his shirt was finally rolled up, she tried hard not to gasp at the huge deep purple bruise which spread over quite a large area of his ribcage.

"Well, he certainly knows how to punch." Sophie tried to keep it light.

"That he does," agreed Greg, "Sophie… "

She felt him lean closer and, suddenly unnerved by his closeness, Sophie put his shirt down hastily. Getting up to move back to her chair, she spoke too quickly. "I'm sure it'll be fine. If you're worried nip to the doctor's. Though to be honest they don't do anything for broken ribs these days anyway."

Suddenly, the front door opened and Sophie heard a familiar voice coming from the hall.

"Hey, Soph, the Christmas cavalry has arrived! Get those glasses out 'cos we've got lots of magnificent bottles here!"

A giggling Gemma and Bob almost fell into the room. Seeing that Sophie wasn't alone, Gemma recovered quickly from her fit of laughter.

"Oh, sorry Soph, didn't realise you had company."

"Gem, this is Greg." Sophie said feeling a little confused by what had just happened.

"Nice to meet you, Greg," Gemma grinned. "Now, are you another lost soul in need of alcohol, this fine Boxing Day? Don't worry we have plenty!" Gemma waved one of the three bottles she was clutching.

Greg got up. "No, it's fine." He smiled. "Thanks for the generous offer but I was about to go anyway."

Bob chipped in. "Please don't go on our account, mate. Stay and have a drink. To be honest, I could do with the odds being more in my favour anyway. You don't know what these two are like together when they've had a drink!"

Greg looked uncertainly at Sophie for a minute. Sophie felt herself blushing for the first time in years. Making up his mind, he began to put on his coat. "No really, I ought to get back and at least say hello to some of my relatives. Nice to meet you, Gemma and… "

"Bob." The two men exchanged a handshake.

Sophie led Greg to the front door and turned to face him. She smiled and tried to keep her voice light.

"It was really good to see you, Greg. I hope tomorrow goes well."

He smiled. "Yep me too." He stepped out on to the doorstep and looked at her for a few seconds, obviously trying to decide what to say. "I'll text you soon, Sophie. Perhaps we could get together for another cuppa or something stronger this time?"

"Er, yeah," Sophie really wasn't sure what she was committing herself to and felt all of a sudden like running away. "… that would be nice."

She watched as he drove off.

When she returned to the living room, Gemma was busy pouring a glass of wine for her. "So that was Greg, eh? Hmmm very nice."

Sophie punched Gemma's arm light-heartedly. "It's nothing like that. He's just been a really good friend." Sophie watched as Gemma arched her eyebrows. "No, really. Look, he had a tough day yesterday and needed a chat. That's all, Gemma. I know how your mind works, my friend."

"Well, I'm just saying he's very easy on the eye and there was a definite spark of something in this room when we walked in. Don't you think, Bob?"

"Hey, leave me out of it. I know nothing of these things you call feelings!" he smirked.

Sophie sat down with her glass thoughtfully. He was just a friend, wasn't he?

33

The rest of the Christmas period crawled by in a mass of leftovers and alcohol. Before Sophie knew it, it was January and her first day back at work.

She had gone through the usual rigmarole of a back to work interview and meeting with occupational health to check that she was fit for work. Sophie had wanted to laugh hysterically when she'd had to assure them that she was 'back to normal'. The reality was she would never be the same person again. How could she be? However, the woman behind the desk, despite her patience and soft caring voice, probably wouldn't really understand, so Sophie had simply sighed, given the required reassurances and a date was set.

When the day arrived, she got up early. It was dark outside and inside the house the atmosphere was just as dismal.

Sophie and Chloe sat in silence over breakfast. Sophie was worried how she would cope today. After all, the last time she had been at work she had collapsed with panic in the cupboard and been dragged out by Mark. Not really her finest hour.

Meanwhile, Chloe was busy worrying about her mocks this week. Despite working hard over the whole of Christmas, she was convinced she hadn't done enough revision and was going to fail everything.

All in all neither of them felt like there was much to look forward to really.

Once Sophie had seen Chloe off to school with lots of kisses and plenty of lunch, she cleared up the kitchen and got ready to go. It felt weird that life was getting back to normal though she actually still felt far from normal. She had survived Christmas and all the annoying happiness that had seemed to surround her. But when New Year, which she had spent quietly with her

Chloe, had finally arrived, Sophie had breathed a huge sigh of relief. That was that, now she didn't have to keep plastering a smile on her face to avoid spoiling everyone else's fun.

As she grabbed her bag from the hall, her eyes went to the beautiful picture Chloe had got her for Christmas. Her heart lurched. The last time she had been going out to work, she'd had both of her daughters at home. Would that ever be the case again? She doubted it. Sighing and fighting back tears, after all she really didn't want to look a wreck on her first day back, Sophie closed the door behind her and headed into work.

At least today she would be surrounded by friendly faces. Anna was in and so was Mark. Both had texted her to wish her luck and said they were looking forward to seeing her. Greg had also been in touch to check she was alright about her impending return. She was touched by everyone's concern.

Feeling quite anxious as soon as she stepped into the hospital, Sophie hurriedly made her way to the locker room and got into her scrubs. Obviously, she just needed to get on with the day and keep herself busy as it would stop her thinking and worrying all the time. It soon turned out that being occupied today wouldn't be a problem as Sophie was greeted with an onslaught of patients almost as soon as she appeared on the ward. It genuinely felt like she'd never been away. It was true the world really didn't stop turning even when you were in your darkest times.

As usual there weren't enough staff so everyone was having to work twice as hard. It was a good thing really, she was so busy sorting out her patients, Sophie didn't have much time to wonder how Rosie was and what she might be doing.

At long last, it was lunch and Sophie could sit down. She looked around her; nothing had changed here, same faces, same décor. But for her everything was different. As she got out her lunch box she remembered the phone call she had received from her mum which had started the ball rolling. Was it really only a few months ago? It seemed like a lifetime. She was trying so hard to be normal today but on the inside she knew she was struggling. It would only take one wrong word from someone and she might just run out of the place.

Just then Mark came in. They had exchanged texts at New Year but apart from that she hadn't heard from him since Christmas Day.

"Sophie, glad to have you back." He gave her a hug and perched on the seat next to her.

"Cheers, Mark, it's weird to be back but at least it gives me something else to think about in the day."

"How's Rosie?"

"She's fine, it's me that's a wreck."

"Well, you don't look like a wreck," Mark said with a grin. He studied his feet for a moment as if thinking about something then looked up at her again. "Are you doing anything after work, Soph? I just wondered if you wanted to grab a coffee and a catch up."

Sophie looked at this kind man who never seemed to give up on her despite all the times she had been short or sharp with him. He genuinely seemed to care. Was a coffee too much to ask? Anyway, since Chloe was having tea at her nan's, she would only be going home to an empty house. Simply more time to sit in Rosie's bedroom alone, thinking about her and wishing that she was still at home.

"Actually, do you know what, Mark? That would be… nice."

Mark's face lit up. "Brilliant, I'll meet you at the entrance later on."

"Hang on, how do you know I finish at the same time as you?"

"I checked." He winked.

Sophie couldn't help smiling to herself.

***

The afternoon was just as busy as the morning. Sophie had forgotten how exhausted she normally felt when her shift had finished. Everything was aching and actually she really felt like just going straight home for a hot bath. She couldn't let Mark down though, he didn't deserve that.

Sophie was just passing the staffroom on her way to the locker room when she heard her name. She stopped to listen for a moment at the open door. It was two women. One of the voices she recognised, the other was new.

"So, this is that Sophie's first day back then?"

"Yep."

"She's been off ages, hasn't she?"

"Yeah, ever since her little girl went into care."

"I heard about that. Some sort of home, wasn't it?"

"That's right. I mean, she wasn't taken off her or anything like that. She actually sent her there, terrible isn't it? Imagine having to do that."

"Yeah. Awful. She must be feeling rotten, no wonder she's been off. Do you know her well?"

"Only a bit. It's funny, she didn't seem like the sort of person who'd do that."

"Things must have been bad though, mustn't they?"

"Suppose so. I don't think I could do it though, even if things got really bad. Could you?"

"No, don't think so. I mean it's a big thing to send your kid away isn't it? Does it happen often do you think? Are autistic kids actually that bad then?"

"Don't know really. I've got some experience because my cousin's boy's autistic. Mind you, he's still in the local school and he talks and everything. He's no trouble at all really, just makes funny noises and doesn't like you to look at him. I don't think our Sue would ever send him away."

"I don't really know much about autistic kids but, I mean, you watch 'Rain man' and it doesn't seem that bad does it? He was just a bit strange wasn't he? Still, I suppose if things were that awful at home with that Sophie's kid at least they'll be easier for her now that she's gone."

Sophie had been listening, rooted to the spot, fury quickly building. The phrase blood boiling seemed very apt at that moment. She wasn't sure what was worse, the total ignorance of extreme autism and what it was like to live with it day in, day out, or the fact she was being talked about at all. She couldn't stop herself bursting in.

"Have you both quite finished?"

Two heads whipped round. Guilty looks settled on their faces instantly when they saw who it was. They stood up to face a shaking Sophie.

"Sophie, we… " began the first woman, who Sophie now recognised as Carol, a health care assistant that she had chatted to on occasion.

"How dare you?" Sophie hissed. "Neither of you knows anything about me, or my daughter or actually my life. I don't have to justify my decision to you pair of… of… bitches."

"But we were saying that we feel sorry for you," the second woman chipped in. Dressed in the same uniform, so obviously a health care assistant too, she was twisting her hands, clearly mortified by the whole situation.

"I don't want your sympathy. I don't want anything from you except for you to shut up and mind your own business. You don't know… " Words failed her. Sophie had had enough. Leaving the two women standing there, embarrassment plastered all over their faces, she marched into the locker room, grabbed her things, slammed her locker shut and stormed out.

By the time she had reached the entrance, angry tears had started springing from her eyes. She just couldn't believe what she'd heard.

True to his word Mark was waiting for her by the main entrance just next to the coffee place. When he saw she was crying, he immediately rushed over.

"Hey what's up? Has it been a bad first day?"

"You could say that." Sophie wiped her eyes. She'd wasted enough tears on those witches. "Let's just say that I could do with a sit down and a drink."

"No problem. Do you want to get a table and I'll go and get us some coffees then? Cappuccinos okay?"

"Lovely." Sophie sat down and racked her brains for the last time a man had bought her a drink.

By the time Mark had been served, Sophie was starting to calm down. As he walked back, carrying the drinks carefully, Sophie looked at Mark as if she'd seen him for the first time. The fact that her eyes weren't now looking through a veil of tears certainly helped.

He walked with an air of confidence. Fairly tall and well-built, Sophie guessed that he was probably in his mid-thirties. Black wavy hair which curled into his neck, a dark complexion and deep brown eyes that you could get lost in, made the word 'rugged' spring to Sophie's mind. When he sat down and smiled, Sophie noticed the crinkles around his eyes and decided that they were a good sign – a man that smiled *a lot*. The romantic in her thought he had the look of a gypsy. And the fact that he was in his thirties, and supposedly neither married nor in a relationship, added to his mysterious aura.

"Right, come on then, what's upset you?" Mark asked.

Sophie told him what had happened and saw the concern in his face as he listened.

"Bloody hell. You need to just forget them, Soph. Let's face it, Carol's just a woman who thinks she knows everything about everything and apparently now she can add autism to the list. And well, the new one is Jan. I'm not a gossip or anything – I'm a man after all," he laughed, "– but word on the grapevine is that she left her last place after having a fling with one of the porters. Unfortunately, his wife also worked there and you can guess what hit the fan when it became public knowledge. So she hasn't got any room at all to pass judgement on you or anyone else for that matter."

Sophie tried to smile. "Wish I'd known that when I was busy erupting at the pair of them." She paused and took a deep breath. "The worst thing is, I'm now left wondering if everyone else thinks the same as them. You know, that I shouldn't have put her in that place. That I should have kept her with me no matter what. That I should have tried harder…"

Mark frowned. "No," he said emphatically. "No, definitely not. Everyone else knows you too well to think anything like that about you. Look, they're just two sad women with nothing better to do than gossip about other people's problems."

"Okay," Sophie sighed, not entirely convinced. After all, everything they had said, she had already thought it about herself, so why wouldn't other people?

She spotted a helmet down by Mark's chair and realised he had been holding it when she'd met him. "I didn't know you had a motorbike."

"Ah, just one of the things you don't know about me." He laughed.

Needing to lighten the mood, she asked him, "So, come on then, tell me. What else don't I know about you?"

"Aha, now that could open a whole can of worms!" Mark leaned back in his chair and pulled his hands through his hair. "What do you want to know?"

"W – ell … I know you've got a sister, but what about the rest of your family?"

"Let's see… well… I lost my mum when I was a teenager, so there's just me, my dad and sister."

"Oh, I'm so sorry."

"It's okay, I know that you know all about loss, eh? It wasn't easy, but we all pulled together. We're quite close now really."

"That's good. Family's important. I know that much. So what about the whole serious relationship thing. Did you never fancy it?"

He looked at Sophie thoughtfully with those chestnut eyes. "I did once. I don't know maybe again someday, but at the moment I'm happy with just me. If someone comes along, they come along. I don't think you can control that part of your life really. I think that's why I would never do the online dating thing, I just think you've got to leave some things up to fate."

"True... Mind you my friend Gemma's just met a lovely man online."

"Hey, I'm not saying it doesn't work for some people, it's just not the way I do things."

Sophie regarded him thoughtfully. "You do seem quite laid back."

"I suppose I am. I try to be anyway. I don't plan too far in advance, I think that's the secret."

"So, where did you work before here?"

"Ha, I feel like I'm in an interrogation now!" Mark laughed.

"Sorry, I just – "

"No, no it's fine, I'm joking. I'm flattered you're so interested. Well let's see, I trained in Sheffield so I worked up there for a while and then I spent a few years travelling. I had a relationship go wrong, badly wrong, and after that I felt like I needed to disappear for a bit, so I did. Then a bit turned into a lot and I guess I was just too happy in the sun to come back."

Sophie found herself wondering what could have gone so wrong with his relationship to send him all over the world. "So, come on then, where did you go? Make me jealous," she laughed.

"Loads of places. Most of Europe, Australia, New Zealand and did a little bit of America. I'd like to go back there someday actually. So much to see there."

"God, you're a bit better travelled than me. So what brought you back finally?"

"Well, my dad was diagnosed with cancer last year and I couldn't leave my little sister to cope on her own especially since she's got kids to look after too."

"Oh I'm so sorry." Sophie realised she was so focussed on what was going on her own life, she sometimes forgot that other people had difficult things to cope with too. "Is he okay?"

"You don't have to keep apologising for all the bad things that happen in my family!" he laughed. "Anyway, yep, he's on the mend. I suppose with cancer there's never really a proper end though, you just have to cross your fingers and hope for the best really."

"And you've never been married?"

"Nah, figured I've got a bit of time yet!"

Sophie groaned. "If you want to bother that is… "

"I'm guessing from that you didn't like being married then?"

"Let's just say it didn't work out. It's okay we're at least on speaking terms now." Sophie found herself telling Mark all about Liam. Weird really since she didn't like talking about her marriage too much. She only left one detail out. Sophie found that he listened intently, fixing her with those chestnut eyes.

When the obviously irritated assistant came by to wipe a nearby table, Sophie glanced at her watch. She couldn't believe that they'd been talking for an hour.

"I think we'd better make a move. It looks like they're getting ready to close up now anyway."

"Ah yes, that's why they keep giving us the evil eye then!"

They walked to the car park together. Before he headed off to his bike, Mark turned to face Sophie and rested his hand on her arm "I've really enjoyed this, Sophie."

"Me too." She meant it. For a while she had been able to fly away from all her worries.

"Sooo… would you like to do it again? Maybe go out for something to eat with me sometime?"

Sophie looked up at this lovely man. Then a picture came into her mind. An image of Rosie in her room, miles away, on her own, while her mum was here chatting to a man.

"Mark, that's a great idea and you've been such a good friend, but… "

"Argh, I don't like buts."

"Maybe in a few months, it's just that with everything that's happened with Rosie, I just don't think I'm ready to start anything. I just can't focus on anything but my girls at the moment."

"Hey, it's only dinner, but I understand of course, and you know what, I'll wait…until you're ready that is."

Sophie smiled. He really was a lovely man.

A few minutes later, she watched him roar off on his bike. Sophie was just about to drive off herself when she heard her phone go. It was a message from Greg of all people.

'Hope your first day went well. Would be lovely to meet up soon for a chat.'

Would it?

34

Sophie attempted to put out of her mind the novel idea of two men interested in her. She kept them at arm's length as the next few months disappeared in a whirlwind of activity. There were visits to Rosie, increasingly busy and demanding work at the hospital, helping Chloe keep on track with her GCSEs and finally a really important event which was looming.

Sophie was busy planning for Rosie's thirteenth birthday in March. She was determined to mark it just like every other parent would mark their child turning thirteen. Why should it be different for Rosie just because she was autistic? Actually, she had found it good to have a real focus. It had lifted her out of the mire that she had sunk into when Rosie had gone away. Finally, a good event to look forward to.

Sophie had spent a long time thinking about how they could all celebrate Rosie becoming a teenager. She'd asked both Chloe and Gemma for their advice about what they thought would work best and she'd even asked Liam for his thoughts. After all, it was only fair since he was firmly back in their lives now and visiting Rosie regularly. He had been really enthusiastic about some sort of celebration and even agreed to pay half which would definitely help since the journey there and back to Rosie's home was costing her a fortune in petrol. They had all finally decided on a family party in a pub's small function room near the home. This meant that Rosie could be brought quickly – long journeys could be stressful – and taken back promptly if she got distressed. They would bring all of Rosie's favourite food and music and invite everyone who was important to Rosie.

The morning of Rosie's birthday was one of those beautiful March mornings that signalled the end of winter and promised you that spring was definitely on the way. Sophie and Chloe loaded the car up with the presents, balloons etc. Sophie felt that wonderful build of excitement at seeing Rosie soon though it was tempered with just a little anxiety at how she would be. Rosie would either love it or hate it. The trouble was if she hated it everyone would know about it.

The journey up there was as usual long, though the amount of times she had done it now, Sophie felt that she could probably do it in her sleep. Liam met them there and as soon as they arrived they set to work transforming the room into a paradise for Rosie. They had chosen decorations with pictures of characters from all Rosie's favourite cartoons and they put balloons and banners everywhere. The staff in the pub had put on a fabulous spread and arranged lights and music.

It could not have gone better.

Emily brought Rosie and when she walked into the room, the look on Rosie's face would be imprinted on Sophie's brain for a long time. All the work had been worth it and Sophie was thrilled to see her so happy during the afternoon. She giggled at the familiar pictures on the walls. She loved the lights and the balloons. She ate plenty of food and sat for a long time cuddling into Sophie while tapping the balloon near her face. Emily, just like the rest of the wonderful staff at the home knew just what balance to strike, she sat there happily, ready to help if things got tough, but let Sophie be Mum and take care of her daughter today.

It was a great atmosphere. Everyone that Sophie had invited cared about Rosie, the only exception being Natalie. She had been a 'needs must' invitation since to invite Andy and the kids without her might just cause a family rift which she could probably do without. Sophie had decided unequivocally, though, that if she became annoying she would be ignoring her for the afternoon.

As usual, Sophie was grateful to her mum. Diana was busy helping to make everything go smoothly. She had bought a beautiful cake that had been specially made for Rosie which now took pride of place on the buffet table. It was huge and in the shape of 'Shrek'. Rosie's face had lit up when she had seen it, which of course made Diana's day. Sophie's dad, on the other hand, although trying his best, was clearly uncomfortable. Ian was sitting stiffly in the corner trying to bear what he called the 'horrendous' music that youngsters listened to these days. Sophie had given him permission to escape to the car if it all got too much for his sixty-eight year old ears. Chloe kept popping over to give him a hug and attempt to chat to him over the music.

Gemma and Bob were here with Alex and Jess. Bob had quickly become a permanent fixture in Gemma's life and Sophie was glad. She had never seen her friend so happy and much to Gemma's relief, he got on well with her kids too. Sophie smiled to herself at how loved up her friend and boyfriend were, since Gemma used to laugh at other couples who insisted on public displays of affection. Tough Gemma, who had always sneered at romance, claiming that love simply did not exist, had now become a complete convert.

As her husband was working, Mark had brought Anna, though, as she'd told Sophie later, she had categorically refused to go on the back of his bike. Sophie had been surprised when on entering, Mark had handed her a huge present for Rosie. It had turned out to be a brightly coloured beanbag, just right for Rosie's room at the home. Impressed with his thoughtfulness, Sophie hadn't been able to stop herself throwing her arms round him, a gesture which had left him looking both thrilled and stunned. Anna and Mark were now sitting near the dancefloor chatting and every now and then Sophie would give them a wave and a smile.

Greg was here with Robbie. He had arrived half way through as, like Sophie, he preferred to limit the amount of time he took his son anywhere different. Robbie, who was vigorously jumping up and down to the music, obviously loved the dancefloor but every now and then, he would stop dancing and dash over to the buffet table to take another handful of crisps, cramming them in his mouth quickly before anyone would notice. Whenever she saw him do it, Sophie would smile over at Greg who would reply with a grin. He had brought Rosie a basket of all different types of chocolate. Another thoughtful gift which Rosie had been delighted with, though in the end Sophie had to hide it before Rosie scoffed the lot and made herself sick.

Busy dancing with his kids, Andy genuinely seemed to be enjoying himself. He, Saskia and Nathaniel even tried to encourage Rosie to dance with them, though of course typically it was only for a few minutes at a time, and completely on her terms. It always gave Sophie a thrill to see Rosie making a connection with her family, for however short a time.

It was clear that Andy was a good dad, Sophie just wished he would be a bit stronger with his irritating, domineering wife. In fact, while the rest of her family were having fun, a sour-faced Natalie sat awkwardly in the corner. Fully made up and looking completely out of place, she was busy on her phone for most of the afternoon. Every now and then she would get up, totter over in her heels and pick at the buffet with her nose very definitely turned up. Sophie decided the food probably wasn't organic enough for her.

Liam had brought his mum, who was polite and obviously making an effort but just looked bemused by the whole affair. She just couldn't understand why Rosie kept running off from her whenever she went near. Eventually she gave up and simply talked to Chloe who was 'normal' and could talk back about ordinary things like school and exams.

Sophie was sociable, more sociable than she had been for a while. She moved around the room and spent some time chatting to different people. However, she didn't linger long with anyone, and she hoped everyone understood the simple fact that this was Rosie's day and Sophie just wanted to be with her and make her happy. The horrible feeling that she had abandoned her daughter to the care of others simply never went away and she always felt she needed to make up for it somehow.

Sophie enjoyed the whole afternoon, but there was one perfect moment in the middle of the afternoon that she would never forget. Rosie was right in the centre of the dance floor, the lights were shining on her transforming her whole body into a multitude of colours. Gripping a balloon in one hand and a special toy, which Chloe had bought her, in the other. She was swaying to the music with a broad smile on her face and, even though Sophie couldn't hear, she knew Rosie was giggling to herself.

Rosie looked happy.

Settled and happy.

Sophie realised that Rosie hadn't had a meltdown for a few weeks. Oh, she was sure that there would be more in the future but they were in a really good phase at the moment and Sophie was determined to savour it. She also realised something else. Sophie couldn't remember the last time she had cried. The tears which had been a daily occurrence for Sophie hadn't appeared for a few weeks. Her heart swelled as she watched her beautiful daughter, so grown up now, who had coped with such a monumental change in her life. Her little girl, for that was what she would always be, couldn't understand the world, she couldn't understand people in the world but she was doing her best. She was here, with all these people, all these sounds, and coping.

She was shaken out of her reverie by a familiar voice.

"Sophie, this is great. She's really enjoying it, isn't she?"

It was Greg.

"Yes, thank goodness. So is Robbie though, by the looks of it." Sophie laughed as she saw Robbie again make a dash for the buffet.

"Yep. I hope you didn't want any crisps left, though, as he seems to be demolishing them all by himself. It's one of his current obsessions. He keeps wanting a bag of them right at bedtime which is leading to some humdinger showdowns at the moment."

"Oh I'm sorry, Greg." She really was. Sophie knew all too well how difficult it was when your autistic child got an obsession you couldn't control.

"Don't be. They handle him well at Thorpe Cloud and, well, it's par for the course isn't it? In our lives I mean. At least, he's surviving in a room full of people now. Not so long ago this situation would have totally freaked him out."

"I know what you mean. Even though Rosie's happy at the moment, I can still feel myself on high alert for any meltdowns today. Autism's just a minefield, isn't it?"

"Ha! Understatement. We could actually do with a manual being handed to us when we get the diagnosis. "

"I know, mind you, can you imagine how thick and heavy it would be?!"

Just at that moment, Robbie headed for the door.

"Sorry, Sophie, duty calls, better make sure he doesn't make a run for it!" Greg smiled as he turned and raced after his son.

Sophie was just about to tuck into a piece of cake when she was aware of someone pulling the chair out to sit down by the side of her.

Liam.

"It's worked out pretty well, hasn't it?" he said as he sat down next to her.

"Yes, I'm really glad we did it. I was a bit nervous about how she'd be, though, to tell you the truth."

Liam suddenly looked quite serious. He leaned closer towards her and instinctively, Sophie moved away. "Sophie, I wanted to tell you something while we're on our own."

Sophie went cold. He didn't want to give it another go did he? They had been getting on better so perhaps he had got the wrong idea. Sophie thought quickly about what she could say.

"The thing is, I've met someone."

Sophie wanted to laugh with relief. "Liam we've been divorced for years, you don't have to tell me about every relationship you have. I mean, I'm sure there have been quite a few, eh?" she smirked.

Sophie noticed that Liam was shifting around in his seat and looking fairly uncomfortable now.

"Well, the thing is when I say I've met her, I actually mean I've been seeing her for quite a while. She's called Siobhan and the thing is... we've... er... decided to... er... get married."

"Right... " Sophie wasn't quite sure what she was supposed to say to that. Was she supposed to offer congratulations? Her blessing? It was quite a strange situation. "Well, my God, Liam, that's... that's big news. Has Chloe met her?"

"Yeah, just the once though, when she was over in February."

"Funny, she never mentioned anything."

"I think she was worried that you had enough on your plate and she didn't want to upset you."

"Oh please, I got over you a long time ago, Liam." Sophie couldn't help it if her smile came out as a sneer.

"I know you did." Liam sighed.

They were both silent for a moment. Sophie idly wondered what this other half of Liam's might be like. Probably young and pretty, like she had been once upon a time. Sophie supposed she'd better say something nice.

"Well, I suppose that's good... for you I mean. Er... I hope you'll be very happy. To be honest, I didn't think you'd ever get married again!"

"Yep, neither did I." Did Sophie imagine a hint of regret then?

"Anyway, we think the wedding will be fairly soon and obviously I want Chloe and Rosie to be there."

"Obviously. But how is that going to work? I mean we can't take Rosie to Ireland."

"I know. So Siobhan has agreed to get married in England near Rosie's home. You know, to make things easier."

Sophie was speechless. They were going to tailor their wedding around Rosie so she could be included. Sophie looked at her ex-husband with a new respect.

What a funny feeling. The father of her children was moving on.

Just then, she heard a brisk Irish accent behind her. Sophie turned to see that Mary had joined them. As usual, this diminutive old woman was smartly turned out with her hair tightly pulled together in a pleat at the back. Looking completely on edge in this environment, giving the impression she would far rather be at some sort of church function.

"Sophie, hello, I've been meaning to come over and have a word with you."

Liam, who'd obviously had his fill of his mother, soon made his excuses and left. Sophie glared at him as he made his escape and left alone, her heart sank. What did her ex- soon to be someone else's mother-in-law want? If it was going to be unpleasant then she would very quickly be walking away. Sophie was determined that nothing was going to spoil Rosie's day.

"So, what can I do for you, Mary?" Sophie was immediately on the defensive which was probably evident in her voice.

"Well, Sophie, it's just that I wondered whether… maybe… perhaps I could go and visit Rosie in the home. Would that be allowed?"

Sophie gasped slightly and couldn't hide her shock. "Really?"

Mary frowned, "Well, yes, I am her grandma after all. I don't want the poor wee child to think I've forgotten her."

"Er… yes of course, Mary, well, that would be wonderful. I mean, God, it would be actually fantastic for her to have some different visitors. She probably gets tired of me!" Sophie's attempt at humour was lost on Mary who just maintained her usual serious expression and simply leaned forward.

"There was just one thing, Sophie. Could I ask you something?"

"Ask away."

"The thing is… well I'm not sure. I just don't have a lot of experience with children like Rosie and so… "

Sophie had never seen Mary so lost for words before and was wondering where this conversation was going.

"So, anyway, I wanted to ask your advice. What exactly do you do with her while you're there? Because well, I have tried talking to her but she just runs away from me. Is that usual? Should I follow her and try to play with her? Or should I wait for her to come to me? Do you think I should sit with her and maybe try to read a book? I just don't really know." Mary's face had crumpled a little and Sophie could see she was completely confused as to how to interact with her autistic granddaughter. It didn't surprise her, a lot of people must feel bewildered when confronted with this complex and always confusing condition.

Sophie took Mary's hands. She felt so touched by the kindness this hitherto quite formidable woman was showing to her special needs daughter. "Oh Mary, don't worry, just go and be with her. Let her lead you."

"But does she know me, Sophie?"

"Do you know what, Mary? I have a feeling our Rosie knows much more than we give her credit for. I think she understands us, I think she definitely knows who we all are and… and I think… I know she likes being with us."

Mary suddenly, and quite unexpectedly, grabbed a stunned Sophie and pulled her into a tight hug. "Oh Sophie, this must have been so hard for you, pet." Mary had never been so demonstrative. After a few seconds though, she was released and patting her hair, Mary regained her composure. "Well, I look forward to seeing her soon. Shall I take her some chocolate, do you think?"

Sophie smiled warmly, "Mary, I think that would be wonderful." And she meant it.

As she wandered over to dance with Rosie again, Sophie thought about her conversation with her frosty mother-in-law and was left with a very clear realisation that sometimes, despite what you always thought, people really did surprise you.

35

Spring had definitely arrived.

As March became April, suddenly Sophie found herself waking up to sunshine streaming through the windows transforming the house into a warmer and brighter place. The harsh sounds of the crows had been replaced with more tuneful birdsong.

Everything felt as if it was changing.

On a particularly warm morning Sophie realised that she now had no reason to shove the washing into the tumble dryer and she should really hang it out. That of course meant that she had to venture out into the garden. It was a heart breaking thought since she had spent the whole of the winter trying to avoid it. It was just too painful to see the trampoline on the dense lawn which Rosie had spent hours at a time bouncing on. Standing there in the long grass, never used, it seemed so lonely, just waiting, like the rest of them, for Rosie to return.

Sophie took a deep breath as she walked up the path with the full basket. She gazed around, astonished, not for the first time, that how even in the lowest periods of your life, everything still carried on. Now, new life had erupted in the garden transforming it, from a drab place full of skeletal bushes, to one of colour and vibrancy. Looking around her, she decided that there was probably too much life. It was extremely overgrown and would need a lot of work to sort it all out.

As she pegged out the washing, Sophie became lost in her thoughts. In her memories, afternoons in the gardens with the girls when they were little had always seemed to be bathed in beautiful sunshine, the two of them running around happily enjoying their toys. Of course the realist in her knew that was probably not true. Many an afternoon had not been perfect with meltdowns over paddling pools, food, anything really. It was just that Sophie seemed to be plagued by all the wonderful happy memories which nagged at her trying to remind her that she had made a terrible mistake sending Rosie away.

She hung up the last pair of jeans and decided that, since she had a free morning, there was no time like the present to start sorting out the wild mess. She dragged the lawn mower out of the rickety shed, which she knew was probably on the verge of collapse, and set to work.

The morning seemed to fly by and to Sophie's amazement she actually enjoyed herself being outside. There was something lovely about feeling the sun on your back and the smell of cut grass. It made her feel young again. Well, certainly younger than she had felt in months.

Once she had finished cutting the lawn, Sophie set to work on the weeding. She realised that she had really neglected the garden over the last few years, simply cutting the lawn whenever she got the chance. Little wonder really, since between working, looking after Rosie and sorting the house, time had been so short.

Even after only a morning's work, Sophie was pleased to see how the garden was beginning to look better. After ripping out some of the huge weeds, she'd actually uncovered quite a few shrubs that she'd forgotten about. Now they had been freed, Sophie hoped they would add more colour to the garden.

In the next few weeks, whenever Sophie had some free time and the weather was good, she would spend it in the garden. To her surprise, she really was starting to enjoy gardening. Something that she had only ever thought of as a hobby for older people like her mum and dad, had suddenly begun to interest her and she wasn't sure why. Maybe it was the physicality of it, ripping out weeds, digging, raking, which helped to get rid of all her frustration. Possibly it was seeing things that she had planted as mere seeds developing slowly and coming to fruition. Or perhaps it was simply being outside in the peace and quiet away from everything. Whatever the reason, Sophie couldn't wait to get into the garden and was thrilled to see that it was now really starting to take shape; it was something she was beginning to be very proud of.

Chloe came out one evening carrying cups of tea for the both of them and they sat and drank it on the rusty old patio table. Sophie made a mental note to buy a new one next pay day.

"It's looking brilliant, Mum."

"Yes it is isn't it? I think we could get it looking really lovely this year. The only thing is… " Sophie studied the hedges, "… I'm not sure I'll be able to cut those hedges, they've got really tall and I don't trust myself up that high with a set of hedge trimmers."

"What about Grandpa, he loves doing jobs for us."

"No," Sophie said firmly, "I'm not going to ask Grandpa because, even though he doesn't think he is, he's getting too old to get up on ladders. I don't want to be responsible for him breaking his neck."

"Well, why don't you pay someone to do it? Someone must know a gardener."

Sophie laughed. "Good idea, Chloe. All that studying must be paying off!"

The next day at work, Sophie just happened to mention it, when Mark almost leapt out of his seat proclaiming that he was quite happy to do it and she shouldn't even think about paying someone. Sophie had mixed feelings. She certainly appreciated the offer, but she didn't want Mark to get the wrong idea. Or was it the right idea? Sophie wasn't sure of anything these days.

A few days later, Mark was there at her door ready to start. Gemma just happened to be there too and could hardly contain herself when she saw him walk into the garden with his shorts on.

"Oh my God, gorgeous man with a powerful tool alert!" she hissed.

"Ssshhh," Sophie hissed back. "He'll hear you! He's just being a friend, that's all."

"Well, I wish I had friends like that. And he rides a motorbike! Oh and look at those legs. Good God, Soph, what are you waiting for? He clearly adores you, why don't you go out with him?"

"It's not that simple. I'm not ready for anything like that. I've got to concentrate on Rosie."

"Well, if you're sure. Just remember they don't make 'em like that very often," Gemma grinned.

"Just go home to your man and stop interfering in my love life."

"What love life is that?"

Gemma hugged her and disappeared next door.

Mark worked like a Trojan, only stopping for the odd cold drink. At one point he got so hot he took his shirt off. Sophie tried to keep herself busy so she wouldn't have to keep catching a glance of Mark's muscular body with ribbons of sweat running down it. Sophie knew that Gemma would be outraged when she realised that she'd gone home far too soon.

When he'd finally finished they sat together with a diet coke on the new patio table that Sophie had treated herself to. She looked in wonder at how the smart trimmed hedge had put the finishing touches to her fabulous new garden.

"You've done a brilliant job, Mark, it looks amazing."

"No worries, Soph, I know it makes me sound like an old man but I quite like gardening. I tend to look after my dad's as he's not really up to doing it these days."

"It's funny, I never used to like it but I'm loving it this year. I suppose I've got more time though now," Sophie's laugh was hollow.

"It shows. You've made it look beautiful out here."

Sophie smiled and their eyes locked for a minute.

She had to ask. "Tell me to mind my own business if you want, I just wondered what happened to send you all the way across the world?"

"I told you my relationship went bad." Mark looked down at his glass clearly uncomfortable,

Sophie immediately felt guilty. "Sorry, I shouldn't have asked. Forget it."

He looked up. "No, it's fine, I'm over it. I mean, I don't want to be back with her or anything, it's just a bit painful to think about that's all. I ended up not just losing her you see, I lost my best friend too."

The penny dropped. "Oh, you mean... "

"Yep, such a cliché isn't it? The girlfriend, actually let's get it right, fiancé, and the best friend. He'd just come back from travelling, was staying with us for a while and hey presto, one affair. I was just about to ask him to be my best man as well. I suppose he turned out to be just that, didn't he?" Mark said drily.

"Oh, Mark... "

"It's okay, I'm not the only one in the world to have been hurt, eh? At least, I heard on the grapevine that they got married so I didn't lose her to a quick fling. They were actually *in lurve*. Suppose it makes it a bit better though I definitely didn't think so at the time. I remember hurling quite a few things at the wall."

Sophie couldn't imagine this man ever being angry.

"What about you, Sophie, seeing as we're being so honest. Has there been anyone since Liam?"

"No, too busy." Sophie smiled. "God, when we broke up the girls were small and I was up to my eyes in sorting them out every day, cleaning the house, going to work. Sorry, but a man was right at the bottom of the list." She laughed. "Anyway, it would take an extra special person to understand about Rosie."

"Well, I'm not extra special or anything but.... still waiting you know, Sophie... " he grinned with a wink.

Sophie looked away. "Mark, I'm sorry… "

"Hey, don't worry, whenever you're ready. I've got the perfect restaurant picked out, you just say the word." He sighed and got up. "Anyway, thanks for the drinks, I better get off now. My sister's bringing the boys round and there'll be hell to pay if Uncle Mark's not there!"

"Well, thanks again, Mark, I really appreciate it. Are you sure you don't want anything for all that work? A gardener would have charged a fortune."

He looked thoughtful. "Just that meal… " He winked again and was gone.

36

The sunshine seemed to have injected a little more enthusiasm into Sophie's soul in other ways. She had made what she felt was a monumental decision. She had decided to book a holiday for herself and Chloe for when her exams had finished.

It would be the first holiday they had had abroad for years as, since Rosie's diagnosis, Sophie had been too terrified to take her too far away from home. The idea of putting Rosie on a plane had been frightening. What if she had a meltdown in the air? What if Sophie couldn't get her on the plane at all? The potential problems were endless and that was just the journey. Actually arriving at the destination would throw up a whole set of new issues. So, Sophie had always settled for a week in a holiday camp in England. Somewhere they could get to easily and back from quickly, should they need to.

Sophie had thought long and hard about booking a holiday. She didn't want anyone to think she was suddenly jetting off now she had got rid of her troublesome daughter. She couldn't bear anyone imagining that she was pleased that she was free. Sophie knew she would sacrifice all the most exotic holidays in the world just to have Rosie at home. However, when she had talked to Gemma about it, she had laughed and told her that anyone who knew Sophie would never think that and to 'stop fannying around and book the damn thing!'

So, Sophie had gone ahead and found a reasonable self-catering week in Crete. A week would be more than enough as Sophie didn't think she would be able to manage any longer away from Rosie, it would be hard enough not being in the same country. Once she had booked it, she felt a thrill of excitement and pride that she had arranged something so lovely for her Chloe. Anytime the guilt hit her, Sophie would make herself picture what she thought Chloe's face would look like when she told her and remember her oldest daughter deserved it after working so hard, despite everything that had happened this year. In fact, Sophie had decided that if her diligent daughter didn't get a bunch of As, she would be having words with the exam board herself.

Just as she had imagined, Chloe was thrilled when a few weeks before her first exam, Sophie presented her with an envelope marked 'A Present for Chloe'. Her face had literally beamed when she saw where they were off to. Chloe hugged Sophie tightly proclaiming her 'the best mum in the whole world.'

37

The weeks leading up to the holiday whizzed by.

Chloe's exams began. It was a nerve-wracking time. Sophie was struggling to watch her daughter head off into a tense situation and not be able to help her. She kept her going with plenty of tea, snacks and moral support and made herself available every night to test her, though most of the time Sophie hadn't a clue what Chloe was answering. She was absolutely sure exams hadn't been as hard when she was young.

As the weeks wore on, Chloe started to look more and more tired and pale. Sophie was so glad that she had taken the plunge and booked a holiday. Her exhausted daughter would certainly be ready for it.

Finally, the last exam was over and Sophie and Chloe both breathed a huge sigh of relief. She wasn't sure who was the most thankful, her or Chloe. After all, Sophie felt as if she had been in that exam room with her daughter every step of the way. Naturally, Chloe was convinced she had done terribly and failed all of them. So to cheer her up, Sophie had promised that she could have a few friends round for a get together. As long as it would only be a few and there would be absolutely no mention of it on Facebook.

In the end, it had turned into a lovely evening. Chloe had invited a decent set of kids who seemed polite and respectful. They were all in good spirits and it was great to have a noisy house again. It had been so quiet since Rosie went and Sophie realised that she had missed the sound of giggling and laughter that seemed to follow Rosie wherever she went.

Sophie ordered pizza and had bought a selection of DVDs for them to watch. After a while though, she felt like a spare part and decided that they were sensible enough for her to leave them and head off to Gemma's.

Gemma answered the door with a glass of wine in her hand. "Hiya babe!"

"You've started early." Sophie smiled.

"This, my love, is for you! I figured you might need it after coping with a house full of teenagers for the last few hours!"

"Ah you're a saviour," Sophie laughed taking it from her. "Mind you, it's been fine. They're all lovely girls and no trouble at all."

"Well, I think you deserve it anyway, just for being you!" Gemma hugged her and dragged her in. "Now come in, it's been ages since we had a good gossip."

It was like old times. Sophie found herself laughing and feeling more like her old self than she had in months.

"Soooo, have you heard from ex-hubby then? Is the wedding of the century still going ahead?"

"Oh yes, so Chloe tells me. I don't have a lot to do with it really. That would be just too weird."

"Hmmm very sensible if you ask me." Gemma nodded sagely. "Judging by mine in particular, these ex-husbands are a strange breed, it's best to ignore them if you can."

"Ha. Actually, they're coming up to fetch Chloe tomorrow. They're taking her out for a meal to celebrate the end of her exams. It's a posh hotel and they're staying over. Chloe's so excited."

"Oooh, so you're going to meet the lovely Siobhan then?"

"It seems so. I'm surprised she's coming to the house. I wouldn't have thought that she'd want to meet me."

"Oh, come on, she'll be feeling just a little bit threatened by you and wanting to check you out. After all, whatever happens us original wives had them first. We've had their babies and there's nothing they can ever do about that."

"What is the protocol with second wives then? Am I supposed to be friendly or mean?"

"I think you're supposed to be bloody grateful that she's got him now and you haven't!"

Sophie looked serious for a minute. "Thanks, Gemma."

Gemma stopped mid-sip looking confused. "What for?"

"For always making me laugh and just, you know… " she sighed, "just being there. I'm not sure I'd have made it through the last few months without you."

"Are you scared the plane might crash? Are you trying to get your goodbyes in?" Gemma giggled, like only Gemma could.

Sophie couldn't help joining in. "We-ell, it is a while since I've flown!" She looked serious again. "Honestly, Gemma, you're a brilliant friend, you know."

"Oh God, you're going to make me well up in a minute." Gemma grabbed her hand. "Hey, we've been there for each other haven't we? That's what friends do."

Sophie was quite impressed that when she went home later the girls had tidied up the pizza boxes and the house still looked fairly presentable. Obviously not to her standard, but nothing a good hoover wouldn't fix.

38

The next morning Chloe was up bright and early getting ready for her night away. Her trip to Liam's had worked out well actually since it had coincided with the night that Sophie had promised to go for a few drinks with work for Anna's birthday. If it had been anyone else, Sophie would have said no, it being so close to the holiday, but Anna had been so lovely since she'd gone back to work that Sophie felt that she had to make an appearance.

She was just putting away the breakfast dishes when she heard a loud knock. Before answering, she checked her hair in the mirror, after all she didn't want to be the archetypal bedraggled first wife. Planting a smile on her face, Sophie threw open the door.

There they stood on the doorstep, hand in hand, her ex-husband and his beautiful wife-to-be, Siobhan.

The new woman in Liam's life was just as Chloe had described. Her hair was long and dark and she had a sheen to it that could only have come from extremely expensive hair products. Her clothes were immaculate and seemed to float over her slim figure. Sunglasses were perched on the top of her head and Sophie was willing to bet that they certainly weren't from Primark. With a touch of embarrassment, Sophie quickly glanced down at the cropped trousers and t-shirt that she had pulled on this morning. It was all she could find that looked half decent since most of her good clothes were packed.

What was it about second wives? Sophie wondered. It was as if men seemed to want to go right back to the beginning again, to what their partners were like before they had been scarred by children. They now seemed to crave the original, untarnished version.

Siobhan reached her hand out with an air of confidence and broad smile which indicated that nothing terrible had ever happened to her. The silky smooth Irish lilt which followed was almost like poetry.

"Hello, I'm Siobhan, it's lovely to meet you."

"Er, hi I'm Sophie." Sophie shook her hand hesitantly, unsure of what to do or say now "Do you want to come in for a minute? Chloe's just flying around as usual, getting her bits and pieces."

"Well –" Liam started nervously. He was obviously acutely aware of the unusual situation emerging. The ex-wife with the new wife. What on earth could possibly happen?

"Thank you, Sophie that would be great." Siobhan glided in. "You have a lovely home," She smiled surveying the room.

Sophie thought she probably didn't mean that. It was, after all, a very ordinary three bedroomed semi, not like the four bedroomed detached house that Chloe had reported Liam and Siobhan had just bought and were in the process of doing up. Sophie observed Siobhan sitting awkwardly on the edge of the aging sofa, the faded colours not really matching her obviously designer clothes.

She desperately wanted to hate this beautiful young woman. Even though she certainly no longer wanted Liam herself, she was finding it so painful to see him move on. However, there was something about this young woman, which made it impossible for Sophie to dislike her. Was it her soft voice and manner? Was it the fact that she did nothing but smile? Or was it the fact that she was altering her wedding plans to accommodate her husband's autistic daughter?

"So… " Sophie thought she'd better make some attempt at conversation, "is everything set for the big day?" Sophie was fully aware how odd it was asking your ex-husband and his wife-to-be this question, but really, what else was there to talk about?

"Oh, yes," Siobhan gushed, "it's going to be perfect. We can't wait, can we, Liam?"

Liam looked at her, eyes shining. Sophie winced a little when she remembered that once upon a time he used to look at her like that. "No, it's going to be great."

"Did Chloe tell you that we're having her and Rosie as bridesmaids?" Siobhan asked.

"Yes she mentioned it." Sophie thought back to the squeal which had come from Chloe's mouth when she'd got the text last night.

"Chloe really is a wonderful girl, Sophie." Siobhan continued.

Sophie felt herself swell with pride. "Thank you."

"I also met Rosie the other day."

"Yes, they'd mentioned you'd both been up."

"She's really special isn't she?"

"Yes, she is. Very, very special." Sophie hoped she meant that.

Siobhan squeezed Liam's hand. "We had a great time with her, didn't we Liam?"

Sophie tried not to laugh. In actual fact, Emily had reported that during Liam's and Siobhan's visit, Rosie had spent most of her time either trying to prod Siobhan with chocolate fingers or run away from her. To her credit, Siobhan hadn't got stressed about it, she had just laughed. Sophie knew you weren't supposed to think this but she'd decided that Liam had chosen well.

Chloe chose that moment to burst into the room.

"Dad!" Chloe hugged Liam.

"Hi Chloe," Siobhan moved over to put her arm round a slightly resistant Chloe. "I managed to get you that lipstick you saw the other day. You know that shade you said you loved?"

"Oh yeah, thanks, Siobhan," she smiled. Chloe turned and raised her eyebrows at Sophie.

Sophie understood at that moment just how hard it probably was for Siobhan. Just a tiny bit of Sophie felt sorry for her replacement. She would forever be trying to earn the love of two children who already loved Liam's first wife unconditionally.

Liam, who had clearly had enough of being in the same room as his ex-wife and wife-to-be, hurried Chloe along. "Right, come on then, Chlo, we'd better be off."

When they all moved towards the door, Sophie thought everyone inwardly heaved a sigh of relief that this awkward meeting was nearly over.

"It was good to meet you finally." Siobhan smiled and held out her hand again. Sophie shook it then watched as Chloe and her new step-mum wandered over to the car. Would she get used to this eventually, Sophie wondered, another woman in her child's life?

Before he too headed out of the door, Sophie held Liam's arm. "So you'll bring her back Saturday afternoon, won't you? She's still got loads of packing to do."

Liam turned to her. "Course." He smiled, that lovely smile that Sophie knew so well. "Have a good holiday Sophie, you deserve it."

In a quiet voice, Sophie couldn't help but say to the only other person who loved Rosie like she did, "I feel guilty, you know."

"Don't" He smiled and stroked her face. "No more, Soph."

And they were gone.

***

Sophie sat with a cup of tea in the silent house after they'd left and thought about her meeting with Siobhan. Without doubt, it had been peculiar. She hadn't known how she was going to feel. Obviously she and Liam had been divorced for a long time but he was still her first love and the father of her children and that was a big thing wasn't it? They had shared so much at one time.

In the end, it had all been fine. She was glad to see that Liam had moved on and was finally happy. They had both managed to let go of what had happened so many years ago. Sophie had realised that if this last year had taught her anything it was that you really had to live in the moment and not dwell on the past, because you never knew when things were going to change forever and the future you thought was going to happen could be ripped away from you.

39

Too late, Sophie realised that she would need to change into something presentable for her evening out with work. She didn't possess many expensive smart clothes, a hangover from living with an autistic child who constantly threatened to cover you in something colourful or sticky, so leggings and tops were usually the most practical option. And anything dressy she had was now sitting neatly in her case ready for Crete.

With about ten minutes to spare before the taxi arrived, Sophie finally managed to find a miniskirt, she had forgotten about at the back of her wardrobe, and a smart T-shirt that went with it well. Together with her straightened hair and full make-up, she didn't think she looked too bad.

The pub was overflowing with familiar faces when Sophie arrived. Anna was very popular so most of the department had come. The combined noise of their voices and the karaoke, which was just starting, made for a vibrant and raucous atmosphere. Judging by the amount of hysterical laughter, everyone seemed to be well on their way.

Sophie managed to push her way to Anna and give her a kiss and a hug.

"What time did you get here?" Sophie shouted in Anna's ear.

"About an hour ago," she yelled back, "but it's happy hour so everyone's gone a bit mad!" Anna leaned in closer and nudged her, giggling. "Hey, Mark's been asking if you were coming. Is there something going on between you two?"

"No, we're just friends."

"Ha! Friends! I've seen the way he gazes at you. You sure he knows you're *just friends*?"

"Ye-es. Anyway, I'm going to get a drink. Want one birthday girl?"

"Nah, I've got two already and I'm already feeling a wee bit squiffy!"

Sophie took one look at the mass of people surrounding the bar and knew it was going to be almost impossible to get served anytime soon. Fortunately, just then Mark spotted her and he was already being served.

"Drink, Soph?" he shouted over the by now almost deafening noise.

"Ooh yes, white wine, please," she called back.

He grinned and turned back to lean on the bar as Sophie tried not to notice just how gorgeous he looked tonight in his jeans and shirt.

A few minutes later he handed her a crisp white wine that seemed to go down way too easily. Sophie tried not to think how even with the staff only metres away, with the two of them standing there facing each other, it felt so much like a date.

"So," Sophie began in an effort to erase not exactly an awkward silence since the pub was full of noise, just an awkward moment.

"Hang on, I can't hear you, Soph, do you want to go outside? We'll only have the smokers to contend with there."

Sophie nodded and followed Mark outside. It was an idyllic, balmy June evening, when after months of huddling inside, the whole world seemed to have moved outside in to the bright sunshine. Sophie was surprised that, given this was a busy inner city pub, there was quite a large, pleasant decking area full of flowering baskets. As there were plenty of tables, Mark led her to one well away from the people who were out there already.

"This okay?"

"Yep, fine." Sophie sat down and took another gulp. She couldn't shake the nervous feeling she had in her stomach, even though she saw this guy virtually every day at work. It was just such a different situation and the addition of alcohol rather than a cup of coffee made it seem all the more serious.

"So, how's things with you then?" Sophie asked.

Mark smiled. "Well, not much different from when I saw you yesterday really."

Sophie laughed, feeling a bit silly. "Well, it seemed like a good conversation opener in my head!"

"We can go back inside if you're finding it too uncomfortable out here with me alone." He laughed too. "I just thought there was no way we would be able to have a decent conversation in there. You can barely hear yourself think."

"No, no it's fine. It's nice out here. I think I'm growing out of noisy pubs to be honest. Give me a quiet country pub any day of the week, where you can relax and think."

"I knew we had lots in common." Mark took a sip of his pint and looked at her over his glass. As he put his glass down he moved forward. "Can I just say that you look really lovely tonight, Sophie?"

Sophie was suddenly aware of the shortness of her skirt and the tightness of her top and felt a little bit exposed suddenly. She wasn't used to hearing things like that anymore.

"Er... thanks," she muttered drinking more wine. At this rate she would be completely drunk before it was even dark.

"So, how's Rosie?"

"Oh she's okay. Up and down, though thankfully mostly up at the moment. I still miss her like mad every day. "

"I guess you will. I mean I haven't got kids but I've seen my sister with hers and I can't imagine what it would be like for her if she didn't have them with her."

"It would be terrible for her," Sophie said softly.

Silence again.

"Anyway, I'm going to see her tomorrow before me and Chloe go away. I just hope she's in a good mood because I'd hate the last time I see her for a week to be a horrible time."

"I'll keep my fingers crossed for you. You know, I think you've been amazing this year. The way you've coped with everything and you can still do that lovely smile."

"Stop. You're making me out to be some kind of a saint! Anyway, I'm not sure I have coped really. Sometimes I feel like I stumble from day to day just sorting whatever rubbish life has decided to throw at me on that particular day."

"Well, hopefully the worst is over now."

"No it isn't. I'll never stop missing her, you know," Sophie realised she had snapped. "Sorry, I just get fed up of people telling me it will get better when it won't ever really. I'm just wading through that's all."

"No, I'm sorry, I guess I'm just trying to say the right thing and failing miserably." He smiled warily.

"You and everyone else. Hey don't feel singled out if I snap at you, I'm horrible to everyone these days."

"You're not horrible."

Sophie looked down at her hands. She'd always found it hard to accept compliments but now she was totally out of practice at receiving them.

"Did you ever want kids, Mark?"

"Maybe one day. I suppose I would have to meet the right person first."

Another awkward silence.

Luckily, at that moment a few of the others began to drift outside and moved over to their table. Sophie had mixed feelings. It felt a little bit easier having a few more people in the conversation but she had enjoyed Mark's company and it felt good to have someone look at her the way Mark had and still was. Sophie could feel his eyes on her and occasionally she would turn and catch his eye. The smile that would instantly light up his face was both kind and incredibly sexy.

Before long, driven out by the noise and the heat, most of the hospital crowd had moved outside to join them. Eventually, they had taken over the entire beer garden. Even though she'd been reticent about coming, Sophie had to admit that it was actually a great atmosphere, so she stayed a lot longer than she had originally intended to.

By the end of the evening there was just a select few left, all people that Sophie liked and got on with. Despite her reservations about the evening, whether it was the company or the copious amounts of alcohol that she had consumed, Sophie felt quite relaxed.

At some point, when the music in the bar had died down, the staff were very obviously clearing up and the conversation had moved on to a drunken debate about the state of the NHS, an exhausted Sophie looked at her watch and decided it was time to go home. She phoned a taxi then gave a quick wave to Mark who was currently being besieged by almost the whole of the female staff who were left in the garden. He grimaced at her and held his hand up. Sophie wasn't sure if it was a wave or not but, as she was starting to feel the effects of way more wine than she usually drank, she didn't want to hang around to find out.

She moved over to Anna, who by now was completely drunk and resting her head on one of the surgeon's shoulders looking like she was about to go to sleep. Fortunately said surgeon was gay and would make sure she got back to her husband safely. Sophie felt herself sway slightly.

"Hey Anna, I'm going to get off now."

"Sophie," Anna raised her head, slowly opened her eyes and pulled Sophie to her, almost falling on top of her in the process. "My lovely friend, you are so brave, do you know that?" In a big voice to the rest of the small crowd still there she announced, "Sophie is soo brave, do you know that?"

"Shhh, Anna," Sophie smiled and wriggled out of her friend's grip. "Look, I'm not back at work until after my holiday, so I'll see you then, okay?"

While Anna continued to tell anyone who was actually still capable of listening, her friend's tragic tale of autism, Sophie tried to walk in a straight line out to the front of the pub to wait for the taxi. Just then she heard a familiar voice behind her.

"Hold up. I'll wait with you, Soph."

As they reached the front wall, she turned and grinned. "I thought you looked a bit busy, didn't want to disturb you for a farewell."

"Wish you had, mate. They wouldn't stop going on about my bike. How fast it goes, whether I've taken a woman on it. God, I'd forgotten what a crowd of drunken females sound like!"

"So, have you?" Sophie laughed.

Mark gently stroked a stray hair that had fallen across Sophie's face. "Well, you see the problem is that there's only one woman that I want to take on it… "

Mark's arms wound round her pulling her close. His lips brushed hers gently. His eyes were wide open and seemed to be searching hers. He pulled back and sighed, those brown eyes still staring. She felt the stirring of something that had laid dormant for a long time; desire.

She moved towards him to finish what he had started. His hands rested on the base of her spine. Sophie felt as if she could stay in this spot with this lovely man forever. As he moved his lips away he looked at her; Sophie had forgotten what it was like to have a man want you as much as he obviously did.

"Sophie," he breathed softly, "you are so beautiful…"

For some inexplicable reason, a tear fell from her eye. All of a sudden she felt so sad. "Do you know how long it has been since anyone called me beautiful?"

He nestled his head into her neck and whispered, "Do you want to come back?"

There was no reason she couldn't. Chloe was safely with her dad and so there was no one at home to hurry back to. But that was the problem. That picture popped into her mind again. A little girl, because to Sophie that was what she would absolutely always be, a little girl in a bed on her own a long way from home. Sophie realised she just couldn't.

Sophie pulled away. It suddenly all felt too fast. "No," she whispered, "… no. I'm sorry Mark, I can't, I just… I… well, I need some time to think."

Mark groaned quietly and his arms fell by his side. "God, Sophie you're driving me mad," he frowned. He dug his hands in his pocket and leaned on the wall. "Just to be clear, that's not a definite 'no' then, just a 'not now'?"

Sophie smiled at him. "It's a 'let me think things through'. Look, I'm going away the day after tomorrow and I need some headspace." She couldn't stand the disappointment on his face. "I'll call you when I get back, is that okay?"

"He got up, hugged her tightly and kissed her cheek. "I'll be here. Waiting."

40

Although Sophie began the following day pondering on what had nearly happened with Mark, the events of the day firmly pushed it to the back of her mind and she suffered a setback which nearly sent her into the depths again.

Sophie had been visiting Rosie as often as she could, sometimes twice a week. She was amazed at how well she was doing. She had been taking part willingly in lots of different activities. She had been pony trekking, bowling, swimming, riding on a trike, and even a very short residential trip where she had actually been canoeing. Rosie seemed to be coping so well that when Sophie went to see her for the last time before she and Chloe went on holiday, Sophie had broached the idea, with the staff, of a home visit at some point in the future.

A home visit was something that Sophie had been desperate to begin ever since Rosie had gone away. The possibility of having her daughter at home again in her own bed, just for one night even, had been the light at the end of a very long dark tunnel.

Except the staff at the home were not in favour of it all. They felt it was too soon to even be thinking about that and that it would be very unsettling for Rosie. They didn't seem to give any indication that it was something that would be happening anytime soon. Sophie felt that she just couldn't argue with anything that wouldn't be good for Rosie and left the home devastated.

She began to drive home but after a few minutes pulled over to the side of the road. With tears in her eyes and her hands shaking she didn't feel like she could carry on much further. She rang the only person she knew would understand.

Greg.

When he heard the misery in her voice he told her to come to his place immediately. Sophie virtually collapsed into his arms when he opened the door. They had only met a few times since Rosie's party, usually just for a coffee if their visits had coincided at the home. Every time she saw him though it felt comfortable, he was proving to be a real friend.

"Oh Sophie, don't cry." Greg led her into his lounge. "Sit here for a minute while I get you a coffee."

Sophie sat there and stared into space for a while thinking over the last year and everything that had happened. It was almost too much to bear. What had she done?

It only took minutes for Greg to return clutching two cups of coffee. He put them on the table and sat next to her.

Sophie turned to him. "She's never coming home is she? I've lost her haven't I?"

"No you haven't, honestly Sophie."

"But I sent her away. It was my fault."

He clasped her shoulders firmly. "Do you think I would willingly have given up my boy? Don't you think I fought like mad to keep him at home? But eventually it was dangerous. I didn't know what he was going to do next and I was frightened, Sophie, really frightened. I said everything that you've said to yourself but at the end of the day I had no choice. It just wasn't a choice, Sophie and neither was yours. And that's what you've got to hold on to." He let her go.

Sophie nodded silently, tears streaming down her face.

"But it hurts like hell doesn't it?" he whispered.

It did.

Sophie knew he was right. She had spent so long feeling guilty about the decision but finally she realised that it wasn't a decision at all, because if it had been then she would never have made it. It was simply something she had had to do. To protect Chloe, to protect herself and to protect Rosie. To make Rosie's life better.

And it was. Better.

Different maybe but definitely better. Everything Sophie was feeling was about her and her guilt. She thought of all the things that Rosie had done in the last year. Places she had been to that Sophie could never have taken her to. She thought of the wonderful moments they shared now instead of the showdowns that had been a daily occurrence before. Before she went away, Rosie had spent her days struggling with the complexities of normal life and so had Sophie.

Greg passed her a tissue.

"It's just that every time I think it's starting to get better, I feel like I get crushed again. I don't know how much more of this I can take. It's like a, like a… " She struggled to find the words between her tears.

"Rollercoaster?" offered Greg.

"Yes, except this one is no bloody fun and I want so much to get off."

"Trouble is, you'll just have to keep going 'cos that's what we do isn't it, us parents of 'special' children? We have to because if we don't then who will?"

"I'm just so tired."

"I know you are."

"And so sad."

"I know that too. I do understand Sophie, I really do. Sometimes, I look at everything that's happened and I wonder why or even how I still get up in the morning. But you just have to because the alternative is giving up and I'm not about to give up on Robbie and I'm pretty sure that you'll never give up on Rosie. Right?"

"Never."

"Well there you are, not much choice then is there?" He grimaced. "You know, not only are our kids special, let's face it we must be too, you know. I mean let's be honest, we really have to go the extra mile don't we. Love, patience, humour, you name it."

"Well, definitely humour!"

"God," Greg laughed, "the things that we have to laugh at on a daily basis that other people would cry and give up over."

They both sat quietly for a moment drinking their coffee. Sophie was surprised that the house was so comfortable. She'd half-expected an architect's house to be all space age and minimalist or something. Instead it was actually lovely. It was spacious and modern but with homely touches and, like Sophie's, it was also covered in photos of his child.

"So, come on, are you looking forward to your holiday?" Greg asked, obviously trying to change the subject.

"Yes and no," Sophie replied. "I mean it'll be lovely spending time with Chloe, but I'm going to struggle being so far from Rosie. I mean I can't exactly rush home if anything happens can I?"

"It'll be fine. Just go and enjoy the rest. God knows you both deserve it."

Sophie found herself wondering what Greg would be doing for a holiday. Did he have someone special tucked away somewhere. He'd never said.

"How's Robbie?" Sophie asked.

"Fine, well, being a teenager and not just that, a teenager with autism which is definitely getting to be an interesting mix." Greg laughed. "He made me laugh the other day. I took him out for a pub lunch and while I wasn't looking he finished the pint belonging to the old guy on the next table. He'd left it when he nipped to the loo."

"Ha! That could be an interesting combination autism and alcohol!"

"Yes especially as he didn't seem to mind the taste. He asked for more. He nearly had a meltdown when I refused. So I had to placate him with crisps until our meal came."

"What did the old guy do?"

"Oh, he made some comment about the rudeness of the youth of today and how they couldn't be controlled. I did try to explain that he was autistic but like most old people he didn't really get it. I got him another pint to shut him up which he seemed happy with. I think I'm just going to have to give that pub a wide berth from now on though."

Sophie chuckled. "Life's so challenging for us isn't it?"

"You think you've just got it figured out and everything changes."

"I've decided you never figure out autism. Even the so-called experts haven't a clue."

"Bloody exhausting isn't it?"

Sophie leaned back on Greg's extraordinarily comfortable sofa. "Yep, Greg, it is. I'm well and truly wrung out." In a surprise move, Greg took her hand.

They both sat there quietly for a moment holding hands. It felt so good but Sophie was completely confused. She thought of Mark and how lovely he was yet, here she was in another man's house holding his hand. Should she tell Greg about Mark and vice versa? Somehow it didn't feel wrong though. Did that make her a bad person? What should she do?

Finally Greg let go and took her mug off her. "Another cuppa?" he asked quietly getting up.

"No thanks, I'd better go. I've got a million and one things to do before our flight and besides, Chloe'll be back in a while." Sophie stood up and realised too late that as Greg hadn't moved, they were now only centimetres apart.

They seemed to stand like that for ages but in reality it was only seconds.

Greg leaned forward, his blue eyes never leaving her face.

Gently, he stroked her cheeks and cradled her face. "Sophie, you know I care about you, don't you?"

All of a sudden, she felt years younger and much lighter than she had in a while.

"Greg… " Sophie didn't know what to say.

"It's okay, you don't need to say anything back," he said softly smiling, "I just needed to tell you. I'll settle for friends because they don't come much better than you." He hugged her.

They stood for a while, arms around each other. Sophie so aware of his strong body which seemed to envelope her. She had never felt so safe. Could she tell him? Could she unload what was always on her mind? That guilt she just couldn't get rid of. Sitting there in the corner of wherever she was. She needed to tell someone before it ate her up.

Sophie took a step back and held Greg's hands. "Can I tell you something, Greg?"

"Of course, anything." He squeezed her hands.

"You've got to promise me you won't hate me, though," she sighed.

"Sophie, I could never hate you." Greg chuckled.

"Promise me," Sophie urged him.

"Okay, okay, I promise," Greg reassured her.

Sophie slumped on the sofa and looked down at her hands. "Everything has been my fault," she said softly.

"What do you mean?" Greg sat down next to her.

Sophie looked up at him and gulped. "My marriage going wrong, Rosie going, everything has been my fault."

"Why do you say that?" Greg frowned, obviously confused.

Sophie took a deep breath and spoke quickly wanting to get the words out. "Liam was working so much. I mean, he's always been a driven man, you know wanting to be the best and well he was spending more and time at work. I did understand but at the same time I was so lonely. He was never home and I just felt like he wasn't interested anymore." Sophie clasped her hands together. "Anyway, there was a porter at work, Neil. We hit it off straight away. He was so funny, always making me laugh. We would chat a lot and after work often meet for coffee. I was getting closer and closer to him. The thing is nothing ever happened. I wouldn't let it. But it could have. One night when we were sitting there giggling, I realised that it had been so long since Liam and I had just sat and chatted or laughed together. I realised that I just didn't love him anymore. I cared about him but I wasn't 'in love' with him. It hit me like a thunderbolt"

"Oh Sophie."

"So I thought the fairest thing was to tell him. I thought it was unfair living a lie. I thought that was the worst thing, you know to stay with someone you didn't feel anything for anymore. Of course, that was before Rosie's diagnosis when I actually realised what the worst thing in the world was."

"I'm guessing he didn't take it well?"

"No. He left. He simply ran to Ireland. He said I broke his heart."

"But Sophie marriage break ups happen all the time. At least you were honest before you actually did the deed."

"Oh, don't worry, we never did the deed. I realised pretty quickly that Neil had only filled a gap. I didn't love him. But don't you see what I did, Greg?"

"What? What did you do?"

"I made it impossible to keep Rosie. If we had stayed together, I think we could have muddled through. We would have coped and she wouldn't have to have gone into a home. You see it's all my fault." Sophie collapsed in tears.

"Oh my God, Sophie how can you think that? You only did what you thought was right. How can you predict what would have happened if Liam had stayed? I know lots of people who have put their children into residential homes even though they have been together. Two doesn't necessarily mean better. If you play the 'What if' game you'll always lose."

"You don't think I'm to blame then? You don't think I'm a terrible person?"

Greg's face erupted into the warmest smile. "No, Sophie, I definitely do not."

Sophie felt as if a tremendous weight had been lifted from her shoulders.

41

From that moment on, Sophie couldn't stop thinking about Mark and Greg and the situation she had unexpectedly found herself in. Throughout the packing and last minute holiday preparations, it had whirled round and round in her head.

As Gemma had put it in her inimitable way. "Bloody hell, Soph. It's like buses, isn't it? No men for years, then two come along at once!"

What on earth was she going to do?

Sophie knew. She would go on holiday with Chloe and try to forget about it.

For now.

42

The holiday with Chloe was perfect.

When they'd arrived at the airport, Sophie tried to put everything to the back of her mind and allow herself a little bit of excitement at the first proper holiday she had had for years. As a girl she'd always felt that bubbling in the bottom of her stomach when they had arrived at the airport or ferry port. It was that wonderful feeling of escaping from normality for a while, where usual rules of bedtimes and homework didn't exist. It had been a while since she had experienced that sensation, since whenever they had set off anywhere new with Rosie, the only feeling in her stomach was intense fear of what could happen when they were all outside their comfort zone.

The journey had gone smoothly and they had finally arrived at their destination in the early hours of the evening. The hotel was impressive composed of immaculate white walls and pristine marble floors. The sort of place Sophie felt was way too good for her. Then when they were shown to their room, Sophie had to stop herself exclaiming out loud as it too was faultless. Spacious with two immense bedrooms and a balcony with an amazing view out to the beach, it was so much better than either of them had expected. Sophie felt that it was truly like another world and Chloe could hardly contain her excitement at being able to spend a week in a place like this. A deluxe static caravan was the best they had managed up until now.

Before they had even unpacked, an excited Chloe dragged Sophie down to the bar and they both sat watching the most incredible sunset with a cold drink in their hands. Sophie tried not to imagine what Rosie might be doing and just simply enjoy this moment with her Chloe.

Sophie and Chloe threw themselves into the holiday and their week on this beautiful island was wonderful. Sophie was determined to make it fabulous for her daughter who had never complained all those times when her friends, who compared to Chloe led fairly normal lives, jetted off all over the place for their summer holidays, while they had to make do with holiday parks in rainy Devon.

Every day, they woke up to sunshine streaming through the thin white curtains and would spend the day either by the pool or at one of the local beaches which looked like something out of a travel brochure. Sophie did wonder whether she ought to do more exploring but they both decided it was simply too hot. In fact, to say it was hot was actually an understatement. Chloe hadn't known heat like it on the few holidays they had had in Britain and Sophie had forgotten what it was like to be so hot that you had to get in the water to cool off, so hot that the sand burnt your feet, and so hot that the sweat simply ran down your back.

So instead of being intrepid explorers, they settled for lazy days on sun loungers reading books and sipping cocktails. Chloe would often let out a deep sigh and proclaim that this place was 'actually heaven.'

As the week went on, Sophie found herself slowly unwinding in what did indeed turn out to be a piece of paradise. It helped that she was watching Chloe having a brilliant time, the pale tight expression her tired daughter had worn throughout her exams had given way to a golden, relaxed glow. She had made friends with a few other teenagers in the hotel and would often meet them at the pool. Sophie noticed that Chloe was particularly good with the younger children in the hotel showing endless patience when playing games with them. It gave Sophie a pang as this is what she would have been like with a sister if things had been different. In fact, watching the families here together on holiday was the only time when Sophie would be dragged down for a moment. Their laughter and happy smiles were enough to trigger the old feelings of jealousy and sadness that she no longer really had a family with her all the time.

Lying in the sun, Sophie often found her thoughts wandering to Mark and Greg. Of course she'd had a few texts from each of them though thankfully they had all been light and friendly and so Sophie had tried to reply with the same tone. It was difficult as she knew she really couldn't let things continue as they were with both of them, it simply wouldn't be fair to leave them both hanging and she had a feeling that neither of them was now going to be content with just friendship. The trouble was she liked them both and enjoyed their company. They had certainly been a huge help this past year and could she afford to lose either of them? It just went round and round in her head, an unsolvable problem. In the end the thoughts would exhaust her and she would sit up, sip a little of her cocktail and make conversation with Chloe. She just hoped that at some point the decision would be made for her.

Once the temperature had cooled, Sophie and Chloe spent the evenings wandering into the nearest town and sampling the local food. Although it was a fairly quiet resort there was still a good selection of tavernas to choose from and Chloe found it fun selecting a different one every night. They made a deal that they wouldn't eat the same dish twice so searched every menu for something different every night. Sophie also fell in love with the Greek people who couldn't do enough to help, both in the hotel and in the town.

The only fly in the ointment was the fact that she missed Rosie terribly, though she tried not to show it. Every evening without fail she rang the home to check on her. The staff would give Rosie the phone and Sophie would talk to her. She could hear her giggling or trying to say some words. They reassured her that she was perfectly happy, but Sophie found it hard to let go of the feeling that if things had been different she would be in this beautiful place with two daughters and not just one. In quiet moments, Sophie tried desperately not to dwell on the fact that life was so unfair.

The night before they were due to fly home, Sophie found a particularly lovely tavern in which to have dinner, overlooking the sea. The meal was delicious and after they finished they just stayed at their table gazing at the ocean well aware that tomorrow they would be saying goodbye to it all. Chloe turned to Sophie and laid her head on her shoulder.

"I've had a brilliant time, Mum. Thanks for booking this holiday."

Sophie stroked her head. "You are so welcome, sweetheart, I've loved spending the week with you."

And she had.

Sophie had decided that whoever had said that you couldn't be friends with your children had got it so wrong. Chloe had been great company. The two of them had gossiped together, laughed together, people watched together and chatted about Chloe's plans for the future. Sophie felt so proud of the person her elder daughter was becoming.

"I know you've missed Rosie this week, Mum. I have too, but you know it's been nice seeing you like this for a change."

"Am I very different then?" Sophie frowned.

Chloe tilted her head as if to study her mum.

"It's your face. I mean you're always really pretty, Mum… "

Sophie laughed.

"It's just that you haven't got that worried look all the time now. You're… you're like you used to be ages ago." Chloe smiled and seeing Sophie's suddenly serious expression hurried on. "Sorry, I mean, you look more relaxed and just, I don't know, sort of happy. I'm not blaming Rosie, I mean it's not her fault and I love her so much too, Mum, it's just that there's been so much to worry about hasn't there?"

Sophie rested her head on her hand. "Yes, there certainly has, honey."

Chloe continued, "The thing is, Mum, I don't think you *should* worry so much. I mean Rosie's happy at the home and more settled now. We actually have nice times when we see her now. It's not all shouting and stress."

"You don't blame me for sending your sister away then?" Sophie said quietly.

"No, honestly, Mum, I don't. I mean, I didn't like her going because I really miss her, but she was so angry and you were getting hurt all the time. I was starting to get nervous about what she might do next, whenever she had a meltdown. "

"It was frightening, wasn't it?" Sophie agreed.

Chloe sighed, "I don't see what else you could have done."

And there it was. Everyone had told her, but hearing it from Chloe's mouth sent a lightning bolt through her. Sophie couldn't have done anything else. She hated it. It was horrible not having her at home. It was terrible having to visit her own daughter in a home. But…

She couldn't have done anything else.

The next day, just before they left for the airport, Sophie was passing the mirror in the apartment and caught a glance of herself. She realised that a very different woman was looking back at her. The golden tan certainly helped but there was something else. It was just as Chloe had said. Sophie realised that the pained expression which she had worn for as long as she could remember had been replaced with a more peaceful one. It was like she had been dismantled and put back together. Never ever to be the same again. She would after all never completely forgive herself. But there was an acceptance now that she had done the best she could at the time.

43

The plane landed on time and after the usual checks at the airport, Sophie and Chloe were pleased to see a smiling Gemma waiting in the car park. Chloe raced up to hug her.

"Gemma!"

"Well hello, my gorgeously tanned unofficial niece! How are you doing, sweetie? Was it brill?

"Yeah, it was fab!" Chloe grinned and waved her camera. "We've got loads of photos to show you."

Gemma pretended to groan. "Hmmm, I might well be busy for a few nights then." She slung her arm around Sophie's shoulder, "…and what about you stranger, did you enjoy yourself, honey?"

"Oh yes. Missed Rosie like mad, mind you, but I managed to ring her every day. Not sure she even knew I'd gone really."

"Ah, typical teenager then. Right! Back to mine for a cuppa, you look like you could murder one."

"Sounds good." Sophie agreed.

It was a short drive from the airport to home so it wasn't long before they were all sitting in Gemma's kitchen with tea and biscuits. Chloe was busy entertaining Alex and Jess with tales of exotic beaches and some of the kids that she'd met.

Gemma clinked her mug with Sophie's. "Here's to being back from wonderful holidays and back to normal life!"

"Ooh you make it sound so exciting," Sophie laughed.

Gemma leaned back from her friend looking thoughtful.

"You know, you look different… something… I don't know what it is… "

Sophie smiled. "It's probably just the sun's lightened my hair or something… "

"Maybe… "

"So any gossip?"

"Not really. Oh, Linda down the road's got a new bloke, saw him leaving when I was on the way to work the other day."

"Another one? She gets through a fair few, doesn't she?!"

"Well, now, you can talk sweetie." Gemma smiled wickedly. "Sooo have you thought any more about the two extremely handsome men in your life?"

Sophie groaned. "Oh don't. I feel terrible. This just isn't me. They're both really lovely. I can't believe I'm in this situation. I just never dreamed… "

"How do you feel about them both?"

"I don't know. I mean, obviously I really like them both but as for anything more I'm just not sure. Maybe I should just say no to both of them and stay friends. I mean I've done alright without a man all these years, haven't I?"

"Well yeah, but like you said they're both great guys. I mean there's nothing hugely wrong with them and let's face it, just how often does that happen? Wouldn't you like to have someone in your life?"

"But I've got my girls and they've got to come first."

"Soph, love, that doesn't mean you can't have someone else too. Look at me, I've got Jess and Alex and they're my world and most definitely come first but it doesn't mean I'm not allowed to have some time on my own with Bob. It isn't against the law you know!"

"I know it's just… "

"It's just, you can't let yourself be totally happy can you, honey?"

"I… "

"You do deserve it, you know."

"I'm scared to… "

"Let yourself be happy?"

"Gemma, stop analysing me!"

"Sorry can't help it! I just know you so well, babe."

"It just feels wrong somehow."

"Why?"

"Well, me being happy when Rosie's… "

"Rosie's what?"

"When Rosie's away."

"Where she's happy?"

"Yes, but –"

"… and settled?"

"But –"

Gemma gripped Sophie's shoulders. "Stop feeling guilty, Sophie. We've all told you but I'm going to tell you for the millionth time and maybe it might finally go in, you did the right thing."

Sophie looked at her friend and in a small, trembling voice replied, "I know."

"Now, tell me again, why you can't be happy?"

Sophie smiled weakly. Could she? She looked over at her beautiful Chloe looking so well and animated, giggling with Alex and Jess hunched over her phone. She suddenly felt a tremendous desire to ring her other daughter.

Leaving Gemma finishing her tea, Sophie disappeared into the living room to make the phone call. When the phone was answered, Sophie was glad it was Emily as she was always so friendly.

"Hi Sophie, did you have a good holiday?"

"Yes, lovely thanks, just got back actually. How's Rosie?"

"She's in a great mood. She's just had tea and ate everything apart from the peas - too green as usual – and now she's chilling with her books in the lounge."

"I think I can hear her." It was true, Sophie could hear the familiar repetitive sounds that Rosie made with her books.

"Can you put her on, so I can speak to her?"

"Yeah sure."

Sophie heard Rosie's sounds getting louder as Emily obviously moved in to the room with her.

Loud giggling came down the phone.

"Hi Rosie, it's Mummy. Mummy says I love you."

More sounds on the line.

"Is that kisses for Mummy? Blow Mummy some kisses." Sophie made some kissing sounds for Rosie. Was she imagining it or was Rosie trying to do it. Just recently it had sounded as if she was trying to say the words 'I love you' down the phone. Sophie wondered if she was imagining it, but the truth is she heard it so much from Sophie she could well be trying to copy it. Sophie hoped so anyway.

"Mummy will see Rosie tomorrow. Okay Rosie?"

More half formed words and giggles.

Just then, Emily came back on the line. "Sorry Sophie, she's run off now."

"Aw that's okay. She sounds so happy tonight."

"Yeah she is, I just hope it lasts when it's brush your teeth time!"

Sophie laughed. She made the usual arrangements to see Rosie the next day – she couldn't wait to see her - and put the phone down. She felt relieved that her week's absence didn't seem to have distressed Rosie in any way. She smiled to herself when she pictured Rosie sitting on the floor in the lounge at Thorpe Cloud House surrounded by all her favourite books, safe and happy. She also felt the familiar excitement at the thought of seeing her tomorrow for lots of cuddles.

44

The next morning, Sophie left Chloe in bed and was up early to make the now familiar trip up to Derbyshire.

As she got in the car, she felt strangely lighter. Was it because the sun was shining? Was it because she would soon see Rosie again? Was it the effect of the holiday? Was it because she was looking forward to a few hours gardening later? Or was it because she had finally realised what she should do about Mark and Greg? It didn't matter, she just felt better.

Just then she heard her phone.

It was a text.

Not just that, it was a beautiful text. Thoughtful, kind words which showed that he cared.

It was time to take a chance. Sophie wrote a reply accepting his offer of dinner, fully realising it was actually much more that she was accepting.

She thought twice, then pressed send.

It was time to live again.

Epilogue

Two Years Later

Sophie watched as Chloe searched for the key in her bag. She leaned on the car and looked around her at the place where her older daughter would be spending the next few years of her life. Not too shabby, she thought, for student accommodation.

It was always meant to be. Given the soft, kind girl she was, Sophie had always firmly believed that Chloe was destined to go into a caring profession. So, here she was, happy and excited, about to start her nursing degree in Sheffield. Sophie never stopped feeling amazed and proud that Chloe had managed to wade through one of the most difficult times in their lives to become this confident, stunning eighteen year old, ready to embark on adulthood.

Sophie thought back to a couple of years ago when Rosie had left home and how devastated she had felt. Today was very different, it was how it was meant to be. Chloe was going at the right time, completely ready and grown up, not at the tender age of twelve. Sophie sighed. With both of them gone, she was dreading the empty house that she was now going to be rattling around in, but she realised that life had to move on. And, over the last two years, it had. For everyone.

To everyone's complete surprise, Natalie and Andy had split up. It had turned out that the saintly Natalie had been having an affair with Andy's extremely boring but incredibly affluent boss. Sophie had always suspected that her sister-in-law had had her eyes permanently on the prize. Initially, she had felt sorry for Andy, who'd always seemed devoted to his wife, but as time went on he was looking more like a man who had been reprieved. Just lately he'd started deep sea diving, another hobby to go with all the other weird and wonderful things he'd done since his release.

Gemma really did seem to have found her soul mate and appeared to be living proof that happy endings did indeed exist. So, nearly a year ago, even though she'd always sworn she would never get married ever, *ever* again, she had tied the knot with Bob. Dressed in a stunning white dress with her red hair cascading down her back, Sophie had never seen her friend look happier or more beautiful. It had been a wonderful day and she had even managed to bring Rosie to the reception for a couple of hours. Luckily, the perfect marriage hadn't robbed Gemma of her wicked sense of humour, so they still shared evenings with copious amounts of wine, laughing at the world.

Liam and Siobhan had also been married a year. Chloe had shown her some of the pictures of the wedding on her phone and Siobhan really had looked gorgeous. Sophie had noticed the smile of pure happiness on Liam's face and was truly glad that he had found someone who could make him happy again. Siobhan had recently let slip to Chloe that she wanted a baby so Sophie was now bracing herself for news that Liam would be having another child. Part of her was dreading it, the intense feeling like he would be replacing their lost child with another one occasionally washed over her. However, the sensible part of her knew that Liam wouldn't think of it like that and she shouldn't either. It really was just more proof that life very rarely stuck to the plan. Sophie certainly understood that more than most.

It had been a long journey to get to where she was.

As she opened the boot and began taking out Chloe's stuff, Sophie thought about just how far they'd all come. Much like a bereavement, she supposed, she would never lose the sadness in the pit of her stomach that she couldn't live with her daughter and be with her all of the time. However, she had found a way through and was managing to live.

It was, without doubt, a very different life to the one Sophie had imagined, but it was a good life with lots of wonderful things in it. She had met some amazing and inspiring people along the way. One of whom was helping her unload the boot.

Mark.

In the end it had to be Mark.

It was true that kind, strong Greg would always understand what she had gone through in a way that no one else ever would. Like Sophie, he knew autism inside and out and there would never have had to be any explanations needed, but in the end she decided that they were both still suffering so much, life with Greg would have been just too sad. Just too much. Fortunately, they had been able to remain good friends and they both knew each of them only had to pick up the phone and they would be there in an instant. Robbie was preparing to start a new phase in his life and go into supported living and, as every new phase brought its difficulties, Sophie had a feeling she would be getting some calls soon.

 Mark, this beautiful man who had told Sophie that he would have waited for her forever, had been like a breath of fresh air in her life. He made her laugh in a way she never thought she would again and more importantly he knew that Sophie would always put her girls first. He understood that, although she loved him deeply, he would always come second to Chloe and Rosie and he was content with that.

Although, Sophie had never been happier with anyone and Mark obviously adored her, each of them had kept their own houses. He wanted to stay with his dad who still needed help and she hadn't been ready for anyone else to move in and fill the gap that Rosie had left. Sophie wasn't sure she ever would be.

And Rosie. Rosie had bloomed into a beautiful young woman. At times Sophie found herself wondering what she might have been doing now if she hadn't been autistic but she tried not to think like this too often.

Rosie was, as always, wonderful Rosie. Sparky, naughty, funny, independent, strong-willed, clever and beautiful. She still had her ups and downs – peaceful phases, terrible phases – after all there were no fairy tale endings with autism. However she was more settled and had progressed so much. The home had given her structure, routine and everything she had needed at the time when she had needed it most.

Sophie put the final box in Chloe's room. Mark was busy setting up the printer while Chloe was putting clothes in her wardrobe. Sophie and Mark had planned to settle her in, then head to Thorpe Cloud House which was only a short distance away to see Rosie. One of the reasons Chloe had chosen Sheffield was so that she could be near her sister.

Sophie sat on the bed and gazed at her older daughter, about to embark on the next part of her life. Feeling herself being watched, Chloe turned and smiled. "You okay, Mum?"

Sophie smiled back. "Yes, I am."

Acknowledgements

I need to say thank you to some great people who have made this book possible. Huge thanks go to my wonderful family who are always so supportive of my writing and spur me on when self-doubt creeps in. A big thank you to Kath Middleton for some excellent proofreading. I don't know how you spotted all those errors, but I'm very grateful that you did! Enormous thanks also go to John Marrs for answering my constant stream of questions so promptly and expertly. John you are my guru! Finally, a special mention must go to my beautiful sister Lyndsay, whose experience inspired this book. Your courage and strength in the face of a difficult decision is an example to us all.

About the author

Kate Hughes is a primary school teacher of more than twenty years. Her passion for reading from an early age has finally led her to making her own contribution to the world of books. She lives in Derbyshire with a husband, three feisty daughters and a lively lilac tortoiseshell cat.

This is her second novel.

Also by Kate Hughes

Mr Brown's Suitcase

Letter from Kate

Hello Reader,

I would like to thank you so much for choosing to read Home and I sincerely hope that you enjoyed Sophie's story.

Writing this novel has been a true labour of love. Autism has affected my family profoundly over many years and I have had to watch those I love cope with it and make decisions which most of us will never have to contemplate. Although this is a work of fiction, through Sophie's story I wanted to show the devastating impact that extreme autism can have on not just the parents of the autistic child but the entire family. I hope I have gone some way to improve your understanding of this difficult condition.

If you did enjoy the book, I'd be really grateful if you could take the time to write a review. I'd love to know what you think and it may also help other readers discover my book.

Best wishes,

Kate.

You can connect with me on Facebook and Twitter.

Printed in Great Britain
by Amazon